"I've been waiting a long time for the sequel to *Burying Daisy Doe*. We've all been waiting! And here it is at last! Ramona Richards has never failed to draw readers in with her characters, her suspense-filled plots, and her master storytelling abilities. *Circle of Vengeanc*e reminds readers, once again, who the queen of suspense really is!"

—**Eva Marie Everson**, best-selling author and president of Word Weavers International, Inc.

"A well-plotted dual time masterpiece that will keep you turning the pages well into the night. I think this is my favorite Ramona Richards story out of all of the ones I've read. I'm eagerly looking forward to the next one!"

—**Lynette Eason**, best-selling and award-winning author of the Extreme Measures series

"Ramona Richards kept me up late turning pages once again! I read *Circle of Vengeance* late into the night, sometimes because I just had to see what happened next and sometimes to see if I was right in how I read the clues that Star Cavanaugh unearthed. This is a twisting, turning generational story that pits innocence against evil, the past against the present, and the weak against the strong. I can't wait to see what cold case Star is embroiled in next!"

—**Jodie Bailey**, *USA Today* best-selling author of *Deadly Cargo*

"*Circle of Vengeance*, Ramona Richards's second book in the Star Cavanaugh Cold Case series, was impossible to put down—I stayed up until one a.m. to finish it. Anxiously awaiting the next one."

—**Patricia Bradley**, author of the Natchez Trace Park Rangers series

CIRCLE OF VENGEANCE

Books in the Star Cavanaugh Cold Case Series

Burying Daisy Doe
Circle of Vengeance

A STAR CAVANAUGH COLD CASE

CIRCLE OF VENGEANCE

RAMONA RICHARDS

Circle of Vengeance

Published by Kregel Publications, a division of Kregel Inc., 2450 Oak Industrial Dr. NE, Grand Rapids, MI 49505. www.kregel.com.

Library of Congress Cataloging-in-Publication Data
Names: Richards, Ramona, 1957- author.
Title: Circle of vengeance / Ramona Richards.
Description: Grand Rapids, MI : Kregel Publications, [2022] | Series: A Star Cavanaugh Cold Case ; 2
Identifiers: LCCN 2022008684 (print) | LCCN 2022008685 (ebook) | ISBN 9780825447471 (paperback) | ISBN 9780825478628 (epub) | ISBN 9780825469596 (kindle)
Classification: LCC PS3618.I3438 C57 2022 (print) | LCC PS3618.I3438 (ebook) | DDC 813/.6--dc23
LC record available at https://lccn.loc.gov/2022008684
LC ebook record available at https://lccn.loc.gov/2022008685

ISBN 978-0-8254-4747-1, print
ISBN 978-0-8254-7862-8, epub
ISBN 978-0-8254-6959-6, Kindle

Printed in the United States of America
22 23 24 25 26 27 28 29 30 31 / 5 4 3 2 1

For Julie,
for never giving up, no matter what

CHAPTER ONE

Sunday, May 14, 1995
Lake Martin, Alabama

THE LITTLEST GIRL squealed, the high-pitched sound rocketing over the water to the twenty-foot walkabout boat anchored less than a hundred yards offshore. Beneath the bow bimini top near the front, two sets of binoculars popped up as Lee and his uncle Chase observed the Marshall clan at play. The extended family of Edmund and Margery Marshall scattered across the long sloping lawn that reached from the lake's edge to the sprawling family compound on the hill above. The boat had drifted closer to shore from when Lee and Chase had first anchored, but it was only one of a dozen or so floating in the fish-filled inlet near the Marshall compound. They were, as Chase had said, "Hiding in plain sight."

On the grassy shore, three generations of the affluent Marshalls had gathered for a leisurely picnic on this quiet Sunday—the patriarch and his wife who had worked to make the wealth, the three children who were helping build it, and the grandchildren who would never have to worry about it. Those grandchildren dashed about between the two Marshall brothers, who tried to toss a football back and forth without tripping over one of their offspring. The tallest of the cousins—a boy not yet a teen—was clearly torn between joining his father and uncle and continuing to torment the younger ones with a lizard he'd caught.

Lee lowered his binoculars and slumped in the front passenger chair of the boat, bored as only a seventeen-year-old boy can be. The promised excitement of following his uncle, a private detective, around on one of his jobs had sounded thrilling. Instead, they had watched as the little girl and her cousins—all under twelve—scampered about in a game of tag for almost an hour.

"Tell me again why we are watching a bunch of rich white folks without a care in the world." Lee had a hard time keeping the envy out of his voice. He didn't care. He could list a dozen things he'd rather be doing.

His uncle took a long breath, a sign of his growing impatience. Sitting behind the wheel of the boat, he twisted, glaring at Lee. "I told you. Background. You see the little girl, the youngest, in the *Little Mermaid* T-shirt."

Lee peered through the binoculars again. "Yeah. The one who looks about five?"

"Yes. Just turned. Today is her birthday. Her name is Hope. She belongs to the youngest of the Marshall kids, the strawberry-blond studying on the blanket."

Lee lowered his binoculars to study his uncle, the sharp angles of the man's face, the crinkled skin of a rough scar that peeked from beneath the collar of his polo shirt. "That blond looks like she's my age. She can't be more than seventeen."

"Eighteen. Just enrolled at UAB."

Lee took another look. He couldn't believe the blond was old enough to be enrolled in the University of Alabama at Birmingham, much less—"And she's got a five-year-old?"

Chase lowered his binoculars. "Yes. What of it?"

The tone in his uncle's voice did not invite an answer to the question. "Nothing. Just unusual, that's all."

Chase lifted the binoculars. "Gen—the woman—isn't involved with the girl's father, but he likes to keep an eye out. And Gen's started dating a new guy she met at UAB. Daddy doesn't like it. Wants to know what's going on."

"So he hired you to keep an eye out?"

"It's what I do."

Right. The ink on Chase's new license as a private investigator had barely had time to dry. "Is the new guy here?"

"Not so far."

Lee raised the binoculars one more time, trying to take in the entire scene. The old man—obviously the eldest Marshall—stood at the grill with a soda in one hand, flipping burgers, hot dogs, and steaks. His wife spread plates and flatware on the picnic table, anchoring a stack of napkins with the ketchup bottle. Two dark-haired young women, probably the brothers' wives, tried to help the older woman, without much success. The kids continued to race about the long lawn that sloped down to the shimmering lake and the Marshall boathouse and dock, making enough racket to wake the dead.

Serene. Happy. The very picture of the American dream.

As they watched, a tall man carrying a cake box emerged from the main house, his long strides carrying him closer to the Marshalls. Spotting him, Gen bounced off her blanket, the books she'd been studying scattering over it. She ran to the man, greeting him with a generous hug and a kiss on the cheek as he struggled to keep the cake box level. Gen's pale complexion and reddish-blond locks made for a sharp contrast to the man's dark skin and hair.

"That's the new guy?"

"Yes. Nicholas Eaton." Chase's teeth ground together, the gritting sound making Lee wince.

Eaton? Lee lowered the binoculars again. "Like the hotel-chain guys? Those Eatons?"

His uncle's voice was tight. "Yes. Oldest son. At UAB working on his MBA."

"I guess rich attracts rich."

Chase jerked the binoculars away from his eyes, his face a twisted mask of anger. "It's not about the money."

Lee scooted back against the hull, trying to move out of range of his uncle's ire. He pushed his dark hair off his forehead. "Of course not."

"He does not want his little girl raised by a"—Chase stopped, swallowing whatever he had been about to say—"a stranger."

"So now what?"

"Now I gather the info, and we wait."

"For what?"

Chase returned to watching the idyllic scene through the binoculars. "For the right time."

Lee dropped it. He wasn't sure he wanted to know the next answer—the right time for *what?* He too continued watching the Marshalls. Eaton and Gen had settled back on the blanket, their heads together as they studied one of her books. The oldest cousin had given up on the lizard and had joined in the football toss. The old man had loaded a platter with meat as his wife rounded up the family.

Lee rolled his shoulders. The tension radiating off his uncle made him nervous, fidgety. He'd been eager to come along, to learn more about his uncle's new private investigation business. It had sounded exciting, like one of those adventure movies he loved. But this . . . was not that. He knew Chase had not told him the whole story. He also knew that if Chase had anything to do with this, that family was about to have their rich-people peacefulness turned topsy-turvy. And Lee didn't want to have anything to do with that.

But he had a bad feeling he was in it for the long haul.

CHAPTER TWO

Present Day
Pineville, Alabama

JILL TURNEY FIDGETED. I waited for her answer, trying not to watch her foot. Jill sat, legs crossed, on a bistro stool at the front of my Overlander, the Airstream travel trailer that was my temporary home and office. Professional, polished, and poised, a lawyer in her prime. Her dark hair remained in a neat, tight French braid, but her floral-embroidered Kate Spade boot bounced like an impatient child in church, making her entire body tremble. Her fingers twisted the strap of the matching handbag, which she clutched in her lap.

We had met a few weeks ago, and now Jill had finally decided to hire me. When she had made that announcement a few minutes ago, I asked one direct question. "What do you want me to do?"

"Isn't it obvious?"

"No. Tell me what you want me to do."

She couldn't answer. Her foot gyrations increased in strength, and the Overlander rocked. *Hmm.* I obviously needed to check the stabilizers underneath. I had, after all, recently had an issue with a local raccoon who liked the underside of my trailer. The cooler temps of autumn had made him braver, enough so that he'd already tangled once with Cletis, the orange campground tabby. That had been a fight to raise the dead. It definitely had dragged me out of bed at two in the morning. Cletis had won, but I'd had to wrangle him to the vet for stitches.

I sighed and sat down on the edge of the recliner, which was on the opposite side of the trailer's living room from the bistro stool. "Look,

Jill, you've been gone from Pineville a long time. I know this thing has plagued your family—"

The foot froze. "This thing?" Her voice rose in pitch. "This *thing*? You mean the murdered woman found in Daddy's barn? The murder they tried so hard to blame on Daddy that it ruined all our lives? You mean that *thing*?"

Well . . . yes. Finding a dead body on someone's property does tend to affect how people view folks.

"Jill—"

"Ricky's been arrested. Again."

Ah. Jill's brother. Twelve years her senior, Ricky Turney was as well known to local law enforcement officials as Otis was to Sheriff Andy Taylor in good old Mayberry. And for similar reasons.

"Your parents called you."

Jill nodded, a short, clipped snap of the head. "They don't have the bail money, so of course they called me. They don't even know how much it'll be this time, since it's not exactly his first offense. He won't be arraigned until tomorrow, and I'm tempted to leave him there to rot." She uncrossed her legs and clamped both feet on the floor. "I am *so* tired of this, Star! It has to stop. Now!"

"Um, rehab—"

She waved away the suggestion before I could get it out. "No good. He won't go, or if he does go, he won't stay. He's going to kill himself, or even worse, someone else."

"He drives while under the—"

"Of course he drives! Mama can't stop him, and Daddy won't. Daddy would personally love it if Ricky took out half the county. But it's not even really the booze, you know?"

"How so?"

"It's that woman! She ruined my family, and she's going to get my brother killed! Even my own psychiatrist tells me that Ricky and I will never be normal as long as that's hanging over our heads. The 'root cause,' she called it. Root of all our evil."

"You see a psychiatrist?"

"Star!"

I straightened. "You have to say it, Jill. I'm not a mind reader. You and Ricky have toyed with this since I got to Pineville. Since Mike introduced us and you found out I was a private investigator. But I can't ask. And I cannot assume. You have to tell me, tell me exactly what you want from me."

She sat completely still, staring down at her hands. "You know I work with investigators every day. This shouldn't be so hard."

"That's work. This is family."

She closed her eyes. "Yes. You understand. Family is different."

Boy howdy, was that an understatement. I'd arrived in Pineville earlier this year in an attempt to solve my own family cold case. It had almost gotten me killed because my judgment had been clouded by family intrigue. And I'd left this small Alabama town, planning to resume my former life in Nashville, only to return for another case. Then another. That I'd ended up staying in Pineville longer than I had planned astonished a lot of people. Including me.

Part of the reason I had lingered now sat in front of me, trying to finally work up the nerve to say the words she'd hinted at for several months. I'd met Jill when the local chief of police, Michael Luinetti, had introduced us not long after my first case was resolved back in the spring. She'd been in town only for a short stay, during one of her many trips home to bail out her brother. I'd met Ricky as well, although he wasn't coherent at the time. He referred to Jill as "the one who got away," meaning she'd escaped small-town Alabama for the lights and corporate world of Chicago. The story they told me about the unsolved crime on their family farm riveted me, so I embraced the idea of working with them. But Jill had to be specific with what she wanted me to do.

Jill took a deep breath and finally spoke, her voice still carrying the twang of her north Alabama roots. Law school and four years in Chicago had dimmed it not one whit. "I want to hire you to solve the murder of Genevieve Marshall Eaton. I want you to find out who really killed her and clear my family's name of this curse."

*

Michael Luinetti looked up from his computer, his face calm, his dark-blue eyes flat. This was a rare event. The German side of his blood usually lost out to the Sicilian side when it came to his expressions. "You want what?" Even his voice remained level, if disbelieving.

I leaned against the doorframe of his office, using my foot to push the windowed door labeled "Chief of Police" farther open. "I was wondering if you could share anything your department has on the murder of Genevieve Eaton. I understand it's still an open case."

He blinked, and I could almost see the investigator part of his brain tumbling the request over a few times. I waited, knowing he'd put it together. I usually brainstorm out loud. Mike prefers to remain silent as the facts click into place in his brain.

Mike and I have, as they say, history. That we spend a lot of time together is regular fodder for the local gossip mill. It makes us a good team and comfortable partners with our work. And good friends.

Well, OK, we're more than friends. We just try not to be too obvious about that part of our relationship while I'm standing in his office discussing dead bodies.

One eyebrow arched. His tell. He had it. "Jill Turney has finally hired you to clear her father."

"Yep."

"You are never getting back to Nashville. You know that, right?"

This had become a running joke between us. After solving the cold-case murders of my father and grandmother last year, I'd returned to Nashville to heal and recoup. I had to come back to Alabama to retrieve the Overlander my grandmother had given me. Mike had immediately introduced me to two potential clients, his not-so-subtle attempts to get me to stay in Pineville. But I'd hauled the Overlander back to Nashville, parked it in the backyard of my cottage there, and refitted part of it as a portable investigation unit, complete with some basic forensic equipment. I'd barely gotten the refit completed when I had a request for help on another Pineville cold case. After a second request, I finally rented a slot at a nearby RV campground. I'd only been back to

Nashville twice in the last six months to check on my house. Both times I'd left the Overlander in Pineville. Now Jill Turney had finally made up her mind, and it looked like maybe I'd be staying a little longer.

"I have to go back soon to prep the house for winter." I'd hired a house sitter, a friend who was temporarily out of work, but it wasn't a long-term solution.

"Or you could just rent it for a year." A suggestion Mike had made a few dozen times. He didn't want me to leave Pineville. And to be honest, despite all the work he'd sent my way, this dark-haired Yankee was the primary reason I hadn't left.

History.

This time, however, his words felt different. Almost like a warning. I moved closer to his desk. "You believe this will take a while." The previous two were relatively recent cases and turned out to be quick to resolve. Still . . . "My father was murdered in 1984. My grandmother in 1954. Those were cold a pretty long time."

"Yes, but your father and grandmother were murdered as part of an ongoing conspiracy of corruption, and their deaths were never investigated. Gen Eaton's murder was under a new sheriff and was investigated thoroughly. Not closed, but they weren't negligent. Just a lot of dead ends. It's been cold since 1999. It also happened before the town and the county split and Pineville became a municipality with a police chief. The files used to be in the combined archives, but I wouldn't swear to it now."

"So I'm wasting my time?"

He shrugged. "And possibly Jill's money. I know that case. I went through all the cold-case files when I was first hired five years ago, and Jill asked me to specifically take a close look at that one. It's been reexamined twice, but the detectives couldn't find a new angle. Everything led to the same place as before—right to Kevin Turney's doorstep. They did a good job, but they couldn't find anything that could either clear or convict her father. While technically the case is open, everyone who's looked at it thinks it's unsolvable."

"So if her father is guilty, he did a masterful cleanup."

"But if he's innocent, someone did a lousy job of framing him."

"No one said it would be easy."

Mike finally smiled. "If it was, it wouldn't hold your interest."

"I do like a challenge."

Mike opened a drawer and pulled out a sheet of paper. "Have Jill fill out this request form. She can ask for the files as a family member involved with the case. Have her send it back with a note appointing you as the agent for the family."

I took the form and glanced over it. Standard stuff. "This is awfully . . . official."

A smile flashed across his face, then he smothered it. "We have a new mayor. I like my job."

"Ah." I folded the paper and slipped it into my purse. I leaned one hip against his desk. "And I kinda like you having this job."

"I always knew you just liked me for my money."

"I do prefer a man who has big bucks."

This time his smile lingered. Another running joke. Mike made less than I had as a beat cop in Nashville. Small town, small budget. I leaned closer. "So what can *you* tell me about the Turneys? Not as police chief. Just as Michael Luinetti, observer of Pineville."

"You know the two are pretty much the same."

I shrugged.

Mike pushed away from his computer and nodded at the door. Ah. Back to business. I walked over and closed the door, then sat in one of his 1960s-style visitor chairs.

He leaned his forearms on the desk. "Kevin Turney moved here in the late seventies, kind of a late-blooming hippie type, want-to-live-off-the-grid sort of guy. Nice fella at the time, from all reports. He bought the land, built the house, barn, all the outbuildings. Not sure where he met Willa, but they married in the mid-eighties. Ricky came along. They wanted to have a bunch of kids, their own commune. But if I remember correctly, Willa had trouble having children, so after a few years, they adopted Jill. The farm flourished."

"And everybody was happy."

Mike nodded. "Until one of Kevin's transient workers discovered loose earth in one of the stalls and uncovered a hand."

"Everything went south."

"Yep. That was about 1998 or 1999. Genevieve Marshall Eaton had been missing for about a year."

"Kidnapped? Runaway wife?"

"At first they suspected runaway. Her marriage had seemed sound, but there had been some odd behaviors, missing cash, strange phone calls. But no signs of foul play."

"But . . ."

"Nicholas Eaton insisted that his wife would never do that, never leave him. He's an interesting character. New money, family is in the hospitality business. Has been since the early sixties. Started with one motel and built or bought into hotel chains. He has a dignified, regal presence and is quite no-nonsense. He'd met Gen in college and described her as kind, intelligent, meticulous, and straightforward. Not a subtle or submissive woman. Not given to sneaking around. If she'd wanted a divorce, she would have confronted him with the problems long before it came to the breaking point. The one twist in the case is that something similar had already happened to them."

I leaned toward his desk. "What do you mean?"

"Gen had a little girl, Hope, the result of an assault when she was only twelve or thirteen. Eaton planned to adopt her, but Hope was kidnapped before they married. She was never located. So Eaton did not take well to the suggestion that Gen had brought this on herself. They already had known tragedy and had stuck together. And to all reports, they were a loving couple, quite devoted to each other, despite all they had been through."

"Who attacked Gen?"

Mike shook his head. "No one knew." He paused and shrugged one shoulder. "At least, no one who would talk to the authorities. After a few weeks, the family stopped cooperating, and their attorney simply told the police that Gen needed to heal."

The pieces slipped together in my head. "They found out she was pregnant."

"That was the gossip of the day. They sent her to family in North Carolina for the next few months—"

"More healing."

His mouth jerked. "Yes."

"And she came back with Hope."

"Yep. And Gen disappeared into the Marshall family compound on Lake Martin for a while. Homeschooled."

"So neither case was resolved?"

"Birmingham cops couldn't get anywhere. Eaton hired a PI, who found no trace of Hope but tracked Gen as far as Trussville, then lost the trail. Nothing until she turned up in Kevin Turney's barn."

"Cause of death?"

"Gunshot to the head. Entrance in the front. The wound was clean, small caliber, but she'd been in the muck too long. Not much left of her face. Dental records inconclusive. Too decomposed for fingerprints."

"Forensics?"

"She was buried in a stall that had once held cows but was being used to store hay. It was a forensics tornado before they ever started digging. Toxic is a mild description."

"So . . . DNA for identification."

Another nod. "And her wedding set."

"You mean her rings?"

"Yep. Very distinctive. Nicholas had them custom made. Their matching wedding bands were black onyx trimmed on both edges in gold. Last I heard, he still wears his. Never remarried. Gen's engagement ring was a five-carat black diamond surrounded by smaller white diamonds."

My eyes widened. "And the killer left them on her hand?"

"The murder definitely wasn't about money. Or the fact that Mr. and Mrs. Nicholas Eaton were one of the wealthiest couples in Birmingham. It also could have been expediency. There's not a pawnbroker or fence in the state who would not have recognized those rings."

"So maybe not a kidnapping."

"Not for money, at any rate. Nicholas identified the rings and provided the DNA sample. The results took a while. In the meantime, rumors flew like crazy, and the Turneys got the worst of it. No one could accept an explanation that didn't lay the blame at their feet. Some of the local stores wouldn't sell to them. They stopped answering the door. Ricky was already an alcoholic, trying to work odd jobs, but he gave up. Jill was young, but the bullying at school took its toll. Willa finally homeschooled Jill until she could get into college."

"Neighbors turned on neighbors."

Mike shrugged. "It happens. Things calmed down some after a few years, but it'll never be the same for them. They tried to sell the land a few years ago, but there were no takers."

"Jill called it a curse."

"I'd have to agree. And I can see why she'd want help clearing it."

"Any suggestions?"

Mike leaned back in his chair and looked up at the ceiling, hands clasped behind his head. When he looked at me again, his blue eyes gleamed. His second tell. The challenge had been accepted, the bit caught between his teeth. He'd help me in any way he could. He pushed a lock of dark-brown hair away from his forehead. "If I were starting this over, I'd start with Gen's family."

"Nicholas Eaton?"

"No." He shook his head. "Although you need to talk to him as well. No, start with the Marshalls. Her mom is alive, and Gen and her brothers were extremely close, even though they were a lot older. Jack and . . . I forget the other one. I always suspected this had a lot less to do with Gen's marriage than it did with something that happened in her past. Start there."

"You got it, Boss." I stood. "Still up for dinner tonight?"

"You cooking?"

I looked at him askance, and he laughed. "Baker's it is. I'll pick you up about six."

I grinned and turned. "I might even dress up," I said over my shoulder.

"For Baker's?"

I paused and winked at him. "No, not for Baker's."

His cheeks flushed, and I opened the door.

"Star?"

I looked back. "Be careful?"

His face was solemn again. "And skirt the Turneys as long as you can.

Kevin once took a shot at me before he realized I was a cop. He might have been a nice guy in the past, but he's turned bitter, reclusive, and I can't say I blame him. And don't forget that something got Gen Marshall killed. Jill may have hired you, but she's not the key to any of this. Don't get shot."

"The core of all my plans, Michael, my friend."

CHAPTER THREE

Monday, July 10, 1995
Birmingham, Alabama

LEE SHIFTED IN the passenger seat of the gray Toyota, the pressure in his bladder becoming a steady ache. "I need to take a break," he muttered.

From behind his binoculars, Chase grimaced. "There's a Mason jar in the back seat."

Really? What is this, the 1930s? "And there's a restaurant—"

"And they could be out and gone while you're taking care of business. A PI should not be heard or seen while he's on stakeout. Never leave your post. Too easy to lose your prey."

Prey? What in the world— Lee stared at Chase, squirming again.

Over the past few weeks, Lee's curiosity about what Chase was really up to had worn thin as his uncle had become obsessed with the growing relationship between Gen Marshall and Nicholas Eaton. Football camp started in a month, his senior year loomed, and Lee had come to regret listening to his mother's cajoling words about this being the perfect summer job. He would have made more money flipping burgers—and probably learned a lot more.

He and Chase had only tackled two other jobs, enough to pay a few expenses and Lee's minuscule paycheck. The rest of the time, they had followed Gen any time she left the Marshall compound for anything other than school. Chase had her summer schedule at UAB memorized, and only during her class periods and times at home did Chase let up on the surveillance.

Now they sat on Second Avenue North, across the street from one of the most well-known legacy jewelers in the city, and Chase's mood had soured more than Lee thought possible.

"I won't lose them. If they're picking out rings, they'll be in there for a while."

The sound that emerged from Chase's throat was almost feral. "They are not picking out rings! She would never marry a . . . a man like that."

A man like . . . what? Rich? Handsome? Lee did not want to voice the obvious slur, but something in Chase's tone got his attention. "Are you sure that's what your client would think?"

Chase's head wrenched in his direction, the glare in his eyes dark and frightening, his voice pure gravel. "Get out. Go to the restaurant. Now."

Lee did not hesitate. He grabbed the door handle and dove out of the car. His gait toward the glass door of the trendy bistro was halting as he worked out the kinks caused by hours of sitting in the small Toyota. He gave a noncommittal wave at the hostess as he headed for the bathroom. Afterward, he washed his face and tried to regain some composure before heading back outside.

The gray Toyota was gone. He glanced at the jewelers, but he knew without checking that Gen Marshall and Nicholas Eaton had returned to his BMW and left.

Great. Chase had left him stranded an hour from home. Letting out a long sigh, Lee scanned the street for a pay phone. His mother was going to kill him.

CHAPTER FOUR

Present Day
The Marshall Family Compound
Lake Martin, Alabama

GIVEN WHAT I knew about how the Marshalls had made their wealth—shipping and textile manufacturing—I fully expected what Mike had described as "the family compound" on Lake Martin to recall Southern plantations of a bygone era. Instead, the long and winding drive led to a setting that could have emerged fully formed from Frank Lloyd Wright's most fevered imagination. Surrounded by soaring oaks and southern pines, the central dark-framed structure seemed more glass than wood and stained concrete, with stark angles, arched peaks, and broad balconies. Only two stories tall, it seemed to stretch along the top of the hill for at least a quarter mile, almost as if it had grown out of the landscape. Arched cloisters connected five distinct sections of the home, each with its own entrance and covered stoop. Even though it was still midmorning, light blazed from all windows, competing with the sun overhead.

I wasn't entirely sure where the front door was.

I decided to trust the drive, which reached its apex near a set of double wooden doors beneath an expansive balcony. I parked Belle, my blue-and-white 1966 GMC Carryall, but before I could reach the stoop, the right door flew back and an older woman wearing matching lime-green shorts and a tank top greeted me with a smile and a wave. She was toned and trim, and her long silver hair was pulled back in a ponytail. A green polka-dotted bandanna covered most of it. On her feet were a pair of cross-trainers worth about a month of Mike Luinetti's salary.

"You must be Star!" She stepped back from the door. "Do come in."

As I did, she introduced herself. "Mike called to let me know you were coming. I'm Margery Marshall. Just Margery. Please forgive my attire. It's cleaning day." Before I could say a word, she turned and strode back into the house, talking as she went, her hands animated in the air. "Yes, I have maids. Everyone asks that. A house this size, it's a necessity. One person could never keep it all clean. It would take you a month, and then you'd just have to start over again. Especially when the kids were younger, the boys in particular. I swear they could create dirt just standing still. But there are just some things I prefer to do myself. I used to tell Eddie . . ." She paused for a half second. "That was Mr. Marshall, Edmund—man, he loved the wild architects, Wright, Sullivan—I told him that this house would be impossible to keep clean, and he told me that's why rich people had maids and such, so they could have their big houses. He was such a cutup, that Eddie. I miss him."

I wondered if Eddie ever got a word in edgewise. I had followed Margery through a marble-floored foyer, past a sunken living room with mid-twentieth-century furnishings, down a narrow hallway with four closed doors, and into a glass-walled sunroom filled with a maze of tall green plants, shelves holding a selection of violets and orchids, and an over-cushioned set of wicker furniture.

"We'll be more comfortable in here over that stuffy living room. Never did like that room, but Eddie considered it essential for entertaining his clients. And we're less likely to hear all the clanging and banging of the maids." Margery paused, pushed her shoes off without untying them, and settled into the corner of a wicker settee, tucking her feet underneath her rear.

According to the police file Mike had given me, Margery Marshall was seventy-three. I couldn't sit like that now, and she had three decades on me. "So . . . Mike called you?"

"Of course! I do not go around inviting just anyone into my home. But he vouched for you. He said you wanted to talk about Genevieve's murder." She let out a long sigh. "I suppose the Turneys are trying to get out from under this again." When I nodded, she leaned forward. "I can't blame them." Her voice dropped to a conspiratorial whisper. "I never believed Kevin Turney had anything to do with it, not really. He was too good a man."

"So you knew him?"

Her hand made an oblong wave at the side of the chair. "I know they live up in Pineville—and that's a long ways off—but you know everyone winds up in Birmingham for one reason or another. When he first moved here, he wasn't much of a farmer. Lots of dreams but not much knowledge about actual farming. Idealist. Like so many of us were in the seventies. So he joined a couple of clubs, took some classes." She waved at the plants, as if greeting old friends. "We wound up in the same gardening club. Nice man. Good man. I liked him—he was fun to talk to and really listened to me, liked my ideas. We'd have coffee. Talk. Dream. He wanted to do so much with that farm of his. So I knew something just wasn't right about all that. Everybody knew it wasn't right. But I mean, a body doesn't wind up in someone's barn by accident."

"So you don't mind talking about your daughter?"

Margery actually paused, her lips pursed, and for a brief second her eyes had a thousand-yard stare. It passed rapidly, and she focused on my face again. "Have you ever lost anyone close to you?"

I nodded.

"Something bizarre happens afterward. At least it did with me. With us. After all the initial consolations and casseroles and carousels of potted plants end, people seemed to be embarrassed by the death. By your grief. No one wants to talk about the lives that had been so precious and short." She straightened. "It's like they wanted to ignore that my beautiful Gen and Hope had ever existed. No mention of their birthdays or questions about the case. If I brought them up, people flinched and looked away. So yes, I want to talk about my daughter and granddaughter. I will tell you everything you want to know and then some."

I had no doubt about that last part. "What do you believe happened to Gen? The reports I've read indicated that her behavior had changed before her disappearance."

She shrugged. "No idea. And the good Lord knows I've run it through my brain often enough. Gen and Nicky were so happy in the beginning, so in love. Giddy, almost like schoolchildren. Nicky adored her, showered her and Hope with gifts. He didn't care that Hope wasn't his, that she was a child born of rape. He took her into his heart. But losing a child does something to you, and losing a child to violence pushes that to a whole new level. Gen became convinced Hope was alive, and she couldn't let it go. She became obsessed, and obsession of any kind is a poison."

"Why did she think Hope was alive?"

Margery fell silent a few moments, then she unfolded and stood, gesturing for me to follow her. She padded out of the sunroom in her socks, heading down yet another hallway. This one was short and took a turn to the left into a much longer passageway, where the walls were lined with family photos.

It never failed. I've yet to be in a family home of any kind—from the wealthiest society mavens to the poorest blue-collar workers—where there was not some kind of family gallery on the wall. For a long time, I didn't fully understand this, until the last memories of my father faded into smoke and vanished—he'd died when I was not quite three—and all I had left of him were the few photos my mother kept.

When we loved, we wanted to remember. Photos lasted longer and were more distinct than most memories.

Margery flicked a switch on the wall, and an entire network of track lighting illuminated the gallery. Most of the framed photos were formal portraits made in a studio. Several at the entrance to the hallway were of the four original family members: Edmund, Margery, and their two sons. As we walked down the hall, a baby appeared in Margery's arms, then the baby turned into a little girl with bright eyes and reddish-blond hair. The boys grew. Wives appeared, then grandchildren.

Then a baby appeared in Gen's arms, when she looked to be a child herself. Margery rested a hand gently on that frame. "I offered to hold Hope for her so it wouldn't be so obvious that she was far too young to have a child. She refused."

"You never considered ending the pregnancy?"

Margery shook her head. "Edmund and I discussed it. Obviously it was an option. We did not want to, but we had to bring Gen into the conversation, even at her age. We presented all the pros and cons. She took them all in with the solemnness of an old judge. She asked if she could take a few days, which surprised and dismayed us. Surprised that she would be so rational and calm at her age, but Gen was always what my mother—God rest her—called an 'old soul.' We also believed that her taking the time would mean she would want to end it. She didn't. She took us up on our offer to help her, provide the support she needed."

Margery touched her daughter's face. "She became determined to do what needed to be done. I homeschooled her for a year, then she went back and finished high school. Walked that stage to get her diploma with her peers."

"Do you know who Hope's father is?"

Margery stilled, her face a mask. "You mean who Gen's rapist was."

"Yes."

She stared up at me, her eyes narrow. "We would have told the police about that monster if we knew!"

"Not if it created more upheaval for Gen once she made her decision."

Margery turned back to the picture, stroking Gen's face again. "You do understand family, don't you? Mike said you did." She took a deep breath and straightened her shoulders. "She couldn't remember enough to identify him. And, after a while, we just wanted to focus on Gen."

She moved to a section where the pictures were less formal, a collage of random snapshots. Her hand rested on one that showed Gen pushing Hope on a swing, both of them caught mid-laugh, hair flying. Hope appeared to be a gregarious, lively child with dark hair and skin and ice-blue eyes that glowed, even in the photo.

"She's lovely," I murmured.

"Indeed."

"Unusual coloring, with those eyes."

"And that, Star, is why Gen became obsessed." Margery faced me. "When Hope was kidnapped, it was from here, down near the lake. Everyone just knew she had drowned, but the searchers never found a body. Eventually they stopped looking, and Gen and Nicky tried to deal with Hope's presumed death. They married, built a life."

She sniffed, glanced back at the picture, then started back down the hallway toward the sunroom. I followed, waiting. As much as she wanted to tell me about Gen and Hope, this couldn't be easy for her. Margery retook her seat and retucked her feet, her eyes holding that thousand-yard stare a few more moments.

She finally took a deep breath and swallowed hard. "A lot of the local communities around here celebrate the Fourth of July on some day other than the Fourth, so as not to compete with the big show at Vulcan Park in Birmingham. Some of them are almost as big. Nicky had to be out of town—he regularly visits all the properties his company owns. Gen went to one of those celebrations in Pine County. And she saw Hope there."

I stared at her. "She was positive?"

A nod. "Swore on her life. Same coloring, with those eyes. A little girl on one of the midway rides that was part of the celebration. The Ferris wheel. But by the time she got to the ride, the girl was gone. Gen turned that fair inside out—even badgered the ride operator until he called security. But there was no sign of a little dark-haired girl with those bright-blue eyes. The security guards claimed she was insane. The police tried to take her seriously, but how could they? How often do grieving mothers see their dead child in a crowd? It's not an uncommon experience. Eventually, one of the Pineville officers told me she was hallucinating."

"And no surveillance cameras the way they have today."

"No. But Gen would not let it go. She said she watched the ride four more times, not believing it herself. She was not hallucinating. After that, she prowled playgrounds, schools, day care centers, all over Pine County. The cops got to know her by name because there were so many complaints filed about her. She called morgues looking for Jane Does, pestered the local hospitals and clinics for information about a little girl like Hope—of course, they would not tell her anything."

Margery looked down at her hands. "Nicky came to talk to Eddie and me about having her committed to a psychiatric facility. He could afford a private clinic where she could get help. We agreed the time had come, and he planned to talk with her that weekend."

"But she vanished."

Margery nodded and plucked at the hem of her shorts. "So of course the authorities declared she'd either fled or Nicky had killed her. That's the approach they took."

"But . . ."

Margery sat a little straighter. "They ignored everything Nicky told them. Even in the nineties it seemed to matter less that he was wealthy and she was grieving than . . ." She looked away again, her mouth a thin line.

Ah. "Than that he was black."

Her eyes snapped back to me. "Of course! Don't you know? All black men are villains. They all kill their wives." She ground her teeth so hard I could hear them across the room, and her fury seethed. "I hope all those racist fools rot in hell."

"What did Nicky tell them?"

She sniffed again and wiped tears—frustration, anger, grief—away from her face. "You talk to him. Genevieve kept meticulous records, which he only found after her disappearance. She wasn't crazy. She was right."

I stared at her. "Margery, what are you saying?"

"She had found Hope. And she had proof. And that's what got her killed. It had nothing to do with the Turneys and everything to do with who took Hope. And till the day I die, I will believe that girl is alive." She pointed at me. "You find Hope, and you'll find out who killed my daughter."

CHAPTER FIVE

Monday, September 11, 1995
Highlands School
Mountain Brook, Alabama

"HE'S NUTS, MOTHER. Crazy. Insane. Mad as a hatter. Looney tunes. Whatever you want to call it, he is not playing with a full deck. Don't make me do this. Summer is over."

But Lee's pleas had fallen short of the mark. His mother had merely patted his arm and replied, "We must stay close to family. He's all we've got."

A statement that immediately made Lee question the state of his parents' marriage. Chase might be his mother's only brother, but Lee's father was her husband. More family than Chase. But she never referred to Lee's dad when she brought up the importance of family. Whatever. Lee should be used to it by now. It didn't matter. Lee had to play out the role.

Now he sat in an office at the exclusive Highlands School, pretending to be Chase's fifteen-year-old son, a rebellious child who needed the discipline of an elite education based on six pillars of character. Chase, dressed to the nines in a slick suit that looked as if it had been custom fit and shoes Lee had only seen in his mother's fashion magazines, waxed eloquently about his impressions of the school, why it would be a good fit for his son, and if it worked out for Lee, possibly his daughter and younger son—who did not, in fact, exist.

Chase, however, had photos of said kids in his wallet, which he was all too glad to share with the school's counselor, who gave the appropriate praise to the fine-looking family.

Lee wanted to vomit. He slunk lower in his chair, which resulted in a sharp poke from his "father."

"Straighten up!" Chase hissed.

Lee pushed up a millimeter or two. *If I miss football practice for this, Coach will kill me.*

Chase looked at the counselor for sympathy. "He is an excellent student, just rebellious. He needs more structure in his life." Chase, ever the doting father, pulled a folder from the Mark Cross briefcase at his side and slid it to the counselor. "His grades are stellar, and he has done a great deal of volunteer and outreach work with our church and the local community center. He's even helped coach a Little League team. You'll see the testimonies from his coach and pastor just under his transcripts."

Lee didn't want to know how Chase had managed to produce those.

The counselor took the folder and skimmed through the documents, making generous sounds of appreciation. "Your son does seem to be an excellent candidate. Have you filled out the application yet?"

Chase shifted ever so slightly in his chair, straightening his shoulders. "I had hoped we could use the tour to convince Lee that Highlands is the perfect school for him. Then we would complete all the paperwork at home and deliver everything needed by courier tomorrow afternoon."

The counselor took a deep breath. "Of course." He stood. "Just let me tell them I'll be out of the office for a bit." He stepped out and closed the door.

Pay dirt. Lee shook his head. The tour had been the entire point of the visit. To view the campus. To take note of the buildings, their entrances and exits—the location of the playground and the primary school sections. To examine what security measures were in place to safeguard the children of some of the city's richest citizens. To see how those measures could be skirted.

Most of all, to pinpoint where Hope Marshall spent each hour of her school day.

"I'm going to be sick."

Chase's expression evolved from ingratiating to smug. "Relax, Lee-lee. Another half hour and I'll get you home to your daddy. No fear, no foul."

"Don't call me that!"

"You are Kevin Turney's son. Act like a child, be treated like one."

"I am *not* a child. And I don't understand how this helps—"

Chase gripped Lee's forearm, leaning closer, his voice a whispered hiss. "Not your place to understand *anything*. You're here to watch, learn, and play a role. You mess this up, and I'll make sure you and your mother both regret it. Got it?"

Lee winced, a twisting pain shooting up to his shoulder. "Yes, sir."

"Good. Now shut up and pay—" Chase's words broke as the counselor returned, a ring of keys clutched in one hand. "Come with me, gentlemen, and I'll show you how we build and support one of the finest educational programs in the country."

Chase stood, smiled, and smoothed imaginary wrinkles from his suit. "We are looking forward to it." He picked up the briefcase and followed the man out.

Lee lingered a half second, then loped after them, suddenly grasping why his father drank so much.

CHAPTER SIX

Present Day
St. Clair County, Alabama

I FIRST FELT the sensation of someone following me not long after I left the Marshall family compound. It can be hard to pinpoint exactly what that feeling is, that odd sensation almost every cop develops sometime in their career. Just an odd sense that something is not quite right, a prickling at the base of the skull. A first alarm that it is time to pay close attention to all surroundings, every person in the area, spots of potential ambush.

Yeah, I know it sounds like paranoia, but to be honest, that sense has saved more than one cop's life. And the few times mine didn't go on alert, I wound up getting hurt. In one case, almost dead. So I don't ignore it.

Following someone discreetly on a two-lane wooded back road, however, is not a skill many people develop. And the guy in the dark-blue Toyota definitely did not have it.

I had spotted him in the rearview when he pulled out of a field road, which struck me as odd. Traffic on field roads tends to be limited to tractors, combines, work trucks, and other farm-related vehicles. Such tracks do not tend to be kind to low-slung sedans, evidenced by how the Toyota bounced when it pulled out. He kept his distance, but after I took a couple of unexpected turns onto county roads, then backtracked over one, he clearly planned to hang in there with me.

I'd been headed for Birmingham. I had an appointment that afternoon with Nicholas Eaton and planned to hit town early and grab lunch at someplace off Highway 280, in case traffic snarled, as it often did on 280. But I didn't want to lead that car all the way to Birmingham, much less to Nicholas Eaton's office. I decided lunch somewhere sooner might be the better option. I paused at a four-way stop long enough to plug in my earbuds, and I called Mike, who picked up on the first ring.

"How did it go with Margery?"

I turned up the volume on the phone. A 1966 GMC Carryall makes a lot of background noise. "Good. Fascinating woman. She made an intriguing suggestion as well."

"Oh?"

"She said I should focus less on who killed Gen and more on finding Hope. She is convinced that Gen was murdered because she'd found Hope. Said Nicholas Eaton had the proof of that." I filled him in on all that Margery had told me.

"Hmm. So you're on your way to meet Eaton?" I had told Mike my plans for the day earlier.

"Not exactly. How do you feel about meeting me for lunch?"

An almost imperceptible beat of silence passed. "Cruiser or unmarked?"

"Cruiser would be good."

"Where?"

"Bluegrass Barbeque in Moody."

"Ah, wide open parking lot, good visibility. Where did you spot him?"

"Right after I left Margery. He bounced out of a field road like he was driving a four-wheeler."

"What *is* he driving?"

"Never got a real good look. He's keeping his distance, but I took too many turns for it to be a coincidence. Some kind of older Toyota sedan. Corolla or Sentra. Dark blue, maybe mid-nineties."

"Gotcha. I'll call Moody PD on the way, let 'em know what's up."

"Warn them I'll be flying down 411 in their direction in about ten minutes."

"Try not to run over any John Deeres."

"I'll keep an eye out."

I hung up and checked the rearview. Yep, he was still with me. His presence raised a lot of questions. The easiest to answer had to be "Why?"—after all, I had just started a new case, and I doubted Jill had kept that information close to home. This case had obsessed her for years. Finally taking a shot at it was a cause for celebration—or at least a strong sense of relief. But cold cases came with their own set of unique characters and situations.

To many people, investigating cold cases was likely a safe, even boring, way to make a living, despite the efforts of a few television shows to make them dramatic. After all, witnesses forget or die, documents get lost, and dead ends are a fact of life. Such investigations tend to require a lot of time sitting in a chair, reviewing paperwork, and talking to people who often don't want to talk.

But of the many reasons investigations go cold, the primary one is that people prefer to keep their secrets hidden. Excavating secrets can turn up some nasty details. I'd sliced open a few that resulted in attacks, gunshots, and at least one suicide.

"You should let sleeping dogs lie"—one of my grandmother's favorite sayings—had never been my inclination. I liked stirring up stuff. It kept me on my toes.

I maintained a steady speed as I turned onto US Highway 411 and headed toward Moody, a small bedroom community outside Birmingham. The blue Toyota followed.

But *how* had he gotten on my trail? No one but Mike knew I was going to visit Margery Marshall that morning, not even Jill. I did not usually inform my clients about my methods or strategies for solving a case. Just better—and safer—for everyone if they did not know. And I knew Mike would not share the information. Not only did he keep my secrets, he wasn't exactly taking the case seriously, saying I was wasting my time and Jill's money. He had even hinted I was merely humoring her.

This did not surprise me—but it didn't deter me either. Michael Luinetti was a good cop, but he was not a cold-case detective. He also had been a police chief for more than five years, a position that tended to be as much about politics as policing. In the six months since we'd met, he'd attended two citizens' groups a month, cut the ribbon on four new businesses, had regular budget meetings with the mayor and city council, tossed out a couple of baseballs at the local high school, written four grants for new equipment, and overseen three civic events, including a picnic and celebration of first responders at the local splash pad. Last week he got tagged to be the grand marshal in the Pineville Christmas Parade.

I'd also learned he did not take teasing about such events kindly. Then again, he was far less cynical than I was about life in general.

That really left only one answer to the "How?" question, and it annoyed me to the core. He had to have followed me when I left the campground this morning—and I had not spotted him. It wasn't the Marshalls who were under surveillance—it was me. Which meant he probably knew who hired me.

Great. This would require a second look at my strategies on this case, and suddenly Margery's suggestion made a lot more sense. But for now, I just wanted him off my tail.

As I passed the Ebenezer United Methodist Church—the edge of the Moody Police Department's jurisdiction—I spotted two of their black-and-white SUVs parked halfway up the church's hillside driveway. The first one pulled out behind me, hanging back a safe distance. I grinned as the second SUV waited for the Toyota to pass, then slipped in behind it.

The result didn't take long. The Toyota took an abrupt left turn onto Kerr Road, and the second SUV followed it. Interesting. So whoever he was, he knew the area. Kerr Road looped back around behind the high school, and two turns later he could be back on 411 heading north again. Back to Pineville or wherever he wanted to go. If he was skilled at all, he would not do anything to give the Moody officer a reason to stop him. Plus, he'd be back out of their jurisdiction in minutes.

Not bad. Between that—and me not spotting him earlier that morning—I realized I might not be dealing with an amateur. Also not a comforting thought.

I pulled into the parking lot of Bluegrass Barbeque, a rustic restaurant that served a hearty meat-and-three menu as well as barbeque. It sat close to the edge of the road, an indication that it had been there longer than 411 had been five lanes wide. But what had once been a small space now opened up onto the parking lot of an adjacent strip mall. Mike's cruiser already sat near the entrance, and when I put Belle in park, my phone pinged with a message alert. He already had a table on the porch and waved me in.

As I sat, he slid a silverware packet and menu to me. "I've ordered you half-and-half tea."

I shot him a teasing grin. "Thanks for remembering."

"Well, it's been so long since we've shared a meal."

"Not quite twenty-four hours. This could become a habit."

"I'm still hoping so."

"Ha. You're still hoping I'll learn to cook."

His cheeks pinked. "Hope does spring eternal." He cleared his throat. "Your blue Toyota belongs to one Zebulon Rhone. Any ideas who that is?"

"Not a clue. I take it the Moody guys ran the plate."

"Yep. Called me not long after he pulled in behind him. I need to talk to the mayor about upgrading our systems. You should see the setup in those SUVs."

"You could always write another grant." I pulled up my phone and did a quick search on Mr. Rhone. "This says Zeb owns a collision repair shop over in Trussville and has since 1973."

Mike scowled. "Not an obvious candidate for following you all over creation."

The server appeared at our table for orders, which we gave. I had to admit I had developed a weakness for meat-and-three fare. A decade ago I had been married to a lawyer who'd insisted on dining in Nashville's most elite and trendy restaurants. He wanted to see and be seen with the financial and governmental power in the city. I lost track of the "chef's choice" restaurants we frequented or how many "deconstructed" meals I ate. Then and there "farm to table" meant $200 per person—not fresh veggies out of the garden.

It wound up being the worst time of my life, and recovery from that relationship was still in the works. Unfortunately, it meant I was a little gun shy around Mike—who had done nothing to deserve it. I tried to let my guard down as much as possible. Being with Mike was easy. Letting him in was another story. But I tried.

"I knew you'd order the fried green tomatoes."

I brushed his arm with the back of my hand, which made him smile. "Anytime they're on the menu. Would Zeb loan out his cars?"

Mike's eyebrows furrowed. "Not unheard of. Some collision centers keep loaners." He closed his hand over mine. "You going to add him to your list?"

"Will head over there early tomorrow. First tomatoes, then Mr. Eaton. Busy day."

"Want me to go with you?"

I shook my head. "My shadow learned two things today. One, I am talking to the Marshalls. Two, I have allies. So does he, so he won't try anything else today—not until he has a better sense of exactly who those allies are. I'll talk to Jill tonight about who she's told."

"But you'll be on your guard."

The server set down plates of barbeque and veggies in front of us, including a dish of fried green tomatoes. I could feel my arteries hardening. I offered one of the tomatoes to Mike, but he passed.

"I'll do my best. I promise."

"Good. Because it feels like you've started churning the waters on this, and I really don't want to find you buried in Kevin Turney's barn."

My eyes narrowed at him. "Have you changed your mind about helping me with this?"

He shrugged and took a sip of his tea. "Let's just say neither of us should take anything for granted. Watch your six."

He focused on his food then, adding some hot sauce to a mound of turnip greens before handing it to me. Something nagged at him—I could see it in his eyes. But he wasn't ready to say anything yet. Mike was the thinker in our friendship. I'd wait.

"I promise," I whispered.

He glanced at me, a quick smile crossing his face. "Eat your tomatoes, Star."

I tried to ignore the affection in the command, but my eyes watered anyway. Must have been the hot sauce.

CHAPTER SEVEN

Saturday, September 23, 1995
Pineville Memorial City Park
Pineville, Alabama

HE SHOULD HAVE suspected. Should have known there was more to the story than his uncle had let on. In the past few months, Lee had finally realized that whatever was going on with this surveillance of Genevieve and Hope Marshall had a great deal more complexity to it than Chase had ever explained. And Lee's disgust deepened with every new detail he picked up.

Like now, and the moment when he saw Chase squat down and give Hope a snow cone as she left a midway ride at one of those traveling fairs that cycle through the South, setting up in parking lots and open fields in small towns. Genevieve and her mother waited patiently for the ride to end, but they were chatting animatedly to each other and didn't see the handsome dark-haired man who intercepted Hope. She took the snow cone with glee and threw her arms around Chase's neck. He had hugged her tenderly, then sent her scurrying to her mother before slipping back into the crowd and making his way back to Lee's side.

Lee's eyes narrowed. "She wasn't scared at all. She acted like she knew you."

Chase stared back across the crowd at the three Marshalls, his expression noncommittal. Backlit by the late afternoon sun, their faces had become slightly shadowed. "We've crossed paths before."

On the other side of the ride, the two older Marshalls looked down at the snow cone, alarm crossing both faces. Genevieve bent and spoke to her daughter, who pointed to the exit of the ride. Both women scanned the area frantically but focused on nothing. They had no idea what they were looking for. They certainly could not know the two men on the other side of the kettle-corn stall were paying close attention. Chase stepped farther into the shadows cast by the setting sun.

"Crossed paths. How many times?"

His uncle shrugged. "A few."

Lee racked his brain but could come up with only a few possibilities. *When would Hope have been alone? Where would her mother have felt safe enough to turn*—"The school."

"They shouldn't let the children play so close to the back fence."

"Where else?"

Chase remained silent a moment. "They leave her alone too much."

"You've been on their boat dock."

Chase cut a glance at him. "You aren't as dumb as your mother believes." He looked back at Hope. "They should never let her play so close to the water unsupervised. Dangerous."

"And you can't see the boat dock from the house. Your boat is smaller than the boathouse."

"Like I said. Dangerous."

It all fell into place. All the little suspicions, all the hints. Lee stared at him. "How long have you been grooming her?"

After a few moments of silence, Chase sniffed. "Grooming. That's an ugly word."

"How long?"

Another shrug. "A couple of years."

"You're going to take her, aren't you? Take her for her biological father. That's what he wants. That's why you've been so weird about all this surveillance."

Chase didn't move or speak. The cloying smell of the kettle corn began to nauseate Lee, but he was not going to give up now. He wanted an answer. Finally, Chase slipped on a pair of sunglasses as the western sky turned orange, the lights of the midway popping on in a synchronized pattern.

"Doesn't her father deserve to see his daughter? To spend time with her?"

"Sounds like something he should take to court."

More silence. Then, "I'm just going to do what I've been hired to do. No more, no less."

"So you were hired to take her?"

They watched as the two women gathered Hope and urged her away from the ride. Genevieve lifted the snow cone from her hand and dropped it into a trash can. Before Hope could put up a fuss, her mother pointed toward an ice-cream stand. Hope's little face lit up, and she was all giggles again.

Chase jerked to his left, took out his wallet, and bought a bag of kettle corn. He munched as he strode back toward the parking lot. Lee trotted after him, not willing to be left behind again. They got in the car, and Chase offered Lee the kettle corn. When he turned it down, his uncle chucked it out the window, scattering the remaining kernels over the ground. He started the engine and backed out of the space.

"I was not hired to take her. The goal was to find ways that her father could spend time with her without anyone knowing."

"So he can't take it to court."

Chase gave one shake of his head. "No." He yanked off the sunglasses and tossed them up on the dash.

"Why not?"

"Let's just say that would get him in more trouble than it's worth."

"But–"

"That's the end of it." Chase's mouth was set in a thin line, the muscles in his face tense and hard.

Lee gave up. There would be no further discussion, at least not tonight. But it was far from the end of it. And it was time he paid a visit to the Pineville library.

CHAPTER EIGHT

Present Day
Birmingham, Alabama

ACCORDING TO THE local business news, Nicholas George Eaton Jr. was fifty years old and had overseen his family's hospitality company for more than fifteen years. His father—still very much alive, thank you—had retired after a series of car accidents, spent time in rehab, and moved to Florida, where he golfed, played poker, and indulged in a little day trading. In other words, he was wealthy man taking advantage of his money while he was young enough to enjoy it. His son, one of the industry's youngest CEOs at the time of his takeover, had stepped into the role with aplomb, grace, and unparalleled skill.

"Regal," Mike had called him. That would have been the first of many adjectives I would have used. Standing in his office overlooking the Birmingham skyline, Nicholas Eaton reminded me of a Caesar standing in the Colosseum, proud and fierce, ready to give the ultimate thumbs-up or down. His hair, trimmed close to his scalp and high on the sides, had the first hints of gray sprinkled throughout. His face remained almost free of lines, except for a few around his eyes, and the warm, rich brown of his skin showed few imperfections—a mole above his left eyebrow, a thin scar along his right jawline. His suit had a custom fit to it, a soft silk and woolen blend that flowed over a trim body.

Eaton had invited me to his office, which sat atop a mountain south of the city. The building, recently purchased to the tune of three million dollars, was stark white on the outside with a modern and open layout on the inside. The company had not quite settled in, given the number of packing boxes along the walls and the buzz of employees outside the C-suite.

Inside those glass double doors, however, lay a meditative quiet. His office, with its wall of windows behind his desk, felt library silent. The thick carpet helped muffle sound, as did two walls of bookshelves filled with books, memorabilia, and fine art. The remaining wall held only a Cubist painting, that on closer inspection proved to be an original from the Harlem Renaissance master Aaron Douglas. Posh digs indeed.

Eaton greeted me with a gesture to sit in one of two white leather and chrome chairs in front of the desk.

"I appreciate you taking the time to speak with me, Mr. Eaton."

He sat and folded his hands in front of him. He still wore his wedding band. "Please feel free to call me Nick. I suspect we are about to discuss some rather intimate subjects. It would feel odd to remain so formal." His baritone voice held a practiced evenness.

Wow. OK. "Nick. It is an unfortunate fact that investigations such as this can feel intrusive. Nature of the beast."

"Believe me, Ms. Cavanaugh—"

"Star."

"Star. This is hardly my first rodeo. You are the third investigator on the case. While I doubt you will find anything the others did not, I pray you will."

"Let's hope your prayers are answered then."

"What do you plan to do differently? I assume you have read the files on the other investigations."

"I have. And at the suggestion of your mother-in-law, I have decided to take a slightly different tactic."

"Which will be?"

"I'm going to focus less on solving your wife's murder and more on locating her daughter."

Nick leaned back in his chair and studied me. Normally, such a perusal and silence would indicate a resistance, a reluctance to speak, but the calm nature of the man indicated the exact opposite—as if he was deciding what he wanted to say and how he wanted to say it. He was exceptionally *still*. I had met few people who could maintain such a stance for any length of time. His extraordinary focus went a long way to explaining his success as CEO. And I suspected that he and I had something in common.

A hard time letting go.

"You believe she is still alive?" The question held the first inflection in his words.

"What I believe is irrelevant. It's a strategy, and I will follow whatever path the information I have gives me."

"You follow the evidence."

I sat a little straighter. The man inspired proper posture. "More or less. In most cold cases, however, the evidence has already been gathered and examined multiple times. I tend to focus on the people, trying to find new questions to ask, new perspectives to review."

"Would it help to have new information?"

"Of course. But as you said, in a case such as this, which has been investigated twice already, new evidence is unlikely."

Another pause. Then the man reached down, opened a lower drawer on his desk, and extracted two small cardboard boxes and a brown accordion folder overfilled with paperwork. The original elastic binder had been cut away and replaced by two green silk ribbons. He placed it in front of him on the desk, one hand resting on it protectively. "Green," he said, the word a bare whisper, "was Hope's favorite color. Probably because it was also her mother's. I have never known a mother and daughter so bonded together." He fingered one of the ribbons, his gaze lingering on the folder. "When the elastic broke after so much use, Gen used these. They were Hope's hair ties." He swallowed hard and straightened shoulders that I hadn't realized could be any straighter. "This was the information Gen gathered in her search for Hope."

I stared at the folder, trying to fight a growing sense of excitement in my gut. "Did you share this with the other investigators?"

"The first ones, yes, I offered. But they assumed that Hope and her kidnapper—if there was one—had drowned. Remember that many people denied a kidnapping. They assumed we had let our little girl drown. Therefore, they deemed this information useless."

I blinked twice, then narrowed my eyes. "Are you saying that they just assumed the two cases were unrelated?"

He gave a quick, short nod. "Gen had become somewhat . . . unstable . . . during those last few weeks."

"After she spotted Hope at that fair."

"Yes. What had been an obsession turned maniacal. She had been left with PTSD after the original attack but had dealt with that in therapy. But the nightmares returned. The startle reflex. Gen rarely slept, and she began seeing a man in her dreams. She described him as a monster. I finally spoke with her parents about committing her for a short time to a psychiatric hospital, to help her deal with the return of the PTSD symptoms. This, of course, threw the first suspicions back on me."

"Understandable, I'm afraid. With the death of a wife, the husband is always the primary suspect until ruled out. Statistics bear this out as the correct path all too frequently."

"Which is why I am grateful I had an impeccable alibi for the day Gen went missing. I was in another city with about two hundred witnesses." He toyed with the ribbon again. "Then they received an anonymous tip that her family was involved. That her brothers had issues with our marriage because of cultural differences."

Cultural differences. "An interesting euphemism."

A wry smile crossed his face, then flitted away.

"Did, in fact, her brothers have a problem with you being black?"

Nick shook his head. "Jack and Owen were never going to be my biggest fans. They were older, very protective of their little sister, for good reason. Any man would have had a problem fitting in. It took a long time for their suspicions of me to ease, but they did. By the time we married, they were fully supportive of our relationship."

"Could the tip have come from someone with old information about the family?"

Nick hesitated. "Perhaps. It did feel odd that it happened only after my conversations with the Marshalls."

One of my little orange flags popped up in the back of my head. "Did you tell them about the dreams?"

Another hesitation, then a tilt of the head, as if he was considering my words. His response came slowly. "As a matter of fact, yes. Also, they had been reluctant to hospitalize her until I mentioned them."

That orange flag turned red. "Did they know her attacker?"

Nick shook his head. "I cannot imagine they did. Why would they withhold such a thing?"

I knew at least a half dozen reasons why but decided now was not the time to cast those aspersions. Not yet, anyway.

He placed his hand lightly on the folder, his gaze lingering on the ribbons. "Both the Marshalls and the detectives dismissed this as the ravings of a mother crippled by grief and denial. They never looked at it. When I realized the second investigator was going to traverse the same territory, I never even offered it to him." He looked up at me. "Do you want it?"

I sat forward. "Absolutely. And I promise I will take good care of it."

"It is precious to me." He hesitated. "Those last months. I could feel her slipping away, and nothing I did, nothing I tried, no support I offered, made a difference. I obviously have pictures and other items from earlier in our relationship. But this is all I have of those last days. I hope it will give you a better picture of my wife."

He slid the folder across the desk, and I accepted it, pulling it closer. "I realize you were only married a short time, but you knew Gen well, did you not?"

Nick nodded. "Yes. Better than anyone. We tried hard not to keep secrets from each other."

"Was the man in her dreams her attacker? That she remembered who it was?"

The question, which should have caught him off guard, barely raised an eyebrow. "What would that have to do with Hope's disappearance?"

I wasn't buying it. He knew as well as I did what the connection would be. "Nick."

He glanced at the folder again. "After—" He stopped, swallowed hard, then pushed back from his desk. "Would you like a water?" He walked to the closest bookcase and pulled on one of the lower panels. A drawer opened, a light went on, and a condensation fog lifted into the room. He pulled out a small bottle of water and offered it to me. I took it, and he withdrew another one. Cracking open the top, he took a sip, then sat in the other white and chrome chair in front of the desk.

"After the dreams started, Gen began making sketches"—he nodded at the folder—"but could never make them clear enough for any recognition. It haunted her."

I bet it did.

He took another sip of water. "My wife needed help. It will always be a great regret in my life that I did not take action sooner. She kept insisting she could resolve this on her own. I wanted to believe her. And I lost her." He fell silent then, his eyes on some distant place.

I stood. "Thank you, Nick. I will do my best. Do you mind if I call with other questions?"

He rose as well. "Of course. I know you cannot make promises, but . . ."

I lifted the folder and held it against my chest. "I will do the best I can. And I'll keep you informed."

"Thank you."

I turned to leave and had almost reached the door when he spoke again. "Star?"

I looked around at him. "If you and I are right, if this was about Hope, then what you have in your hands is what got Gen killed. Please remember that."

"I will. And that much I *can* promise."

I wound my way back through the aisles of moving boxes to the exit and placed the folder on the passenger side, bracing it with a blanket I always keep tucked behind the seat. I'd just fastened my own seat belt when my phone rang, with Mike's number popping up on the ID. I plugged in my earbuds and answered it.

"What's up?"

"I just got a call from Trussville PD."

"Small-town cop grapevine at work?"

"More or less. Word got back to them that Moody had run the plate on one of their business owners. Slow day, so they dropped by to ask Zeb Rhone if he had any loaners out."

"And?" I slid the key into the ignition.

"Zeb is dead."

My hand froze in the process of turning the key. "What did you say?"

"Zeb's been murdered. Double tap in the center ring. Recent. Sometime after lunch. His body was still warm. The blue Toyota is on the lot. They've impounded it and are going through Zeb's inventory to see if any other cars or license plates are missing."

"So whoever returned the car probably shot him."

"Probably. No one wants to make too many assumptions at this point. Star?"

"Yeah?"

"You've met with exactly three people on this case, and already someone's been killed. You need to figure out exactly what it is you've stirred up, and fast. And you may want to warn your client to watch her back."

CHAPTER NINE

Tuesday, September 26, 1995
Edith Cutler Memorial Library
Pineville, Alabama

LEE JUMPED AS the assistant librarian peered over his shoulder again. "Are you sure I can't help you find something?"

Lee looked up from yet another "Police Beat" column in the seemingly infinite number of bound local newspapers. He wrinkled his nose, and his eyes watered. He pressed a finger below his nose to stave off an impending sneeze. Lee had been flipping through dusty volumes in the periodicals section since he had arrived after football practice.

"For instance, we have an index of all the local papers." She kept her voice at a low stage whisper, even though the library was mostly empty. Tuesday night, a half hour before they closed, meant low traffic through the stacks. "It's behind the desk. You have to ask for it, but it's open to all patrons. Or I could look up any topic and give you a list."

Lee grinned at her. "Are you bored?"

She pushed her glasses up on her nose. Unlike the head librarian—who had been a fixture here since the 1960s—the assistant had come on board a few months earlier, fresh out of college. She was cute in a nerdy sort of way, and she smelled of freshly cut flowers.

"A little," she admitted. "But you also seem really determined to find something. You've been at it all afternoon."

Lee glanced around. "I'm looking for any articles about the Marshall family."

Her eyebrows shot up. "The ones who have the big compound over on Lake Martin?"

He nodded.

"Honey, you're looking in the wrong section. I used to date one of the deputies who work that part of the Tallapoosa County. Anything that happens out there never gets detailed in the standard police columns. Hang on. I'll be right back." She trotted back toward the main desk and disappeared into the room behind it.

Lee stood up, closed the volume of newspapers, and slid it back into the vertical shelf that was its home. A few minutes passed as he wondered if he should check one more volume, but then she returned, a slip of paper and a small box in one hand.

"All the major papers have been on microfilm for years. Word around the librarian circles is that most will be on the internet within a few years, but some declare microfilm will be around a long time. More stable. The local papers are very discreet about the Marshalls. With all the advertisements they buy, they're too much of a cash cow to risk getting on their bad side. The Birmingham papers . . . not so much." She handed him the box and the paper. "Our readers are in the back corner"—she pointed—"but you'll need to be quick about it. We're getting ready to close." She gestured to the paper. "That's the locations you need. I hope it's what you're looking for."

"Thank you, um . . ."

"Clarissa." Her cheeks pinked.

"I'm Lee. So . . . are you still dating that deputy?"

The pink deepened and spread down her neck. "No. He turned out to be a bit of a jerk. A couple of guys around here have seemed interested, but they haven't—"

"Good." Lee clenched his eyes shut. "No. Sorry. I don't mean that it was good that deputy was a jerk to you—"

Clarissa giggled. "I know what you meant. And thank you."

He hefted the box, his own face growing warm. "I'll get this right back to you."

She dipped her head, then turned and headed back toward the desk. Lee watched her go, admiring her as she retreated. She *was* cute . . .

A soft tone sounded overhead, followed by an equally mellow voice. "The library will be closing in thirty minutes."

It jerked Lee into action, and he took a seat at one of the ancient microfilm machines and loaded the reel from the box onto the carousel. He winced at the grating sound the film made as it sped through the machine, a sound made even louder by the silence around him. But given the instructions Clarissa had provided, he slowed, then stopped on an August 12, 1989, article in the local news section of the Birmingham paper. He stared at it, not quite believing the report.

LOCAL GIRL KIDNAPPED

> DADEVILLE—The search continues for a 12-year-old girl abducted Saturday at approximately 3 p.m. She was last seen at the Dadeville Public Library wearing a green T-shirt, white jeans, and carrying a purple backpack. Authorities are searching for a man driving a dark gray Toyota sedan. Foul play is suspected. If anyone has information, please contact the ALEA tip line at 205-555-6400. A reward is being offered by the girl's family. S. K.

Scrawled between the margins of the newspaper columns, obviously before it had been shot for the microfilm, the words "Genevieve Marshall—follow up with bros" stood out in stark relief. Lee's eyes narrowed. Who would make such a note? It sounded like someone was making research notes. So maybe the original reporter?

He glanced at Clarissa's note again, then scrolled on to the next article. This one, dated August 14, 1989, contained a sense of relief in the words.

KIDNAP VICTIM LOCATED

> DADEVILLE—Authorities have canceled the search for a girl reported missing Saturday. The 12-year-old was found in a wooded area near Lake Martin Monday at 5 a.m. Authorities

> continue to search for a man considered a person of interest. He reportedly is in his mid-30s, with dark hair, 6 feet tall, and a burn scar on his neck. A reward for information is being offered by the girl's family. If anyone has any details, please contact ALEA tip line at 205-555-6400. S. K.

This time the scrawled words looped across the article in the next column as well. "G Marsh–raped–her descr–'monster'–bros. ready to kill. Who's hiding?"

Lee read the words over and over, his brain not wanting to accept what he–somehow, deep down–already knew. Dadeville was almost one hundred miles away from Pineville, but it was close to Lake Martin, where the Marshalls lived, and a part of the county where Chase had worked with law enforcement and still had a lot of friends. Friends who might hire him as a PI. Puzzle pieces Lee did not want to fit were finding their spots in his head.

He turned over Clarissa's note, pulled a pen out of his school backpack, and made a note of the articles' dates, then sent both pages to the printer. He rewound the microfilm and replaced it in the box. As he picked up his printouts and headed for the desk, the soft overhead voice reminded patrons that the library would close in ten minutes. He handed the box to Clarissa, who gave him a sweet smile and leaned closer to him.

"Did you find what you were looking for?"

He rested an elbow on the desk. "Maybe. Can I ask you a question?"

"Sure." The pink was back in her cheeks.

"How did you know these articles were about the Marshalls? Their names aren't mentioned."

"Oh." She blinked, then shrugged. "I don't know. They were listed in the index." She gestured to an oversized red volume on the shelf behind the desk.

"There was some handwriting on the articles, like it was there before the paper was photographed." He laid the printouts on the desk in front of her.

Clarissa nodded, standing a little straighter, turning the sheets for a better look. "Yeah, you see that sometimes. By the time a paper got around to turning back issues into microfilm, some issues were missing from their morgue."

Lee scowled. "Their morgue?"

"Yeah. Their store of all the back issues, articles, reporters' notes on famous stories, that kind of thing. If an issue is missing, they scrounge them from wherever they can."

"What about initials at the end of an article?" He pointed them out. "These both ended with the letters S. K."

"Bylines are a privilege, and a lot of the general articles, stuff that just covers local events and such, are staff written, by junior reporters and the like. Sometimes papers let them put their initials at the end for a quick reference or for the reporters' clips."

"So if I went to the paper and asked who S. K. was, someone would probably know?"

She shrugged again, dropping to a lower alto. "Maybe. Young reporters move around a lot."

"Could the reporter have made the notes?"

"Possibly. If he'd kept the copies of that edition for his clips or research."

"Thank you. Oh, and by the way . . ." Lee reached out, took her hand, and kissed the back of it. "I really appreciate your help."

Her eyes shot wide, and this time she flushed all the way to her hairline. Her voice dropped to a whisper. "You're welcome. Anytime." She pulled her hand away slowly, pressing it against her stomach.

With a grin, Lee backed away, then turned and headed out the door. He had a lot more questions and only a few answers, but he decided smart, older—and very cute—women could make hanging out at the library a lot more interesting than he'd expected.

Back in his pickup, he checked his notes and did the math again. He had first seen Hope Marshall back in May, from his uncle's boat, when the Marshalls had been celebrating her fifth birthday. That made her birth date fall in 1990. May . . . nine months from August. Lee closed his eyes a moment as a wave of nausea washed over him, then he opened the truck's glove box and pulled out a pint of Jack Daniel's. He took a swig, shuddered, then took another. He capped it and waited for his stomach to stop roiling.

He did not want to believe the facts, much less his suspicion. But now he knew that the reason Hope's father could not pursue visitation in court was because her father was Genevieve's rapist. Genevieve, who could probably identify him as such. Which was why he had hired Chase Rhone to follow the girl, to keep an eye on her and her mother, so that he could keep his distance.

Images flooded Lee's mind. All the photos they had taken, the study of the school grounds and schedule, tracking Genevieve's movements. Chase getting close to Hope, getting her to trust him. It was all part of a larger plan. Not just information gathering—they had a goal. And Lee suddenly knew, deep in his gut, what it was.

Chase Rhone planned to kidnap Hope Marshall for her biological father. Genevieve's rapist.

Lee opened the door to the truck and left the contents of his churning stomach in the parking lot. He wiped his mouth, shut the door, and reached for the whiskey again. He had some serious decisions to make. He just wasn't sure he was strong enough to make them come to pass.

CHAPTER TEN

Present Day
Birmingham, Alabama

In 1963 an army veteran and Birmingham native named Johnnie Cavanaugh bought a three-bedroom Craftsman-style bungalow in a cozy neighborhood off US Highway 11, just where it turned into First Avenue. There he and his bride raised three children, including my mother, Susan. Sometime in the late seventies, Susan began classes at Samford University, where she met Robert Spire, a navy JAG officer home on leave for the holidays. My grandmother called him "Bobby Spire, the sweet spitfire," and that was the romantic image of my father I grew up with—and idolized. An image only slightly tarnished when I finally solved his 1984 murder earlier this year.

That middle generation was all gone. Gran and I were the only ones left, so I chose her last name when I divorced, instead of Susan and Bobby's. We were always close—I lived with Gran a lot when I was growing up. The neighborhood wasn't as grand as it had been, but the house had a sound foundation, and I helped with the upkeep since my grandfather had died a decade or so ago. When anyone ever asked me where I was from, I said here. This house was as close as I came to a permanent home. I loved my Nashville cottage, but it didn't hold the memories and sense of safety this place did.

Safety being the key word as I arrived at the house after my visit with Nick Eaton. As much as I loved the Overlander I inherited from my grandfather, it was not exactly what I would consider a secure location. And I didn't want anything to happen to the precious collection that

Nick had entrusted to me. Not only was Gran's house out of the fray and away from the investigation, but she also had a fireproof safe. I planned to do my work on Eaton's papers there, take what notes I needed on my laptop, shoot all the documents with my phone, upload the photographs, and keep the originals locked up tight. When I'd called Gran to ask if I could set up shop in her dining room for a few hours, she was delighted. She also said the three magic words guaranteed to make my mouth water and my brain fog with glee: chicken and dumplings.

I couldn't have driven there fast enough.

Gran, at eighty, was like an ancient pixie. She was petite, wise, and full of sharp comebacks for anyone who mistook her for a sweet old lady. Her short silver hair lay flat against her scalp in a cut she referred to as "practical," but it shimmered in the sun as she greeted me from the door of the back porch. "Star, my darling girl!" She gave me a quick wave, then held the storm door open while I gathered my stuff from the passenger seat. "Have you married that Yankee yet?"

This has been her standard greeting for the past six months, ever since she'd met Mike, who hailed from western Pennsylvania. She adored him and obviously believed our relationship was further along than it was.

"Not yet, Gran." I shouldered my backpack, picked up the brown folder, and followed her through the back door. Our footsteps echoed in the back porch my grandfather had enclosed for me when I kept adopting all the stray cats in the neighborhood. He was allergic, but I was incorrigible, so keeping them on the back porch was our compromise. Gran always referred to my affinity for felines as one of my "unique gifts," and I couldn't deny that cats seemed drawn to me—and me to them. I didn't want to coop one up in the Overlander, but Cletis seemed to have adopted me and now spent more time under my trailer than with anyone else in the campground. Even the manager had noticed.

Gran closed the door behind us. "What's the holdup? Surely you haven't found someone else up there in that backwater swamp."

Gran was not fond of Pineville.

"Hardly. But Mike hasn't exactly asked either."

"Let me guess. You terrify him."

"Gran–"

She touched the ribbon-bedecked folder under my arm. "What's that?"

"Something I need to keep safe."

"About the new case?

"Yep."

She headed for the stove, where a giant pot of chicken and dumplings simmered, filling the house with its irresistible odor. She stirred it gently with a wooden spoon.

She waved a hand at me. "Tea's in the fridge. Sweetened the way you like it."

Which meant hardly at all. I set Nick's folder on the end of the kitchen table away from where we would eat and the backpack on a chair nearby. I opened the fridge and pulled out a glass pitcher that had to be at least sixty years old. It had been a wedding present for Gran from one of her best friends. A plastic lid from a dairy whip container rested on the top. "If I bought you a new pitcher, would you use it?"

Gran looked around at me as I added ice to two glasses. "Now why would you do that when the one I have is perfectly fine?"

I lifted the plastic lid. "Maybe one with a lid that fits."

"Stop dreaming up useless ways to spend money. What can you tell me about the case?"

I set the glasses on the table and poured the tea. "Actually, I was hoping you might be able to tell me something about it."

Gran kept stirring, checking on the tenderness of the dumplings with a fork. "Why could I help?"

"Because you've been a news junkie since Walter Cronkite was a baby."

She snickered, put down the fork, and spooned chicken and dumplings into two bowls. "I'm hardly that old."

"When did he sign off the air the last time?"

"March 6, 1981. You were exactly six weeks old, and your daddy had brought home balloons."

I pointed at her. "See?"

"Well, they say that having a good memory is a key to longevity."

"If that's the case, you'll be here after I'm gone."

Gran sniffed and brought the bowls to the table. "Don't even hint at such a thing. Now sit, so I can say grace."

I did, then she did, and we savored some of the best dumplings on God's green earth. I might have even moaned a little. Seriously, they were *that* good.

Gran paused and pointed at the folder at the end of the table. "So what do you want to pick my immortal brain about?"

"How much do you remember about Genevieve Marshall?"

Gran froze, then slowly set down her fork. "Don't tell me you've been hired to resolve that."

"Why not?"

She shook her head slowly. "That poor child. That poor family."

"Genevieve or Hope?"

"All of them." She resumed eating but chewed much slower, swallowing before her next words. "You know what happened to Genevieve when she was a child, right?"

"Yes. Some things are in the police files in Pineville, but more about the murder and the way her body was found in Pineville. Anything else would be with the Tallapoosa County sheriff or Dadeville's PD. I've talked to Margery Marshall and Nicholas Eaton." I gestured to the folder. "Nick gave me that. He said it was the documentation Gen had gathered when she tried to find Hope."

"Such a tragic situation. It occupied the evening news around here for months off and on. It was like they couldn't let it go, let that family have some peace. I was convinced they'd drive the Eatons right out of town. People were even making jokes about it, like searching their gardens for Gen's body. It was awful." She took a sip of tea, but her gaze was in the far distance. "There were a lot of people around here who desperately tried to make it his fault."

"Nick's?"

She nodded. "It had to be the husband, you see, the stepfather"—she gave a slight shrug—"or rather the stepfather-to-be. It was too horrific to consider that a monster who would do something like that was out there, randomly targeting young girls—first Genevieve, then Hope."

"But Hope was much younger than Gen when she was taken. And Mike said police at the time did not consider the two cases related."

Gran gave a scoffing laugh. "The police might not have, but the media surely did. One of them even caught Gen on camera saying she recognized the man she'd chased at the Fourth of July fair. She said it was the same man who had taken her."

I stared at her. "Say that again?" Not even Nick had gone that far.

She nodded at the folder. "I bet it's in there if she truly did. But yes, she said that. It was an offhand moment, one of those ambush interviews when she was trying to get from her car to the courthouse." Gran peered at me. "And the cops didn't say they were connected?"

"Apparently not. Not according to the files—or Nick Eaton. There was almost six years between the events, and the age difference between the two made it unlikely that it was the same perpetrator. Wackos who like five-year-olds don't usually go for pubescent girls."

"Back then the media made a big deal about the fact that Gen had lost her marbles. Grief-stricken. Hallucinating. After all, everyone was convinced that Hope was dead, probably drowned. What if the second attack was not about sex?"

"But if Gen believed that the man who took Hope was the same one who had assaulted her, why would it not—" I stared at my grandmother, who nodded, and the gears in my head finally clicked with a new theory. "You know, Margery Marshall kept insisting that Hope was not dead. That if I could find Hope, I would find Gen's killer. I didn't really know what to make of that, although it gave me a new direction to start in." I pushed my bowl away, wiped my hands on a napkin, and stood up. "Gen wasn't crazy, was she?"

Gran shook her head.

I picked up the folder and the backpack. "Mind if I set up in your dining room?"

Gran gestured toward the door. "Help yourself."

Although we had always eaten in the kitchen—as far back as I could remember—the house had a great room that held both a living and dining area. The dining room, decorated with a Queen Anne set that Gran kept polished to a high sheen, had been intended for entertaining—which my grandparents had never done. Too busy while my grandfather was still working, and on the road too much in the Overlander after he retired.

I pulled my laptop out of the backpack, opened it, and started a document for notes. Then I untied the ribbons on the folder and began removing and sorting items. It was a treasure hunt that promised great reward.

Because if Margery was right . . . and Hope was alive . . .

If Gen was right . . . and Hope had been taken by the same man who had assaulted her . . .

If my grandmother was right . . . and Genevieve was not crazy . . .

Then there was only one possible answer.

The man who had killed Genevieve and kidnapped Hope Marshall was Gen's rapist—and Hope's biological father.

CHAPTER ELEVEN

Saturday, October 7, 1995
Lake Martin, Alabama

LEE WATCHED THE small frame of Hope Marshall bounce each time Chase Rhone's boat crossed over a wave, glee lighting her face. She sat in the back, near the motor, her tiny *Little Mermaid* life jacket encasing her body in a semblance of safety. She clung to the rail, pointing and shouting at sights along the banks.

He glanced at his uncle as the man steered the boat across the choppy waters of Lake Martin, heading for the far side of the lake from the Marshall family compound. "How did you get her to come along?"

Behind his sunglasses, Chase's face appeared void of emotion. "She hates movies, Lee-lee."

"I asked you not to call me that."

"You have to earn a man's name, boy. You haven't."

Lee gritted his teeth and pushed down his anger. "What did you mean about the movies? She sure seems to like *The Little Mermaid.*"

"Because it's Disney. And a little-girl movie."

"So?"

Chase banked the boat to the left. "That family. They don't appreciate what they have. Her mother and that man are off on some kind of date. Her grandfather and his sons are playing golf. Grandmother is supposed to be watching all the kids, but she sets them up in their home theater to watch movies every Sunday afternoon. 'Sundays at the Cinema,' she calls it. Electronic babysitting while she plays at what she calls art. Slapping watercolors on a canvas and pretending she's Andrew

Wyeth or something. Hope hates the movies they choose, so I told her if she could sneak out, I'd take her for a boat ride."

"You taught a five-year-old to sneak out of the house?"

"People take kids for granted. Hope is a smart little thing. She figured out on her own how to get down to the boathouse without being seen. Very clever. Like her father."

"How do you know all this stuff?"

Chase changed the boat's direction again. "Technology, boy. It's not just for playing video games."

The realization hit Lee like a bucket of ice. "You bugged their house."

The boat slowed as Chase eased it up to a small dock, and Lee glanced around. A small cottage stood not far from the shore, but the cove was secluded, surrounded by tall southern pines, hickory trees, shorter cedars, and firs. No road led away from the cabin, but a sturdy four-wheeler sat next to it. On the dock, a golden retriever puppy stood, its tail wagging furiously.

"Puppy!" Hope screamed.

Lee scowled at his uncle. "You really went all out, didn't you?"

Chase paused and hung his sunglasses over the wheel. "Those people. Don't feel sympathy for them. They ignore her. Treat her like an outsider. And they are keeping her away from her father."

You mean her mother's rapist. But Lee didn't have the nerve to say it. Not yet. "Is he here?"

Chase hesitated and shook his head. "She's not ready yet. But soon." He turned toward the girl. "Hope! Sweetie! Help me tie off the boat and we can get you to the puppy. You get to name him." He scooped her up and set her on the dock, letting her hold the end of the rope as he looped the slack around one of the pilings. He murmured compliments and praise as they completed the task, then she turned and fled to the puppy, dropping to her knees and throwing her arms around it. The young dog responded with yips and licks, wiggling so much Lee wondered if it might sling off all its fur. Chase squatted beside Hope, stroking first her hair, then the dog's back.

"You've done this before, you devil," Lee murmured, watching the three of them. Hope suddenly squealed and threw her arms around

Chase's neck, bouncing against him. He laughed and picked her up, heading toward the cabin, the dog trailing at his heels.

"Flounder!" Hope called out, then shook her head. "No! Scuttle!" Chase said something Lee could not hear, then Hope leaned so far away from him she almost toppled out of his arms. He caught her as she giggled furiously, pointed down at the puppy. "Yes! Sebastian! You are Sebastian!"

Sebastian? What kind of name is—ah. The crab from *The Little Mermaid.* Lee sighed and climbed out of the boat, slouching as he headed to the cabin. He should stop this. He should tell someone. But who?

Who would believe him over Chase Rhone anyway? He used to be one of them. A cop. Everyone in central Alabama knew who he was. They would definitely take his side over a teenager's. And what would happen to his mother if Lee turned on his uncle? Chase had already made threats against his parents. Implied there was a great deal about Lee's mother—Chase's sister—that her husband did not know. And Lee knew all too well how much debt they were in, how precarious their whole situation in Pineville was.

Lee tried to stand straighter, but the nausea that plagued him so much these days returned, cramping his stomach with an uneasy pain.

No, he'd have to see it through. At least for now.

CHAPTER TWELVE

Present Day
Birmingham, Alabama

IN LESS THAN an hour, my attitude toward Genevieve Marshall Eaton changed from unstable murder victim to warrior queen. And by the time I got through the material her husband had given me, I felt she'd been done a great disservice by the investigators who had come before me.

Not that those detectives had not done good work. Obviously, I was a fan of the police. I'd been a cop. My best friend was one. Most of my closest friends were. I considered all of them my brothers and sisters in arms. But even the best could develop a set of blinders where both victim and perpetrator were concerned. Preset biases kicked in. Layer on the fact that at least four different agencies had been involved over the years, and the waters had become muddied. From the files I'd read before, I could tell that most of the investigators felt that Gen had been a spoiled rich girl traumatized by her earlier assault. She was seen as fragile and muddleheaded, as if the fog from the first attack had never lifted.

The information in front of me, however, told an entirely different tale. Gen had kept an in-depth and precise accounting of her searches for Hope, online and off. Where she had been and what she had observed. After a detailed record of an event, she followed with her own emotions and reactions, often admitting that her desperation might have colored her interpretation. Among her notes were photographs she had taken as well as "souvenirs": bits and pieces she had gathered, such as a ticket from that Fourth of July fair.

After more than four hours of reading, rereading, and making copious notes, I needed to brainstorm with someone else, but it was after eight in the evening. I decided to sleep on it, and I crashed in Gran's spare bedroom—which had been mine once upon a time. I'd hit it fresh the next morning. I didn't sleep right away—some of Gen's observations swirled in my head, and I knew by dawn they would have started to ferment, the pieces falling into place.

Gran loved to cook, and the next morning I was the blessed recipient of biscuits, gravy, scrambled eggs, bacon, and grits. Despite the urge to take a nap afterward, I called Mike, and he agreed to meet me at the Overlander. Turned out he had news as well, which he wanted to save for our meeting. I uploaded the photographs I'd taken to the cloud, returned all Gen's information to the folder, tied it with the green ribbons, and put it in Gran's safe. I showered and changed into the spare clothes I kept at the house. Then I gave Gran a quick hug and kiss and headed back to Pineville, unexpectedly anxious to see Mike again.

Sometimes it felt as if I were more involved with him than I let myself believe.

It was Cletis, however, who was waiting on the steps to the trailer, his bottlebrush tail letting me know he was most annoyed. I adjusted my backpack on my shoulder and stared down at him. "What?"

His response was a curled lip and a half snarl, half whine deep in his throat. He stood, pacing back and forth on the step, repeating the noise.

"You know, for a cat that's mostly feral, you are getting awfully persnickety."

He hissed.

"Yeah, I get it. Something has upset your world. You're going to have to be more specific."

Yes, as a matter a fact, I *do* talk to all cats as if they are small, somewhat mute humans. My grandfather used to swear they responded as if they understood me.

Cletis leaped off the step and went to stand beside his house. "House" being a loose term for the shelter I'd constructed for him. Since Cletis did, in fact, still behave more like a feral cat than a domesticated one, he would not set foot inside any of the campers or cabins in the campground—and woe be to anyone who tried to confine him. But wanting to give him a home base and some protection—other than the underside of my trailer—for the coming winter, I had acquired an oversized cat carrier and removed the top half. I'd weighted it with sand, then cushioned the interior with soft bedding and a heating pad, which I could control from inside the trailer. It sat near the steps, under the trailer's awning, but I'd rigged it with its own miniature awning so he could still see out even while covered. It had taken all summer and into the first days of fall, but with the cooler mornings and the warmth of the heating pad, he had finally made it his own. He'd scratched the bedding around to make a customized nest, and in one corner he'd gathered a few hickory nuts from the nearby trees. I'd thought he might be part squirrel until I found him chasing one around on the patch of pavement the trailer sat on. They were his toys.

Cats. What could I say.

Now he stood next to the house and snarled at me.

Ah. The awning had been knocked askew, drooping toward the nest, and the angle of the house had shifted. "Well, okie dokie, then. You've messed up your house."

He hissed.

I reached to straighten everything out, then paused. Cletis was a good-sized cat, but he could not have shifted the house, given how I had weighted it. And since his first foray into the base, he'd avoided touching the awning.

He had not done this.

My gaze shot to the trailer door. I had left it latched and locked. Now it was no longer latched. Almost but not quite, as if someone had pushed it closed without realizing it needed an extra bump to latch completely.

Someone had been—or still was—in my home.

I backed away and moved to the far side of the Carryall. I took my phone out of my pocket and dialed Mike's number.

"I'm almost there," he said. "Turning in now."

"Someone has been in the Overlander."

"Don't go in."

"Not on your life."

"I'll be there in seconds."

He ended the call, and I heard the rumble of his cruiser's motor at the same time. It eased slowly in behind the Carryall, and he came to my side, leaving the car running. "What's going on?"

I gestured to the door. "I always make sure it's closed firmly because it has a hitch in the lock. It's not closed now."

"Good catch."

"Cletis told me."

He glanced at the orange tabby, who now stood on the picnic table under my awning, pacing and complaining. Mike hesitated a fraction of a second, but he'd been down this road with cats and me before. "Right. If I remember, you don't have a back door."

"Nope."

"The knob may be locked. Got your keys?"

I pulled the ring out of my jeans pocket and jangled it.

"You unlock and pull it open. I'll go in first."

"Mike—"

"It's what I get paid for."

"And here I thought you got paid for cutting ribbons and posing with small children."

He grinned. "I'll be careful."

We approached the trailer, ignoring Cletis, and I tested the knob. Yep, locked. I slid the key in, turned it, unlocked the door, and jerked it open. Mike, who had waited to the right side of it, his gun drawn, took a quick look inside, front and back, then eased up the steps. Five seconds later he called, "Clear!"

It was a small trailer.

From the front door, the entire space was visible, including most of the bedroom, which did not have a door. The only place for anyone to hide was in the bathroom or the bedroom closet.

I paused to straighten Cletis's bed, then followed Mike inside.

He holstered his gun and returned to the front. He put a finger to his lips and pointed at the shade on the lamp next to my recliner. It sat at an odd angle, and a sense of dread tightened my chest. I would never consider myself a neat freak, but living in a twenty-six-foot aluminum tube had made me tidier than my natural inclination. Mike knew this, knew I'd never let a tilted lampshade sit for more than a minute.

"Take a look around for anything missing or out of place."

A normal police instruction for a moment like this.

I went through the trailer carefully, now looking for clues I might not have spotted before. I noted at least two listening devices, one tucked under the bistro table opposite the recliner and one in the workspace I'd set up halfway to the bedroom. When I straightened the lampshade, I spotted a tiny lens, not much bigger than a house spider, tucked near the ceiling, blending in with a seam in the paneling.

Great. I'd been bugged.

After I pointed out the devices to Mike, he motioned for me to retreat outside, and we got into the cruiser.

"What do you want to do about this?"

I shrugged. "I should be furious, but oddly, I'm not. To be honest, I'm more curious."

He studied me. "You don't feel violated? I know I would."

"Mike, I've been a PI for almost a decade. It's hardly the first time I've been bugged. Usually I just rip them out and go on with business."

"Without reporting it?"

"Why bother? The cops can't—or won't—really do anything. It's a B and E, but nothing was taken. Hard to connect the devices directly with any active case. With that camera, whoever did this will know we found them. If we leave them in place, they'll know I'm not going to say anything useful . . . they won't trust the information even if I do. However, if I pull out the ones we found, the ones they will have seen us locate, and leave any others that may be there, it could be useful as this case goes along."

"If you file a report, I could use our resources to track their purchase."

I paused for a second. "Would they be that stupid, to leave such a trail?"

This time it was Mike who shrugged. "Most criminals aren't known for their smarts. The so-called 'criminal mastermind' is a myth created by comic books and bad gangster novels."

"You're awfully young to be such a cynic."

His blue eyes brightened. "You haven't seen some of the losers I've arrested. Once I found a guy hanging half through the roof of the post office. His goal was to break in and steal all the Social Security checks."

"I take it he's never heard of direct deposit?" I swallowed a laugh.

Mike shook his head, looking away into the trees that surrounded the campground. "Nope. Nor had he done the math. Pineville currently has about seven thousand residents. About ten percent are retirees, most of whom no longer get paper checks. The ones who do don't receive them at the same time. When I tried to explain this, he asked, 'What about checks to the electric company?'"

I snorted. "OK. I'll file and let you do your thing. So what's your news?"

Mike hesitated, then took a deep breath. "Unbeknownst to his employees, Zeb Rhone had installed a new security system, apparently trying to catch people breaking into the lot in order to steal catalytic converters and other parts. There are fairly new cameras all over the lot."

"It caught his killer on video?"

Mike's mouth tightened. "Yes. And no."

"Explain."

He looked forward, staring at the back of the Carryall, his words precise. "The video shows the Toyota pulling in and what appears to be a young man getting out. He went into the office and before Zeb could turn to greet him, the man pulled a gun and shot Zeb. Cold-blooded, no hesitation. Then the man turned and left, heading through the back of the lot and out a break in the fence at the back. He wore a red Pineville High School varsity jacket, a blue ball cap, and jeans."

I heard what he did not say. "The cameras never caught his face."

Mike shook his head. "Unlike the employees, this guy apparently did know the cameras were there. He kept his face turned away. He only slipped up once, giving us a pretty good profile shot."

I waited. "And?"

He looked at my face, watching for my reaction to his next words. "It looks like Ricky Turney."

My eyes widened as I processed this, my brain going numb. I opened my mouth to speak, my tongue pressed against the back of my teeth, but nothing came out. I had seen Jill only three days ago, at which point Ricky was still in jail. I had spent the next day—when Ricky was to be arraigned—reading the files and filing paperwork with Mike as well as the Tallapoosa County Sheriff's Department. I'd made appointments with Margery Marshall and Nick Eaton for yesterday. Jill had left for Chicago after Ricky was released. "So I guess Jill bailing him out wasn't a good idea after all."

Mike sat rock-still. "Not if she told him she had hired you."

I shook my head, my brain cells firing again. I pointed at the trailer. "The man Jill described would never have the wherewithal to do that. To bug my trailer. She acts as if he doesn't have the gray matter to make it out of bed in the morning."

"And you and I both know that being an alcoholic doesn't always equate to spending your life wallowing in the gutter."

True. My ex-husband, a lawyer who had been addicted to both power and alcohol, had made it work, maintaining a high-profile career while mostly intoxicated. But I shook my head again. "Jill really does make it sound like Ricky seldom leaves the house. How was he while in your jail?"

Mike narrowed his eyes. "You really think I spend time with the prisoners?"

"Ah. That's right. You're too busy cutting ribbons."

He scowled, but humor lit his eyes. "I'm never living this down, am I?"

"Nope."

He chuckled and opened the door of the cruiser. "Come with me. We'll gather a few of those devices, then head to the station to report. The lead detective on the Rhone murder is supposed to meet me in about an hour, and we're going to ride over and talk to Ricky Turney. Want to come along?"

I took his hand. "Are you kidding? Wouldn't miss it for the world. You sure the lead won't mind?"

His eyebrows arched. "And miss a chance to meet the woman who brought down the most notorious crime syndicate in Pine County history? He'll love it."

"You're wicked."

Mike leaned close to me. "Not as wicked as I could be."

"Michael."

"Yes."

"Let's pick some bugs."

"Yes, ma'am."

CHAPTER THIRTEEN

Saturday, November 11, 1995
Lake Martin, Alabama

"HAND ME THAT Allen wrench and stop acting as if you've lost your best friend."

Lee, sitting on the floor a few feet from his uncle, twisted around and plucked the wrench from the toolbox to toss it to Chase. "I'm not."

Chase caught it easily and gave Lee a quick glance. "You are. Sourpuss, you look like you've been sucking lemons. I wasn't just bringing her here to play with the puppy."

Lee looked at Sebastian, who lay sprawled in the doorway of the room, his wet fur leaving a distinctive odor in the air, part wet dog, part dead fish. Chase had thrown sticks into the lake until the pup had grown exhausted. "So you weren't just grooming her to meet and spend time with her father, were you?"

"She needs room to play. Hand me the Phillips-head."

Lee did, then pulled his knees up, wrapping his arms around his legs. Over the last two months, Chase had added two rooms to the cabin, plus a bathroom. Lee helped him on Saturdays and Sundays, although Sunday afternoons had always been spent with Hope. It had become almost routine for them to let the boat glide silently up to the Marshall boathouse, where Hope would wait for them, once again sneaking out of "Sundays at the Cinema." Two hours later they would return her the same way.

She now called Chase "Uncle" and him "Brother Lee." She ran the two words together so that it came out "brotherly," which made Chase laugh. Lee, however, still could not get his head around what was going on. Chase talked little about Hope's father these days, and his interactions with the little girl seemed above board—except for the fact that they "borrowed" her on Sunday afternoons. He never acted weird or creepy with her. In fact, he treated her with respect and affection.

Almost as if she were his own daughter.

It was a thought that stuck, one that Lee despised and tried desperately to push away. The implication was too much.

"Does your client—Hope's father—know you're putting together a bedroom for her?"

Chase set the dresser he'd been assembling up on one end in order to tighten more of the fasteners. He reached for the Allen wrench again. "He's paying for it, so yes."

Lee looked from the white Queen Anne half bed to the dresser to the narrow chest of drawers they had already assembled. "He's paying for all the *Little Mermaid* decor?"

Chase twisted one bolt until it squeaked against the wood, the muscles in his arm bulging with the effort. "Yes. Why all the questions, boy?"

Shrugging, Lee looked back toward Sebastian, who had fallen asleep. "Just curious. You act like she's going to be staying for a long time."

His uncle stilled, staring at one of the bolts in the bottom of the dresser as if it were about to leap out at his face. When he spoke again, his words carried a softness that belied their meaning. "Lee-lee, think more about your own family and less about my business. I brought you on to teach you to be a PI. Your mother does not believe you'll amount to much if I don't help you out. There's been no word concerning scholarships, despite all your time in the library, all your applications, all that time with the pretty little librarian."

Lee's chest tightened, and he found it hard to breathe.

"Your mother, bless her heart, was just that kind of disappointment to our parents. All those men before your father. The drugs. All the times our parents had to help her out of trouble. The way our father had to strong-arm your daddy to marry her. He was an outsider, ya know. Not from around here. Didn't know what he was getting into. Still doesn't know a lot about her past."

Finally gasping a bit of air, Lee blurted out, "He loves her!"

The smile on Chase's face was slight, twisted. "Of course he does. Because he doesn't know all the gory details. It would crush him if he did."

Unable to take it anymore, Lee fled, jumping over the dog as he bolted from the cabin, running into the woods. He crashed through the underbrush, the bare branches and briars tearing at him as he shoved through them, until his breath caught and the stinging cuts and slashes on his skin burned deep.

He stopped, grasping the trunk of a young tree, leaning hard against it, pressing his cheek into the bark. *He's wrong! He doesn't know us. Doesn't know what we have.* Lee pictured his father's face, the lank blond hair and rheumy blue eyes, ruddy cheeks. Lee knew his dark hair and eyes came from his mother, his height and bulk. But it wasn't unusual for a child to look more like one parent than other, right? *He's wrong!*

Lee slowly caught his breath. He'd have to go back, even if he didn't want to. The boat was the only way out of this cove.

When he finally made his way back to the cabin, Chase was loading the toolbox onto the boat.

"Feed the dog" was the only thing he said.

Lee did, then checked to make sure the cedar shavings in the dog's house were fresh and the run that tethered the retriever untangled and clear of snags. Chase came by at least once a day to feed the animal, but Sebastian was Hope's pet. No one else's.

Lee dropped down on one of the boat seats as Chase pushed away from the dock. As the engine revved and the boat picked up speed, Chase turned to Lee. "You need to get a check on your emotions, boy, or they'll be the death of you or someone you love. You hear me?"

Lee nodded.

"What?"

"Yes, sir!"

"Good."

Lee watched as the cabin faded in the distance, that feeling of being smothered returning. *Have we broken any laws?* He didn't know. Didn't know who to ask. *Does it matter? After all, who would believe me anyway?*

A niggling thought appeared in the back of his mind then, something he had almost forgotten over the past few weeks. Maybe, just maybe, there was someone who might listen.

CHAPTER FOURTEEN

Present Day
Pineville, Alabama

DETECTIVE LIEUTENANT STEPHEN Hicks peered at me with the same squint-eyed expression of a chemistry student who wasn't sure what he was looking at under the microscope.

"Not what you expected?" I asked.

Behind his desk, Mike snorted. "People who haven't met you tend to believe the press reports about our Amazonian angel. Or Miss Betsy and Miss Claudia's tales of you as a cat whisperer. Or Miss Doris's praises about your—"

"Ah. I get it." After I had helped clear a generations-old network of corruption and graft in Pineville—which had resulted in the murders of my paternal grandmother and my father over the course of almost forty years—the news media had made me out to be some sort of avenging Amazon, making a great deal out of my height and the fact that I survived two attacks on my life while taking down three of the most prominent citizens in town. While I *am* tall—just under six feet—I don't have the bulk or the upper-body strength to be an Amazon. Or the coloring. I have blue eyes and, at least currently, short blond hair.

Misses Betsy and Claudia Hall, curators of the Pineville museum, however, turned my affinity with cats into legendary tales. And Miss Doris Rankin, eighty-four years old and still waltzing around the occasional ballroom with her beloved, had become one of my staunchest supporters in town. Between the three of them, I came off sounding like a crazy cat lady who used to be Wonder Woman.

Detective Hicks, on the other hand, stood maybe five foot eight, with a boxer's build. Rich brown eyes were framed by creased skin that had seen a lot of action over the years, and a slight stubble shadowed his dark skin. This man had not been to bed in quite a while.

"I admit I expected you to be . . . bigger." He held his hands a couple feet apart.

I smiled. "I run. Strong but skinny. You been working on Rhone's murder all night?"

Hicks dropped into one of Mike's office chairs. "How could you tell?"

"You have that cool TV cop stubble."

He rubbed a hand over his jaw. "Yeah, didn't take the time, even though I have an electric razor in my desk."

"A lot of evidence to process?"

"A ton. Zeb had a lot of side action besides the repair work going on, some of it illegal. We're still sorting through it. Took us four hours just to go through the video from the surveillance cameras. My wife is starting to wonder if I've left her again."

I sat in the other plastic chair. "And the guy caught on screen is Ricky Turney?"

Hicks shrugged. "Actually, that was Mike's idea."

I leaned back and looked at Mike, blinking. "Oh really?"

Twin spots of pink rose over Mike's cheekbones, making the bright blue of his eyes pop. He shrugged one shoulder. "Ricky is known for lumbering around town in his high school varsity jacket, even though it's way too tight on him at this point. He was probably around one fifty, one sixty in high school. Now he's close to two hundred. It has a rather distinctive tear on the left sleeve. Auburn fan, even though he didn't attend, so he often has one of their navy-blue caps on." He paused and pulled a screenshot from a folder, sliding it across the desk to me. "Steve sent me this. Who does this look like to you?"

I picked it up, but in truth I wouldn't know Ricky from a tree. I had only met the man once, several months ago. The shot had caught a burly man looking over his shoulder, so his face was in profile and partially shadowed by the cap. The right red sleeve of his jacket was clear and in focus, and there was an odd dark smear on the left, but the rest of the shot was a blur. I could barely tell that he was white. I looked up at Mike, eyebrows arched. "So you concluded this was Richard Turney based on his sleeves?"

The pink on his cheeks spread. "That, and an overall general impression. The Pineville High School changed the design on their jackets a few years after Ricky graduated, so there aren't many of *those* around." He pointed at the photo. "It's a gut hunch, Star, based on my knowledge of Ricky."

Hicks sighed. "It's a place to start. It's all we've got right now."

"Were his fingerprints at the site? Because I know y'all have him in the system."

The detective nodded. "His . . . and a hundred or so others. It's a collision repair shop that also traded in drugs and stolen goods. Zeb was a piece of work."

"So some of those hundreds were also felons."

Mike's words were developing a defensive tone. "You know how this works, Star. One elimination at a time."

"But you're starting with Ricky because the man who shot Zeb was the one following me yesterday morning."

Both men remained silent a moment, then Mike said simply, "Yes."

Great. Here I was trying to lift the "curse" that had settled on the Turney family, and all I'd done so far was add to it.

Mike, apparently, had taken to reading my mind again. This ability had been unnerving at first, but he *was* a good cop . . . and my face wasn't exactly as static as I would prefer it to be.

"Star, it's not going to add to Ricky's problems. In fact, if we can eliminate him, if he has a good alibi, then it could help."

I followed this line of reasoning, and my eyes widened. "If it's not him, then someone wants us to believe it is."

"Seven thousand people in Pineville, remember? Not many of them are forty-four-year-old men who wear their high school varsity jacket. Recently bailed out of jail. A man with nothing to lose."

I stood. "A man who, according to his sister, is usually too drunk to walk a straight line, much less do a double tap hit in the ten-ring."

Hicks rose as well. "So let's eliminate him before my wife thinks I'm gone for good."

Mike picked up his keys off the desk. "I'll drive."

I had never been to the Turney property, but I had visited more than a few failing farms over the years, especially those hidden away in the nooks and crannies of the rural South. A few miles out of Pineville, some of the last of the Appalachian foothills pressed their toes into the landscape. Steep and narrow ridges rose out of the earth, some as much as a quarter-mile high but with little access, and they were often separated by flatlands with room for a few family farms. And while cliffs extended straight up, over the eons, streams and rivers carved out hollows—"hollers"—in a few that allowed narrow roads to be built, often dead-ending at a small farm that had been hewed out of the mountainside.

Occasionally, one of the ridges would be broad and flat enough on top that an entire community of farms would take root. In the earlier part of the twentieth century, these isolated and insular communities could support churches, schools, stores, co-ops, and community gathering spots. With the improvements in roadbuilding, communication, and a county-wide education system, the isolation fell away—and so did the support of the local businesses and churches. But the farms held on. Some specialized in one crop or another—such as tomatoes or soybeans—and thrived. Others . . . not so much.

The Turney farm was clearly one of the latter. The once-white farmhouse, its paint peeling and porch sagging, was nestled into the side of one of those ridges. Streaks of rust marred the red tin roof. The outbuildings—a chicken coop, smokehouse, toolshed, and the infamous barn—were all in similar disrepair and scattered to the left and right of the house. The yard had been mostly churned to ruts of mud, but a small patch of grass clung to life near the steps, which had pulled away from the porch, leaving a gap almost a foot wide between the top one and the first board of the porch. An ancient Buick Regal sat just off the grass, next to a Ford Ranger that seemed to be more Bondo and rust than metal or fiberglass.

On that front porch, a man sat in a rocking chair, a shotgun across his lap. He rocked in a steady rhythm, watching us as the cruiser came to a halt and we stepped out, trying to avoid the mud. Mike stood near the left front wheel, while Hicks took up a similar position on the right. I stood just behind Hicks, all too aware of my status as a civilian without a gun.

In his late sixties or seventies, the man wore mud-streaked canvas work pants, a soiled white T-shirt, and heavy work boots. His hair had apparently been disrupted throughout the day by fingers plowing through it in either frustration or anger, as its spikes and snarls emphasized the scowl on the man's jowly face.

"What y'all want?"

Mike held up his hands. "We just want to talk for a few, Kevin. Can you put down the shotgun, please? I don't relish dodging another load of your buckshot."

Kevin Turney remained silent, just rocking. Then with a half grin, he twisted and leaned the shotgun against the wall of the house. "It was a lot o' fun watchin' you jump like that."

"I'll bet. Not so much fun for me." Mike's words held a wry sarcasm, which Turney seemed to take in stride.

He cackled, then pointed at Hicks and me. "Who're they? You know I don't cotton to strangers up in here."

Mike gestured to Hicks first. "This is Lieutenant Stephen Hicks. He's a detective with the Trussville PD. And this is Star Cavanaugh. She's a private investigator."

Turney's eyes narrowed at me. "You the one my daughter hired."

"Yes, sir."

"Waste o' money."

"We worked that out, Mr. Turney. She only pays for results." Plus expenses, but I didn't feel the need to add that part. Not with that shotgun within reach.

His gaze shifted abruptly to Hicks. "What's Trussville want with us?"

Mike stepped slowly toward the porch. "We'd like to talk with Ricky, if he's home."

The man's shoulders drooped. "What's he done now? Y'all only let him go day before yesterday. Surely he ain't stirred up trouble already."

"Is he home?"

"Willa!" The word was a harsh bellow. "Willa!"

A gaunt woman with unnaturally dark hair appeared in the window behind the rocking chair. "What, you old coot?"

"Tell Ricky to get down here. The law wants to have a chat."

"Already? He ain't done nothing. He's asleep."

"Now, woman."

Willa disappeared, muttering under her breath.

I was beginning to understand Jill more by the minute.

Turney waved a hand at the haphazard scattering of straight-backed chairs and rockers on the porch. "Y'all might as well have a seat. It'll be a bit, and he won't be able to stand long anyway."

I glanced at Mike, who remained expressionless. I had seen him in full cop mode before—it was eerie how still he could be. But this side of him always put me on full alert. He sensed that not all was right with circumstances. "We're fine, Kevin."

"Suit yourselves."

"Do you know where he was yesterday?"

For the first time, Turney stopped rocking. "He's a grown man. I don't keep him on a leash."

"So you don't know?"

"What I said." Turney twisted slightly in the chair, his right arm dropping down on the side closest to the shotgun.

In response, both officers widened their stances and rested their hands on their pistols. Kevin shook his head and put his hand back on the handle of the chair. "I ain't looking for war. Just want y'all to be fair with him."

Mike relaxed. Hicks did not. "We will," Mike said.

A shuffling sound from within the house was followed by the arrival of a man behind the screen door. He wore a half-open bathrobe over a vest-style T-shirt and boxer shorts. At least three days of stubble shadowed his face, and his graying dark hair stood straight up on one side while being matted to his head on the other. He leaned heavily against the doorframe and took a swig from the beer can in his right hand.

I dared not glance at Mike again, but clearly this was not the killer. That man had been clean-shaven. And sober.

"What can I do you for?" The words were barely audible, and he cleared his throat and repeated the question.

Mike answered for us. "Hello, Ricky."

"Chief."

"Can you tell me what you've been doing since you got out on bail?"

Ricky rolled one shoulder and held up the can. "Drinking."

"Just here?"

A slight shake of the head. "Started down at Dewey's." He squeezed his eyes shut. "No, wait." He shivered, an action that seemed to roll from his shoulders down to his feet. "I followed Jilly to her hotel in Gadsden to pick up some stuff she'd brought me." He opened his eyes. "Then she left for the airport. Then I went to Dewey's." Another squint. "No, I stopped at the library first. Then Dewey's." He tried to straightened, but took another pull on the beer.

This tidbit surprised me so much my silence ended abruptly. "The library?"

Ricky squinted again, this time at me. "You the one Jilly hired?"

"I am."

He saluted me with the can. "Good luck."

"Waste o' money," his father muttered.

Ricky's congenial mood shifted so suddenly that this time I did shoot a glance at Mike. The good-old-boy demeanor vanished, and Ricky snarled at the older man. "Jilly's got it. She can spend it however she sees fit. She got out of here. I can't blame her for wanting answers. If you occasionally got out of that chair and actually *did* something worthwhile, all our lives might change."

Kevin Turney was out of the rocker like a shot, screaming at his son. "And if you didn't stay drunk all the time, she sure as shootin' wouldn't have to spend it on you!"

Ricky hit the screen door with the heel of his hand. It rocketed open and slammed into the wall. He threw the beer can with unexpected strength off the side of the porch, hard enough that it hit the top of the Buick Regal and sailed toward the barn. He took two steps toward Turney, who snatched up the shotgun and pointed it at his son.

Both cops snapped their guns out of their holsters as Mike shouted at Kevin, "Turney!"

Ricky didn't stop, grabbing the barrel of the shotgun, yanking it from his father's hands, and sending it along the same trajectory as the can. He grabbed Kevin's T-shirt and pulled him up on his toes. "What did you say, old man?"

With the gun out of the picture, Mike and Hicks pointed their pistols at the sky, fingers off the triggers. "Ricky! Let him go."

Mike's commanding shout finally got through to Ricky. He released his father, shoving him backward and holding his hands wide. He turned to Mike. "It isn't loaded. It's never loaded. Not since he shot at you. I hide the shells." He pressed three fingers to the side of his head. "It's too early for this." He turned and walked to the far edge of the porch, leaned over a wobbly rail, and vomited into the yard.

Obviously a complicated man.

As Mike and Hicks holstered their weapons, I went around them and approached Ricky, ignoring the clods of mud that stuck to my shoes. I waited until he finished, wiped his mouth on his sleeve, then turned back. His eyebrows arched when he saw me.

"What?"

"Why did you stop at the library?"

Ricky gave me a half smile, then straightened and closed his robe, tying the sash securely. "Clarissa."

"Clarissa?" Mike asked. "The librarian?"

"Librarian he's been sweet on since high school." Kevin settled back into his rocker. "He just never had the nerve to put any moves on her. She married someone else."

Ricky winked at me. "She's divorced now. I was sober when I got out. So I dropped by to see her. Always try to when I'm sober."

"Which means he doesn't see her a lot," Kevin muttered.

Another wink.

"What time were you there?" I asked.

He kept his eyes on me, and the clarity in them surprised me. He was not as drunk as he seemed. "Arraignment was at nine. We got to Jilly's hotel about ten thirty or so. So I probably was at the library a little after eleven. We went to lunch."

"She will confirm this?" I asked.

He grinned. "Without a doubt."

Mike stepped beside me. "Ricky, is there any reason someone else would pretend to be you? To try to make it seem like you were somewhere else?"

The grin faded, and Ricky looked at his father, who had a sudden interest in the chicken coop on the other side of the house. "What do you mean?" Ricky asked, his voice hoarse again, his focus still on Kevin.

"Do you still have your varsity football jacket?"

Ricky finally looked at Mike and gave a slight shake of his head. "I gave it away. Gave it to a friend."

"Who?"

"I . . . I don't remember."

"Try. It's important."

Kevin returned to the conversation, his voice softer. He looked at his son, and his earlier anger had dissipated, giving way to an expression of grief and tenderness. A father's look. "If he says he don't remember, he don't. He has blackouts. He gives away a lot of stuff."

Mike took a deep breath, took in both men for a moment, then looked at Hicks, who nodded. "All right." He studied Ricky, who sagged under the observation. "You call me if you remember anything about that jacket. Yes?"

Ricky nodded. "I will."

Mike turned and walked back to the cruiser, as did Hicks. I climbed into the back seat, trying in futility to clean the mud off my shoes as I did. We rode away in silence, traversing the narrow road that had led into the Turney property. As we pulled onto the main road, I cleared my throat, and Mike glanced at me in the rearview mirror.

"What?"

"Ricky isn't what he seems. I don't think he shot Zeb Rhone, but he knows more than he's letting on."

"Without a doubt. On both counts. He's lying about the jacket."

"Agreed. On the other hand, I have a feeling Clarissa will remember all too well the last time she saw that jacket."

CHAPTER FIFTEEN

Wednesday, November 22, 1995
Birmingham, Alabama

LEE STOOD ACROSS the street, arms crossed, feeling intimidated by the six-story structure in front of him. *The Birmingham News*, the preeminent paper in the state, was housed in a red brick and white stone structure that anchored a corner in Birmingham's downtown Central City neighborhood. Even though it wasn't one of the tallest buildings downtown, it did not seem like a place where one simply walked in and started asking questions. Even the terra-cotta nameplate over the door felt forbidding. But Lee knew that was exactly what he needed to do. And he hoped to find someone to talk to about all this. Advice. Sharing without fear.

Clarissa's face came to mind. That sweet, nerdy girl had gotten under his skin. Older, yes, but he didn't care. She *liked* talking to him, when so few people did. He found himself spending more and more time in the library, with the excuse that he needed to study hard for his senior year. One more semester and he'd be out. He needed to bring up his grades. Apply for scholarships. His football coach encouraged him with that idea as well.

All of which were lies. While he had always done well, to the point that he only had to pass two classes this year, Lee didn't hold out much hope for scholarships on either his grades or his performance on the field. But it gave him an excuse to hang out with Clarissa.

But he didn't dare tell her anything about this, about his uncle and Hope Marshall. It would change Clarissa's opinion of him, without a doubt. What would she think of him? Coward? Slacker? *Criminal?*

It would put her in too much danger as well, and he couldn't bear that. Clarissa knew all the players, and if she let so much as a word slip out, it could all crash down on his family. Destroy them all. And he did not even want to contemplate what his uncle would do to them both. As Chase had reminded Lee on more than one occasion, as a former cop, he knew how to make bodies disappear so that no one ever found them.

Lee's stomach flipped, and he fought back a wave of nausea. The bottle of Jack Daniel's in his truck promised it would settle his nerves and his stomach, but not only was that another lie, he also didn't want to start this quest half in the bag.

And that was what this was. A quest, a search into foreign territory for a prize that would resolve the world's problems. And keep Hope safe.

"Let's do this."

Lee straightened his shoulders, checked the traffic, and crossed the street. Inside, warmth washed over him, pushing away the chill of the November day. The lobby was quiet, and Lee hoped there were still a few people around despite the upcoming holiday. School had let out early for Thanksgiving, so this had been the first day he could get away from Pineville without drawing the notice of his parents, his uncle, or his school. He had gotten out of school at noon, but his mother would still be at work and his father out in the fields.

The receptionist looked up from her computer in anticipation. He crossed to her and cleared his throat, pulling the article printouts from his pocket and unfolding them. He pointed to the "S. K." initials at the end of each. "Is there anyone"—his voice broke, and he tried again—"anyone here who can tell me who S. K. is?"

She looked from the articles to his face, then back again. The receptionist was an attractive woman in her mid-forties with a no-nonsense expression on her face. "Why?"

Lee blinked. That wasn't a question he had been expecting. He floundered. "Um . . ."

"Do I need to call security?"

A wash of panic went over him. "No!" He lowered his voice. "No.

Please. I just wanted to talk to someone about these articles. A friend suggested S. K. might be the person who wrote them."

She studied him. "How old are those articles?"

"Um . . . six years. August 1989."

Without looking away from him, she picked up the phone and dialed a number. After a moment, she said, "Is Chris up there?" She listened, then said, "Could he come to the lobby for a few minutes? There's someone here with a couple of questions he might be able to answer." Another beat, and she hung up the phone.

She addressed Lee again. "Someone will be down in a moment. Please wait over there." She pointed at a spot away from her, then turned back to her computer.

Lee did as he was told, trying not to fidget, trying to ignore the lure of the bottle in his glove box. After several minutes he heard the elevator ding, and an older man lumbered toward the receptionist. Without speaking, she pointed him toward Lee.

Lee straightened as the man approached. He looked like a grandfather, shoulders a bit hunched and an unruly fringe of white hair circling a mostly bare skull. His bulbous nose shone like Rudolph's, and his watery blue eyes peered at Lee with curiosity.

"Shouldn't you be in school?"

"Out early for Thanksgiving."

"And you're spending your time off coming here?"

Silently, Lee held out the articles. The man took them, reading the print, then tilting them to read the handwritten notes. His eyes widened, and he peered over the top of the papers at Lee. "These go back a-ways. The Genevieve Marshall kidnapping. Big news at the time. Lots of folks said it was a hoax until her baby was born. Even then some suspected it was family, not a stranger, especially given how they acted. So what do you want to know?"

"Do you know who S. K. is?"

The man nodded. "Scott Ketsler. Staff reporter at the time. Took on the grunt work, the assignments no one else wanted. Scott was a good one. Would tackle anything. He believed the Marshall story would be big news, but the family stonewalled, shut everyone out."

"Does he still work here?"

The man handed Lee the articles. "Nope. Got tired of handling the grunt work, I guess. He's in Colorado somewhere."

Lee's shoulders drooped.

The old man sighed. "Why is this so important?"

"I . . . I just wanted to know what he knew that wasn't in the paper."

"For a school assignment?"

"Something like that. I would need to know pretty quick." Lee folded the printouts and put them back in his pocket, unable to hide his disappointment. "It was a long shot."

After a moment's hesitation, the old man asked, "You want to become a reporter?"

Lee shrugged. "I can't afford college."

His gaze remaining on Lee, he called over his shoulder, "Ruthie, pull out an application, would ya?" To Lee he said, "Just before you graduate, put in an application. You never know what might turn up." Ruthie approached and handed the man two sheets of paper stapled together. He passed them to Lee. "In the meantime, I'll see if I can hunt down Scott. Someone around here may still have his info. How can I get in touch with you?"

"I don't have—"

The man pulled a small notebook out of his back pants pocket, then a pen from his shirt pocket. He handed them to Lee. "Never go anywhere without these, son. Never. You don't know when you might need them. Write down your phone number."

Lee did and handed the pad and pen back. The old man ripped the page with Lee's number on it, then gave him the pad. "Start with this." He shrugged. "I'd give you the pen, but it's one of my favorites. Do this long enough and you'll have favorites of your own. If you ever want to talk about being a reporter, just call here and ask for Chris Mayes." He pointed behind him. "And don't let Ruthie spook you. It's her job to weed out the crazies. She decided you were OK, or she never would have called me."

With that, the man turned and lumbered back toward the elevator. Lee shot a quick smile at Ruthie and fled out the doors, back into the cold.

CHAPTER SIXTEEN

Present Day
Pineville, Alabama

CLARISSA NEWTON, NEARING fifty, was adorable. I could imagine how cute she must have been in her twenties. Her brown hair had random streaks of gray running through it, making it look almost as if she'd had it frosted. It lay in poofy waves that ended just above her collar, and a mauve-and-purple-striped headband kept it out of her eyes. She wore jeans and a mauve cardigan over an *Avengers: Endgame* T-shirt—a modest, comfortable-looking outfit that outlined a trim and firm figure. Red-framed glasses with multicolored earpieces magnified brown eyes that took in every detail of Mike's and my appearances. We had left Detective Hicks back at the station so that he could head home for a nap while we checked out Ricky Turney's alibi.

Clarissa's voice was librarian mellow as she pushed aside a stack of books and focused on us. "Hello, Chief Luinetti. You two do not look like you are here to check out our romance section."

Mike gave her one of his sweetest smiles, which didn't annoy me at all. At all. Not at all. Not even a little bit.

"We want to ask you about Ricky Turney."

Clarissa folded her hands on the counter in front of her. "What about him?"

"Was he in here on Tuesday?"

She looked at me. "You must be Star Cavanaugh."

Mike's cheeks reddened, and I almost laughed. He had not introduced us, and Clarissa had politely called him on it.

"I am."

"Ricky mentioned that Jilly had hired you."

Jilly. As far as I knew, only one person in the world called my client that: her brother. In that moment I would be willing to bet that Clarissa knew that as well. "She did. We're hoping to finally clear this up for the Turney family."

"It would be a welcome change."

"So he was here Tuesday?" Mike asked.

Clarissa nodded but continued to look at me. "Came in about eleven, asked if the latest *Smithsonian* magazine had arrived yet."

This was, without a doubt, one of the more intriguing conversations I'd had since arriving in Pineville. Mike shifted from one foot to the other. Apparently he was feeling it too.

"Did he stay long?"

Her gaze glided from me to Mike. "He read two articles in the magazine. Then we went to lunch. Marca's."

"The one in the truck stop?"

"Ricky is a man of many facets. Not many genuine Italian restaurants in Pineville, Alabama, but Ricky knows where the best secrets are hidden. He brought me back here, and he went from here to Dewey's." She removed her glasses and gingerly scratched an itch under her eyebrow, careful not to smear her makeup. "Which means I won't see him again for a bit. Probably not until you arrest him again."

"Which articles?" I asked.

She replaced her glasses, and this time her smile was barely more than a slight curl. "One was on the human genome project. DNA. Genetics. Proof of relationships. The other, I believe, was on how the study of genealogy has disrupted families. That looking too closely into the behavior of your ancestors is not always a good thing."

"How long have you known Ricky?"

She straightened, pushing away from the counter. She picked up the stack of books she had pushed aside and put them on a cart. Without looking at us, she pursed her lips, considering her answer. "Since he was in high school. I had started working here as an assistant. He was a junior, if I remember. I was the new girl in town, and two of the boys from high school started coming in, flirting with me in that way high school boys do. Enthusiastically if not efficiently. Another couple of men from the community did the same, although they were more adept at flirting. I was flattered. Library science majors are not usually targets on college campuses, where the competition wears Greek letters around their necks. My boss at the time warned me to stay away from all of them. Said they were trouble." She paused and looked up at me, obviously avoiding Mike's gaze. "I should have listened. None of them wound up being real prizes." She focused on the books again. "I married the wrong one, and Ricky vanished after the murder. If I hadn't—"

My eyes narrowed. "Vanished? How?"

The books were still more fascinating than we were. "No idea. Just gone, right after Ms. Eaton disappeared, for like two—no, three—years. Came back after 9/11. By then everything had changed. Family, friends . . . Ricky. His parents had Jilly by then. She and my daughter were best friends in junior high. I'm sure he felt like the whole world had shifted by the time he got back." She glanced at Mike. "Any other questions?"

"When was the last time you saw him wear his high school varsity jacket?"

This one caught her off guard. She stiffened. "His what?"

Mike didn't respond. We all knew she had heard the question. After a moment, she swallowed. "Not Tuesday."

"Was it in the truck when you went with him?"

She paused a moment, then shook her head. "It hasn't really been cold enough yet for it."

Mike moved closer to the desk and slid his business card toward her. "Clarissa, this is important."

She took it, holding it by one corner. "I know. He has blackouts. He gives stuff away. He once took off his clothes in downtown Birmingham and gave them to a homeless guy. Even his shoes. Came home in a jumpsuit from the Birmingham jail. Sometimes the missing time causes trouble. Sometimes it's caused by trouble. But whatever you believe he did, he probably did not do."

"Probably?"

She looked down at the card. "He has blackouts."

Mike leaned closer, his voice low. "Call me if you think of anything I might want to know."

She gave a single nod, dropped the card in a drawer, and turned to the book cart. We were dismissed.

Back in the cruiser, I looked at Mike. "I don't know that I've *ever* had a conversation with that much subtext."

"She wants to tell us more but isn't ready to yet. Let's give her some time." He took a deep breath. "So which do you want to address first? The genealogy or Ricky's arrest record?"

"You take the arrest record. I'll take a look at the bloodlines. Let's see who hops out of the periphery."

He hesitated, then put his hand on my arm. "Family secrets are always the deadliest. But you know that."

Man, did I. The last ones I stirred up almost got me killed. "I'll be careful."

"Because not all the shotguns will be unloaded."

CHAPTER SEVENTEEN

Sunday, December 10, 1995
Lake Martin, Alabama

HOPE MARSHALL SCREAMED. Lee dropped to his knees in the boat, covering his ears, but he could still hear her terror streaming from the cabin. They were screams of fear, of grief. Infinite yells of "No!" and calls for her mother.

At just after four that afternoon, when they were preparing to take Hope home, Chase had pretended to get a phone call. Tears had flooded down his face as he told Hope that her mother, the sweet, caring Genevieve Marshall, had been killed in a car accident. She was gone.

Lee had watched as Hope tried to process what she'd heard. At five, she had no experience with death, not even that of a pet. No concept that there had been people in this world who were no longer around. Chase wound up having to repeat himself multiple times, telling her that her mother had gone to live with God up in the sky, in heaven, and would never be back.

Never. Heaven. More concepts Hope could not quite grasp. She knew what the words meant by definition—she was a clever child—but had no true understanding of the full meanings.

Who of us does? thought Lee. *Who understands "never" until it happens, and you finally get it years later?*

What Hope did understand was that she was not going back to the Marshall compound tonight. Or tomorrow. Or possibly the next day.

And the idea of not seeing her mother over the next few days terrified her. So Hope Marshall screamed. And Lee fled the cabin to take refuge in the boat, his thoughts as bitter as the booze he'd swallowed in preparation for today.

It didn't work, did it? All your careful grooming? Lee's mind filled with images from the past few months, of Chase working to get Hope used to them, to the cabin. Even convincing her that her mother and "Nicky" had allowed all these visits, that they knew Chase and Lee well, that they approved her sneaking out for these Sunday afternoon visits. That her mother knew the cabin held a room created especially for Hope, with furniture perfect for a little girl and drawers full of clothes that Hope had helped pick out from catalogs.

When the screams finally stopped, Lee uncurled from the bottom of the boat and pulled himself onto one of the benches near the back. He sat there staring out at the lake, the waves brushing lightly against the shore and the pilings until he heard footsteps on the dock. He turned, and Chase tossed him the keys to the boat. Lee caught them awkwardly. "What? Where is she?"

"In her room. She'll cry it out, then she'll be fine. Take the boat and go home. It'll hit in the next hour or so, and the state troopers and marine rescue will be all over it. If we're lucky, they'll assume she drowned and it won't go much further than that. But they may come looking in all these backwater coves. You don't need to be here."

"Is her father coming?"

Chase hesitated. "He'll be here."

"You won't–"

"I'm not going to hurt her. I'm not a perv, boy. You know better than that."

Actually I don't. "When do you want me to come back?"

"Next Sunday. We'll be fine until then. And, Lee-lee–"

Don't call me that!

"–tell your mother that I've set everything in action."

My mother? "Why?"

Chase's face reddened. "You just tell her. And no one else. About anything. Anyone else who knows about this will be in as much trouble as you, if you say a word. You got me?"

Lee nodded.

Chase turned and stalked back toward the cabin. Lee untied the boat, put the key in the ignition, and started the engine, easing the boat away from the dock using the slowest speed possible. Hope's screams echoed in his head, and Lee suspected they would echo tonight in his dreams. But before then, he needed to talk to his mother. Clearly she knew something he didn't, and it was time to clear the air.

By the time Lee returned the boat to Chase's house and drove his pickup back to his home, he had a lot of pent-up energy that needed an outlet, and his anger at whatever his mother's involvement was continued to grow by the minute. But when he arrived, the house stood empty. Of course . . . Sunday afternoon. Both his parents would be at their church, attending one committee meeting or another, or taking part in one of the church's outreach programs.

He paced, the energy bubbling over as he muttered to himself. He finally dug into his father's stash of bourbon and downed what easily could be just the first bottle of many if he found no other outlet for his escalating rage. Rage at his uncle, his family—most of all, at himself for doing nothing to stop this barreling train he was on.

Lee had just taken the second long draw on the bottle when the phone rang, double blasts from the one on the wall in the kitchen and from his parents' room upstairs. He strode into the kitchen and yanked up the receiver. "Yes!"

He heard only a long silence from the other end and was about to hang up when he heard someone clear their throat. "Um . . ."

"Yes." Lee tried to keep the frustration out of his voice. "How can I help you?"

"I was told someone at this number was trying to find me. My name is Scott Ketsler."

Lee stared at the phone, the name freezing in his thoughts. Scott Ketsler. S. K. The reporter.

In the back of his mind, Lee felt a shimmer of hope.

CHAPTER EIGHTEEN

Present Day
Pineville, Alabama

BY SUNDAY, MY work area in the Overlander looked like an explosion in a wallpaper factory.

When I was a cold-case detective for the Metro Nashville Police Department, I often took ribbing for what my partner referred to as my "visual" way of working. Every case had its share of files, of course, and with open homicides, most departments have a murder book, usually a three-ring binder with the crucial elements of the investigation. Some teams also use a murder board—normally an oversized whiteboard filled with photos, timelines, and dozens of sticky notes helping to tie everything together. These are standard, but every team develops their own method, whatever works best for them and how their brains work.

When my grandfather had bought the Overlander, the rooms had been—front to back—a dining area, kitchen, living area/second bedroom, and a master bedroom, with a tiny bathroom sandwiched between the last two. When my grandfather renovated it, he'd turned the front room into the living/dining area with a recliner, loveseat, and a small bistro table and two stools. A small flat-screen television was mounted near the ceiling facing the love seat. The middle area had become primarily storage for the innumerable souvenirs he collected from each of his and Gran's trips, along with a couch that converted into a second bed. The master bedroom had remained pretty much as it was in the original design, with some upgrades to the decor.

He'd also painted a six-foot-tall flamingo on the back side of it, in honor of his favorite bird, which has resulted in the Pineville locals referring to my home here as "the beastie." It made for a most distinctive headquarters.

Since hauling the Overlander to Pineville on a semipermanent basis, I'd pulled out some of the cabinets from the middle section and added a small desk with a computer and a printer. But since there was no room for a large whiteboard, I had invested in several rolls of white butcher paper and skeins of yarn. Long stretches of the paper took up almost three walls of the area, with the desk as a central point for all the tidbits of information. My visual way of working was to have as much of the case's information as possible surrounding me. If I wanted to mull over what happened in 1989 or 1995 over 1996 or 1999, all I had to do was turn my head.

I had downloaded the photos I'd made and added them to the notes I had already taken, printing some of them out and taping them to the butcher paper. I tried to weave what we knew so far together from the various periods with the information Genevieve had gathered, so strands of yarn linked connecting elements from each time frame. A timeline for the crimes had congealed in my head, but there was far too much information missing for my satisfaction. A number of names had also popped up in Gen's notes, but they had been out of context with the other information, so for now they were listed on a strip of paper connected to nothing else. They had always been singular, and with a number of them, I wasn't sure if they were first or last names or how to start searching any database for them. "Lee," for instance, always appeared in parentheses and with a question mark. "Scott" appeared in her later notes, sometimes with a "CO" beside it, and I lost track of the number of things that could indicate. The one that really scrambled my reasoning was "Uncle." That one appeared once in a wildly scratched sentence toward the end of her research: "She called him Uncle."

So while some things were taking shape, a lot more information remained confusing. And though I wasn't sure where to turn next, I had a suspicion about who could help me.

So on this bright autumn Sunday morning, I stood in the middle of the room, dressed in navy slacks, a rose-colored blouse, with a navy and rose scarf around my neck, looking at the information we had so far and waiting for Mike Luinetti to show up in his personal car to escort me to church. Because in a small Southern town like Pineville, there was no better place to get the scoop on past events like the oldest church in the area. And Pine Grove Baptist was it. Mike had been a member almost since arriving in Pineville five years ago. He was now a deacon and head of their security team. Miss Doris Rankin—*Miss* Doris to the locals, despite her having been married to Mr. George Rankin for more than fifty years—had drawn me into the church as well, when I'd first arrived back in the spring. Mike and I usually rode together in his Jaguar, which he'd inherited from his father. We made quite the sight, but people were used to our friendship as well as our occasional collaborations on my cases.

I wasn't exactly sure when he and I became "an item," but I'd grown to accept the fact that people saw us as a couple. Fortunately, Mike realized that I came with enough baggage to fill an eighteen-wheeler, and he had so far been content with the slow progression of our relationship.

"Ahoy, the beastie!" Mike's voice from the front door echoed through the small space, and I grimaced.

"Come aboard and bring your inside voice."

He chuckled. "Too early?"

"More like I have a case hangover."

He entered, shut the door, and wandered past the kitchen. "Fill me in?" He took in the butcher paper display. "Wow. You have been busy."

"Genealogy on the web is a wormhole. I got lost three times before I found my way out." I checked the clock on the computer. "I'll have to make a long story short, or we'll be late." I pointed to the different areas as I talked, well aware that we could be overheard on the remaining bugs—if anyone was truly listening.

"There are three major crimes involved in this puzzle, over eleven years, and there are a lot of moving parts. In August 1989 Genevieve Marshall was assaulted near Lake Martin, where her family lived, and had a child as a result. Hope, who was born in May 1990. In December 1995

Hope disappeared from the family compound and was presumed dead at first, from drowning. In July 1996 Genevieve became convinced she saw Hope at a community fair in Pineville, almost one hundred miles from where Hope was taken, and Gen spent the next two years trying to find her daughter, compiling an amazing amount of information. Then in July 1998 Genevieve disappeared. No trace. Until her body was found in the Turneys' barn a year later."

I took a breath and redirected his attention to a different section of the paper. "There were four different agencies involved over the years, including ALEA, but nothing popped. They focused on solving Gen's murder, but every lead went dead. Because the original investigators had questioned whether Gen had truly been kidnapped, her assault was a nonstarter and the family stonewalled whenever that came up. Even though Gen was killed while she was trying to find Hope, the overall assumption was that Gen just wandered onto the farm without an invitation—wrong place at the wrong time—and was shot."

Mike cleared his throat. "Which is why all the suspicion fell on the Turneys. Ricky's always been unstable. Kevin reportedly had been a nice guy, congenial, but he went downhill like a rock afterward—hard to tell what he was like before. Willa's a complete unknown to most people, even though she grew up around here."

I looked at him. "Well, not completely unknown."

His head tilted and his eyebrows arched, his curious puppy look. "Oh?"

"Genealogy is a wormhole. Never know what will turn up. Did you know she was a Rhone before she married?"

His eyes narrowed.

"Yep. As in Zebulon Rhone. Apparently, they are cousins . . . *were* cousins on her father's side."

"Which would make Ricky a cousin."

"Yep."

"And even more suspicious in Zeb's death."

"Yep. Family killing family isn't exactly unheard of."

"But he's no kin of Genevieve. And Thursday we found out that Ricky disappeared after her murder." Mike shook his head. "But he was a kid then. Barely eighteen. Why would he kill a perfect stranger? He could have left for any number of reasons. He'd graduated from high school. Maybe he took a job somewhere."

"Or maybe it was because the girl he wanted married someone else."

"Or maybe we could ask him."

I scowled at Mike. "What? Actually investigate the question? What fun is that?"

He laughed, then pointed to another section of the paper. "What is all that?"

"That, my dear Michael, is the fly in the pie. A tidbit from Gen's research that could turn this on its head."

He peered closely at one note and froze. He then straightened and turned back to me. "She saw her assailant at the same fair she spotted Hope?"

I chewed my lower lip. "Yep. In fact, she saw him more than once. And the older she got, the more clear the memories of that first attack became. She began drawing sketches of him, recalling what she could and keeping a journal about it. Smells, sounds. He'd kept her for almost forty-eight hours. Drugged for most of it, so everything was hazy. She had nightmares—at one point she even questioned her own memories, wondering if she was filling in blanks with what came out in the dreams."

"Which adds credence to the idea that she was not as obsessed or delusional as some folks declared."

"Oh, she was definitely obsessed. But not delusional, just confused. And Nick said she suffered from PTSD, which would have clouded the issues even further." I checked the clock again. "We need to go. I'll tell you more on the way."

I started toward the door, and Mike cleared his throat. "Um . . . Star?"

I looked around, and he pointed at my feet. "Shoes."

"Oh. Right."

He snorted as I padded back into the bedroom and dug a pair of navy pumps out of the closet. I wasn't a fan of high heels, but I did keep them for special occasions.

Properly shod, I walked with Mike to his white 1978 Jaguar XKE, a beauty of a car that his father had worked on for years. The elder

Luinetti had been a mechanic in Pittsburgh, and when he'd had to give up both work and driving due to his health, he'd passed the car to his youngest son. Of the seven Luinetti siblings, Mike, the baby of the family, was the only one who'd inherited his father's gift for engines.

He held the passenger door for me, and I slid in. When he started the engine, only a low rumble and a slight vibration let us know the beauty was awake and purring. He backed out, and the odd juxtaposition of having such a car in a small Southern campground crossed my mind, but it was not unlike the juxtaposition of discovering a former Pittsburgh cop as the head of a small-town police force in Alabama. Mike's journey fascinated me, but while he'd been quick on the snap to flirt with me when I'd first arrived, he'd been slow to share his background.

Admittedly, I'd been a little reluctant to open up as well. I'd arrived in Pineville with a more than substantial chip on my shoulder about the town. It was the site of my grandmother's murder in 1954 as well as my father's murder in 1984, when he had come here to investigate hers. A network of corruption that dated back to the 1920s had covered up both murders and protected the killers. The loss of her husband at such a young age—and in such a way—had devastated my mother and eventually led to her death at only sixty.

I hated this place.

But it surprised me. The people here, the families who had lived with that cesspool for so long, were the ones who had stepped up and helped clean it out, once I had brought down the officials who had reigned so formidably, creating an atmopshere laced with fear. Most of the townspeople were decent folks caught in a bad situation. Even Mike, who had been hired as police chief precisely because he was a young outsider the politicos assumed they could control, turned out to be more than he appeared.

He once told me that my arrival in town, and the discovery about why I was there, had given folks the first iota of hope they'd had in a long time. And that feeling of being trapped, even if the web was a self-made one, was something both Mike and I could relate to. I had escaped mine through divorce and a new career. Mike had left his behind in

Pittsburgh, desperate enough to even leave the remnants of his beloved family.

It made us a good team.

Now that we were away from the trailer, I brought up something we'd both avoided in my workroom. "Did you hear back from your tech guys on the bugs?"

He shook his head. "They said it would probably be Monday at the earliest. They're trying to track serial numbers, so they have to wait for some people to get back with them." Mike had just turned onto the main highway toward the church when he asked, "So what else have you ferreted out?"

"Nicholas Eaton is testing me."

"How so?"

"In Gen's notes, she references not only her assailant but a younger man she saw with him several times. Not during the original attack, but afterward. He was there when she spotted Hope the first time, but she didn't remember it until later, when she saw her assailant again. She records that she sketched both men, but those sketches were not in the material Nick gave me. He's holding some information back, to see how I progress. He told me the other investigators didn't even look at Gen's research, and he believes I might not either. That I just took it to be cooperative."

"Did he give you the files his own investigator had collected?"

I shook my head. "No. Something else I want to ask him about. Did you get a chance to look at them?"

"No. I went over our old files at Margery's request, but there was only a note in there that an independent investigation had been done, that it had turned up nothing new." He adjusted his hands on the steering wheel. "I couldn't even see a new angle from which to approach the case."

I could hear the frustration in his voice. Anytime an investigator—and Mike was a good one—reopened a file, the search for a new direction, a new angle was paramount. That was the way many cold cases were broken—just new eyes on old details. Dramatized forensics shows on television often made a big to-do about improvements in science or pathology, such as new DNA techniques, being the chisel that solved cold cases. But more often than not, it was just the determination of excellent investigators who turned the case sideways and examined it from a new perspective. Good old-fashioned police work.

"Of course not. There have been a lot of accepted elements in this case that seemed to lock it down. Your hands were tied. There is absolutely no evidence that Hope is still alive. With her presumed dead, motive for Gen's murder becomes sketchy and hard to decipher. She had irritated a lot of people with her obsession, but not enough to kill her. The husband had an airtight alibi—and no evidence exists that he hired someone. That doesn't leave much besides wrong place, wrong time. Her body had been in that barn for probably a year, and that's assuming it was put there right after she was killed. They went over the Turney house and property with a fine-tooth comb, but after a year, even blood evidence deteriorates. They found nothing. Did you know that Kevin Turney is descended from English aristocracy?"

Mike's mouth tensed, and the tip of his tongue appeared for a microsecond between his lips, something he did when he was trying hard to be patient—specifically, not to speak.

I couldn't help it. I burst out laughing. "Sorry. I guess that was a rather sudden left turn in the conversation."

"Somewhat. Although I'm gradually getting used to you doing it. Effective as an interview technique. Not so much when trying to explain something."

I wiped my eyes. "Sorry. My mind is about four steps ahead of my tongue this morning."

"Every morning, darling."

I grinned. "Kevin's mother's side of the family came over to the New World in the 1680s. Business opportunities, specifically shipping. They gradually moved down the East Coast to Charleston, then over into Atlanta. That's where his mother met his father in the 1920s. Kevin bought that chunk of farmland they're sitting on in 1970 with money from his mother's family. He had this idea of starting another commune, like The Farm in Summertown, Tennessee, but he wound up marrying Willa, who comes from a conservative farming family. They were planning on having a bunch of kids, but that didn't work out."

"And you found this all out on the internet?"

"Like I said. Research like this is a wormhole. I didn't find as much out about the Turneys and the Rhone thread vanished about four generations back. Apparently they haven't developed the same kind of interest in their ancestors as Kevin's mother's folks. I'm hoping that Miss Doris might be up for a couple of chats this week."

"Would you like for me to see if I can talk to Kevin again? Or Ricky? Without the other one around?"

I braced one hand on the dash as he turned into the churchyard. "Ricky was definitely holding something back."

He nodded. "I'll see what I can work out. You going to revisit Clarissa?"

"Yep, but I want to give her a little time to consider our questions. She's a smart lady, but I think she's avoided facing some things for a long time. And she said something about her daughter I want to follow up on."

Mike parked near the end of a row of cars and killed the engine and slid out. He opened the passenger door and took my hand, aiding my balance as I stood. There was a reason I didn't wear high heels much.

I took his arm, and as we entered the building, I realized the church had become more than a source of community information to me. I looked forward to being with these people, to worshiping with them. And I said a quick prayer that whatever I was stirring up would not put any of them in danger. But I had to go where the evidence led, no matter the cost.

CHAPTER NINETEEN

Sunday, December 10, 1995
Pineville, Alabama

LEE SLUMPED HEAVILY against the wall and slid to the floor, the bottom of the bottle hitting the linoleum with a solid thunk. "I—" He swallowed hard. "I didn't think you'd call."

The voice on the other end of the phone was a pleasant baritone. "Chris said you inquired about some D-section articles I wrote five years ago. My curiosity was aroused. Sorry I didn't call sooner. I've been up in the mountains camping."

"In December?"

Scott Ketsler chuckled. "Snow camping. Everybody asks. But it's exhilarating."

"I bet."

Another low laugh. "So which articles were you asking about?"

"Genevieve Marshall's assault." Lee cleared his throat. "Her rape." The line went silent long enough for Lee to wonder if they had been cut off. "Hello?"

This time the baritone was less pleasant, more wary. "How did you even know those were about Genevieve Marshall? Her name wasn't mentioned. Policy of the paper about minors."

Lee straightened and braced his back against the wall. "I looked at them on microfilm at the library. Before they were photographed, someone had written her name in the margin. There were some other notes there too. That she'd described her attacker as a monster, that her brothers were ready to kill. That sounds almost like they knew who he was. Did they?"

Ketsler took a deep breath and released it slowly. "That's what some speculated. That it had to be someone who knew the family. It was complicated. These small-town crimes. They're always more convoluted than people expect them to be." He paused. "Why do you want to know? Why now?"

"You know she had a kid."

"Yeah. I wanted to do a follow-up story on that, but they shut me down."

"Who?"

"The family. The cops. Even her brothers, who were dead set on revenge when it first happened. Her mother even had the county deputies escort me off the property, threatened to get a restraining order. I knew something was off, but in the long run, it didn't seem worth it. If they just wanted to get along with their lives, let them."

"So you agree. They knew who did it?"

Another pause. "Yeah, they did. That's why it all got shut down. Her description was too on point. I saw the expression on the cops' faces when I tried to push for more information."

Lee tried to wrap his mind around that. *If they knew, why wasn't the man in jail? Why would they protect—*

"Why are you asking about all this?"

Lee glanced down at the bottle. "This could get me in a world of trouble. My whole family."

"Look, man, I don't even know what your name is. Just tell me."

"Her daughter has been kidnapped."

The alarm in Ketsler's voice shot through the phone. "What did you say?"

Fear gripped Lee's chest. *Don't do this!* In his mind he could see Chase's reaction, the violence that would explode against his family . . . against his mother. He squeezed his eyes shut.

Ketsler became more demanding. "Did you really say her daughter has been kidnapped?"

Lee's throat tightened. "Yes."

"When?"

"Today. A few hours ago."

"How do you know this?"

"I . . . I can't tell you that. But I believe it's her biological father."

Ketsler made a choking noise. "The one who raped Gen."

Gen? He called her Gen? "Yeah."

"I gotta make some calls, man. I'll call you back."

This was a mistake. "No. Don't call me back. I . . . I won't be at this number. I shouldn't have done this. My family—just don't call back. Ever." Lee pushed up off the floor.

"Wait. You have to—"

Lee hung up. Beads of moisture dripped down in his eyes, and he brushed them away. He hadn't realized he was even sweating, but his shirt and hair were soaked. His chest hurt, and his stomach roiled. *This was a mistake.* Why in the world would someone halfway across the country be his confidant? A friend? *He's a reporter! What were you thinking?*

But Lee knew exactly what he'd been hoping. That he could find help. To tell someone, anyone, who might believe him. To find a way to stop this without putting his family in danger.

Apparently that was not possible. If the authorities really had known who had attacked Genevieve Marshall, if all this time they had not pursued it and had hidden the culprit, then they would not take kindly to anyone attempting to expose that.

It finally sank in that if he told anyone about what Chase had done, it would all come back on him. They would all turn on him. Chase. His family. The cops.

Lee picked up the bottle off the floor and took another long swig. He was alone. Nothing to be done. Endure. Survive. Get through it, with hopes that no one died.

Especially a girl named Hope.

Her little face came to his mind in that moment, the sweetness of her smile, the bright intelligence in her eyes. Her incredible innocence, the way she clung to Chase, worshiping him as if he had met some need she didn't realize she had.

Lee took another swig. OK. That was it then. If he couldn't stop this, couldn't prevent whatever scheme Chase had in mind for the girl, then it would become all about her. Protecting her. No matter what the cost.

It would all be about Hope.

CHAPTER TWENTY

Present Day
Pineville, Alabama

THE PINE GROVE Baptist Church had been built in an actual pine grove more than a hundred years ago, but most of the pines had given way to the parking lot and adjacent graveyard. The surviving trees, in a sense of true Southern contrariness, were giant oaks that had been around longer than the church. The massive trees shaded the church, towering over the roof and the long, concrete dinner-on-the-grounds table behind it. When the church had been rebuilt after a tornado in the sixties, one such oak had become the ceiling beams for the roof, providing one of the few touches of color inside the sanctuary. The outside was an odd pink stucco, but the interior walls were white. The church also had a sturdy basement-*cum*-tornado shelter, added during the rebuild.

Mike and I entered the church together but separated almost immediately. He went to chat with the security team and the deacons, while I headed down the center aisle to sit with Miss Doris Rankin and her "girls," a cluster of primarily retired businesswomen who still held a strong sway over anything that happened in Pineville. They also knew the best gossip. Miss Doris, at eighty-four, was one of the oldest, and the youngest of the crew had just turned sixty-four. I knew this last part because I had been invited to her birthday party, held at the Rankins' Italianate mansion just off the Pineville square.

After the events of this past spring, Miss Doris considered me an honorary member of the group, without a doubt one of the primary signs of my acceptance into Pineville society. The membership did come with the caveat that I avoid getting any more of her friends killed or arrested.

She was only partially joking. Clearing out the town's corruption had sent several of her friends to prison. Although three of them worked out plea deals and wound up with probation, some of the former prominent citizens were now missing from the landscape.

Miss Doris, unlike many of her peers, had benefited from sixty years of ballroom dancing. Her posture remained ramrod straight and her figure trim. She often flitted through the congregation as if she were about to storm the beaches at Normandy, her shock of red hair perfectly coiffed and pinned. She still wore heels and had purchased her clothes from the finest stores in Birmingham and Gadsden, although she had recently confessed to me that she had discovered the wonders of online shopping.

I just hoped her bank account was up to the pressure.

I slipped in beside her on the pew, and she immediately turned from another conversation to give me a quick side hug. "Any updates on the new case?"

I should have been surprised, but I wasn't. Miss Doris was tied into every "information network" in Pineville. "Not really, but can I talk to you later today?"

Her eyes brightened with curiosity. "Absolutely. Come by the house about three. George will be napping, and all the kids are actually back in their own homes." The Rankins' five children and increasing numbers of grandchildren had a tendency to spend long periods of time living with them. "We'll have afternoon tea and a good old chat."

Afternoon tea. That meant a light lunch for me. Sunday tea with Miss Doris was the real deal and included enough pastries, finger sandwiches, clotted cream, and jam to keep me wired for a week. "I will definitely be there."

"Anything in particular I need to be warming up the gray matter about?"

"Hope Marshall."

Her perfectly manicured eyebrows arched. "So not Genevieve?"

"Her too. But mostly Hope."

"Indeed."

The church's senior pastor, Robert Harris, a gregarious man in his late fifties who had been with the church for more than thirty years, emerged from a door at the front of the church and began greeting people and pressing palms. A shorter man than one might expect, he had a great bearing, a booming preacher voice, and almost always grabbed a man's elbow when shaking hands. He never touched the women, ever, and if posing with them for a picture at some event, he always crossed his arms or clutched his hands together near his waist. I had noticed this immediately and mentioned it to Mike, who merely mumbled, "Some lessons are harder learned than others."

The pastor greeted Miss Doris and her girls with a quick bow, then paused in front of me. "Ms. Cavanaugh, how are you this morning?"

"Doing well, sir."

He hesitated, then cleared his throat.

I tilted my head, peering at him, curiosity blooming. "Can I help you with something, Reverend Harris?"

He leaned a little closer than I expected, enough that I could tell he had used a minty mouthwash that morning. "Can you"—he cleared his throat again—"could you come by the church office tomorrow afternoon. Around one or so?"

I nodded. "I will."

"Good." He straightened and repeated the word louder. "Good! Glad to hear it." He then moved on to other members of the congregation. I watched him, then looked at Miss Doris, who stared at me, then the pastor. Then me. Despite his low tone, she had obviously heard.

"What was that all about?"

"I have no idea. I guess I'll find out tomorrow afternoon." I bent my head toward her. "So does everyone in the county know I'm looking into Genevieve Marshall's murder?"

She grinned. "Pretty much. The drugstore crowd is all abuzz with it. They can't wait to see what you turn up." The Pineville Drugstore had a soda fountain that also served a short order breakfast and lunch menu. Many of the town's movers and shakers ate there almost every day. "Most are rooting for you as much over this as in the spring." Her voice dropped to a whisper. "Some are even taking wagers about how long it'll take you to root it out."

"They do know such bets are illegal, right?"

"Yes, and no one ever bets on Alabama football either."

"Well, betting against the Tide would be a losing proposition."

One eyebrow arched. "No one would ever bet against the Tide."

I grinned. "What are my odds?"

"Currently fifteen to one."

"So they don't have a lot of faith in me."

"Well, it was forty to one last week."

Ah, community involvement. It could be a blessing or a curse to a PI. A blessing because some unexpected information could wiggle its way out of the woodwork. A curse because that information often turned out to be innuendo and gossip—not particularly reliable—and could spook the rats back into their hidey-holes.

I looked around, trying to spot Mike, and finally located him in a back corner, deep in conversation with one of the deacons, his brows furrowed in concentration. I watched as the chat ended, and Mike clapped the man on the shoulder as he walked away. Mike's gaze immediately found mine, and he mouthed, "Talk later."

"Curiouser and curiouser," cried Alice.

People wanted to talk. But the people closest to Genevieve and Hope—the ones who most needed to talk—seemed to be holding something back. And I suddenly realized that Jill could quite possibly be the only Turney who really wanted this thing solved.

Family dramas. Invariably, cold cases bring up a lot of family drama. Even when family members want a crime solved, they don't always like the buried family secrets unearthed. People start to get twitchy the deeper the case goes.

As I settled into the pew again, I whispered, "This is stirring the town up again, isn't it?"

Miss Doris opened her hymnbook, checked the service bulletin for the right hymn number, and turned to it. As she scanned down the words, she said, "You deal in toxic secrets, my dear. You shouldn't be surprised if the air turns foul."

*

Local Joe's, a barbecue restaurant just up the road from the church, was Mike's choice for lunch.

So much for eating light.

For a Northerner, Mike had certainly fallen for some of the more staple Southern "delicacies," such as fried pickles and banana pudding. At Local Joe's, however, he usually went for their brisket. I always opted for a meat-and-three plate, knowing I would have leftovers for dinner.

We didn't speak much on the short ride from the church, and I could tell from the furrow between his brows that Mike's focus was elsewhere. While I tended to brainstorm out loud—or on butcher paper—Mike was a ponderer. He took everything in, turned it over in his head a while, then presented the information only when he was ready. In the meantime, his expression was one of fierce concentration, his blue eyes narrowed and shaded, his jawline tight. He was also one of those men whose five o'clock shadow showed up by lunchtime, and the overall effect was to make his face look drawn.

Knowing he was working through something, I waited in silence. This too was a sign of our growing friendship, at least in my eyes—the fact that we didn't have to talk to be comfortable with each other. My ex-husband had been a slick chatterbox whose constant clattering indicated he was manipulating something or someone, usually me. To this day I'm wary of anyone who can't shut up long enough to take a breath.

I was appreciating Mike's silence with a touch of anticipation with what he would have to say when he turned into the narrow parking lot beside the restaurant. Mike shot me a quick glance as he cautiously edged the Jag between two pickups. "You're quiet this afternoon."

I almost laughed. I didn't, but almost. "I figured you were working something out."

He gave a single nod. "You saw me talking to the man in the back?"

"Yeah."

He glided out, came around, and opened the passenger door. I took his hand, and he helped me out of the car, just as he had at the church. Yes, I was perfectly capable of getting out of a car by myself.

But the Jag was so low-slung, and I was so unused to heels that I had, in the recent past, lost my balance and hit my head falling back into it. While Mike had always been a gentleman toward me and would probably do this anyway unless I protested, it was far more about us both avoiding a trip to the ER than polite chivalry. He was just considerate that way.

Besides, I liked it.

"He's a friend of the Rhone family."

"As in Zeb Rhone, the guy who got shot?" I released Mike's hand and took hold of his arm.

"Him. Apparently Zeb's family has asked the Trussville PD not to pursue the investigation."

I stopped and stared at him. "But it's a murder!"

Mike's mouth thinned, and he nodded.

"They can't stop this, right?"

He shook his head. "The police have no choice but to continue."

"Then why?"

He shrugged. "That's what I've been trying to work out. A victim's family are not the ones who tend to give up on a murder investigation. They're usually screaming for answers louder than anybody."

"Loud and long. In fact, the only times I've known a victim's family to shut down was when—" I narrowed my eyes as I remembered the details on those previous cases.

Mike's mouth twitched, and there was a glint in his eyes. "Yep."

"They're protecting someone. As you said, family killing family isn't unheard of. They know who shot him."

"That's Hicks's supposition. The Trussville guys are not happy with them."

"Anyone actively impeding the investigation?"

"Not so far. Just the rumblings about 'no need to work so hard on this' and 'Zeb was old, had a good life. Let's just move on.' Hicks had to warn them not to interfere."

"It's one of the family then?"

Mike resumed walking toward the entrance. "Possibly. Even Zeb's widow has suddenly gone quiet on them. Hicks went to see her yesterday, and she wouldn't even open the door. Why would you protect someone who had killed your husband?"

The hair on the back of my neck stood up, and I tugged on Mike's arm. "Maybe for the same reason that the good citizens of Pineville protected corrupt officials for more than fifty years."

He looked down at the ground. He, too, had been caught in the web that had kept people silent for all those years. When he spoke, the words were low and harsh. "Fear. That would make more sense. They aren't protecting *him*. They're protecting themselves."

"Did Zeb have children?"

He gave a single nod. "Three girls. All of them have children as well." He looked up at me. "Most of them are still small. Under ten."

"They have a monster in the family. They don't want him riled."

Mike's eyes narrowed, and he reached for my hand, squeezing my fingers. "Star–"

"I know." I knew exactly what he was thinking.

This monster had been following me all over Pine County.

"The Overlander is not safe."

I took a deep breath, but it was shakier than I had planned. "I know. But he acted against Zeb because Zeb could identify him as the driver of that car. He's probably the one who planted the devices because he wants to know what I do. He won't act against me until I'm a threat. If he does, it'll stir up a new investigation, and I doubt he wants that either. He's just keeping tabs for now. And if we can control what he knows–"

"I could lure him out later. I know the technique." Mike squeezed my hand again. "I still don't like it."

I wasn't crazy about it either, but I also didn't want to let someone else drive my investigation. "How about if I focus on the Birmingham side of the investigation for a few days. I'll stay with Gran and see if I can spend some time with Nicholas Eaton."

He nodded. "Good idea. And, Star, I hate to say this, but–"

"I'll start carrying the Glock."

"Just be careful."

I grinned. "Always."

CHAPTER TWENTY-ONE

Sunday, January 7, 1996
Lake Martin, Alabama

"TAKE THE GREEN one. You need the green one."

Lee grinned. "I do? For what?"

Hope pointed. "Remember to stay inside the lines. OK?"

"Yes, ma'am." Lee stretched out on the floor next to Hope, watching her color various scenes from *The Little Mermaid*. The pages from the Disney coloring book had been ripped out and now splayed around her like an oversized halo. She had handed him a green crayon and given him strict instructions on how to use it, which he followed carefully. Hope had become precise in her routines, even her coloring, which Chase had endorsed, saying that it gave the little girl some grounding in her new, somewhat chaotic world.

Lee had not responded to Chase. He didn't speak to Chase any more than he had to. His focus had turned to Hope, and Lee tried to be with her as much as possible over the Christmas holidays. But he had to go back to school tomorrow, and he struggled not to fret over leaving her.

They had moved her twice in the last month as the search for Hope intensified. After his phone call to Ketsler, the news exploded. The announcement of the kidnapping had hit the airwaves that night during the ten o'clock broadcast. Authorities from a half dozen agencies had descended, scouring the area, searching cabins and houses, and dragging sections of the lake. They had traced the call from Ketsler to Lee's parents' phone, but both had sworn no one had been home that afternoon. They never locked their doors, so anyone could have wandered in. They'd had a good dozen farm workers at the time. It could have been any of them. Eventually the cops gave it up as a dead end.

Apparently no one, including his parents, had considered the teenager in the house. Fine by him. Lee had been invisible most of his life anyway. Good time to make use of that.

But when he had been with his parents, Lee had seen Genevieve Marshall on television three times, begging for the return of her daughter. Her family—and Nicholas Eaton—stood huddled behind her, their anguished and tear-stained faces appealing to whatever villain had done this. With no television at any of their locations, however, Hope had no idea that her mother was still alive.

Chase had been right about that. After the initial storms of grief, Hope had seemed to accept everything her "uncle" told her. She had only spent one semester at the ritzy school and did not seem to miss it. Chase's intentions to homeschool her sounded ambitious, but Lee had not participated in the discussion. Instead, he had searched stores for games, puzzles, books, and coloring books for Hope. Anything to engage her.

And for the most part, it had worked. He had also succeeded in teaching her to call him by his first name instead of his middle name, Lee, which the rest of the world did—at least for now. It was their special secret, although it would not be for long. He could not convince Chase nor his mother to stop calling him "Lee-lee"—they seemed to get some sort of perverse glee out of it. Time to change. His first name had a more adult sound to it. Teaching Hope to use it had been the first step of many in connecting the two of them, and in breaking away from his childish past.

Lee took Hope and Sebastian on long walks along the lakeshore and let her swim in the shallows. Chase still controlled Lee's access to the little girl, but recently he had let Lee stay with her when he went into town for supplies. He had left them no means of transportation—he didn't trust Lee that much—but it was a start.

Trust was also the first step in a longer plan. A plan to get Hope back to her family without revealing that Lee was the traitor. He had to be cautious—he didn't want Chase's fury to come back on his family, which it would if this wasn't handled carefully.

So trust first, both from Chase and from Hope.

Trust, then affection. He would be Hope's best friend and Chase's devoted partner.

The endgame to get Hope back to her mother would come later.

"Purple. Take the purple one."

He glanced at Hope. "You want me to work on Flounder?"

The dark curls flew as she shook her head, laughing. "No, silly! Ursula! You need to take care of the bad guys."

Lee grinned and touched her back. "I'll do my best, darlin'."

CHAPTER TWENTY-TWO

Present Day
Pineville, Alabama

SUNDAY TEA WITH Miss Doris was a thing of beauty. It was the one time she tried to keep everything as "high and proper" as they were in her youth, when Birmingham still had debutantes and girls dressed up in skirts and heels to go to football games. At the Rankins' home, this essentially meant a small meal served in the formal dining room on fine china with linen napkins, a lace tablecloth, and a maid who circulated through the room at frequent intervals to replenish the hot water, clotted cream, and jam, along with a variety of narrow sandwiches. I felt as if I'd been transported to Regency England, which I supposed was Doris's true goal.

The conversation, however, was anything but prim and proper, and Miss Doris informed me at the outset that the maid had signed a nondisclosure agreement as part of her employment.

Welcome back to the twenty-first century.

Miss Doris poured a small bit of hot water into the teapot, then swished it around to warm it, as the maid hovered, waiting for final instructions. "Would you prefer coffee?"

"No, thank you. Tea is fine." I knew from experience that Miss Doris made tea strong enough to rival the darkest roast coffee. I suspected I would be working late tonight. "Milk, no sugar."

"No wonder you are so skinny." She nodded at the maid, who left.

I am absolutely *not* skinny, but this was less about my weight than her cook's offerings. I picked up the serving tongs and added a sandwich and two pastries to my plate as Miss Doris poured the first bit of hot water from the teapot into a small bowl, added fresh hot water to the teapot, then dropped in a round strainer full of loose-leaf tea.

"We'll let that steep for a few moments." Near her plate sat a small hourglass, which she turned upside down. As the sands flowed, she leaned back in her chair. "Now. Hope Marshall."

"According to the reports I've read, she disappeared in December 1995. At first presumed drowned, until a tip came in that she had been kidnapped."

"Oh yes, that poor child. The Marshalls were all frantic. Margery blamed herself at first, and so did a lot of other people, including Genevieve. It put a rift in the family that took a long time to overcome."

"Do you know the Marshalls?"

She fiddled with the timer. "Of course. I came out with one of Margery's older sisters. She wasn't a Marshall at the time. A Spencer. Five girls, spread out. Margery—Genevieve's mother—was what they called a change-of-life baby back then, probably indulged more because of it. The Spencers and the Marshalls lived in Birmingham, of course, but in all central Alabama, the people at our level of wealth are a small, close-knit community, especially sixty-five years ago, which is when we debuted. Very insular. All the same clubs, that kind of thing. Even in the nineties we all knew each other fairly well, although we had spread apart by then. Margery came out late, if I remember, not until she was twenty. She was a bit of a wild one. Spoiled. Quite free spirited, but everyone knew she would marry Edmund Marshall. Predetermined, more a family merger than a romance."

I watched her closely. Miss Doris tended to meet everyone's eyes directly, but her gaze wandered as she spoke, flitting from the food to the tea service to the silverware. Her accent had changed as well, from casual Southern to something a touch more posh, with rounder vowels and a lack of contractions. "Why would they blame Margery?"

Her gaze continued to wander a moment, then she stared solely at the hourglass timer, as if hurrying the tea. "She was supposed to be watching Hope. Every Sunday she hosted a movie for all the grandchildren, while Genevieve and Nicholas went out. They were still in school, clashing schedules, so that was their together time. But it was a Sunday afternoon when Hope disappeared. The Marshalls have an in-home theater, but when the lights came on that afternoon, Hope was nowhere to be found. At first, the Marshalls searched the shore, wondering if Hope had fallen into the water, which was frigid. But Hope had already had swimming lessons and was comfortable and strong in the water. They refused to admit she might have drowned. But by the time the tip came in, they had shut down their involvement and their denials piled up. The first responders still searched for her but found nothing." She paused and checked the tea, even though the sands had not emptied. "Do you know the rest of the story?"

"I do. I'm more interested in the family, but I do have what may sound like a strange question for you."

She finally stopped fidgeting and met my eyes. "What would that be?"

"Do you remember if any children were adopted around that time?"

Her eyes widened. "I am sure there were, but, Star, despite what you might believe, I do not know *everyone* in Pine County, much less the surrounding ones—" She stopped. "My word, are you saying Hope is still alive?"

"Margery certainly leans that way. And I'm keeping an open mind."

"How is that even possible? Everyone has assumed she has been dead for more than twenty-five years."

I leaned forward. "Because I believe Genevieve was obsessed but not delusional. She really did see her daughter twice, and at that July Fourth fair the child was with a family. If Hope had survived for that long, then the likelihood is that she wasn't taken by someone who planned to kill her. Whatever reason they took her may have been just as harmful mentally, emotionally, but their intentions were for her to stay alive."

Miss Doris hesitated, noticed the sands had finished, and removed the strainer from the teapot. As she poured two cups, she chewed lightly on her lower lip. She added milk to one cup and handed it to me on a saucer. "But she would be in her thirties now. Why wouldn't she just come back to her family?"

I'd spent a great deal of time pondering this. "She might not remember them. Most people don't have a lot of solid memories before the age of five. And most of the ones we do remember have been reinforced by photographs, conversations, other people's memories of similar events. Separated from those reminders, real memories change and fade . . . especially if an authority figure is reinforcing a different narrative. Other things we remember may, in fact, be dreams or stories someone told us, which become imprinted in our minds as memories. We think they happened, but they never did. Memories can be very fluid."

Miss Doris took a sip of tea, grimaced, and set the cup down on its saucer. She added a teaspoon of sugar, then stirred, staring at the cup. "I have this memory from when I was a child. An orange cat. Big, fluffy thing. I carried it around one day, all day, near Christmas. I remember our tree." She put down the spoon, still watching the tea. "It struck me as odd because Mother never let us have pets in the house. Never. Not even for a visit. But I remember it so well. Its weight, the way it purred in my arms, the feel of its fur. One day I mentioned it to my mother, and she laughed. She explained that it was a friend's stuffed animal. She and her parents had been visiting for Christmas, and when they left, they took the stuffed cat with them." She looked up. "George has always said that I wanted a cat so much I made it real."

I nodded. "I have memories like that. So while it would be traumatic, convincing a young child that memories of a previous family are just dreams might not be as hard as we'd like to believe."

"That's diabolical."

"So is kidnapping a child." I spooned a bit of clotted cream onto a pastry. "All the previous investigations into Genevieve's murder have discounted that it had anything to do with Hope's disappearance because of the belief that Hope was dead. I'm going to work a different angle—that it had *everything* to do with Hope. What if Genevieve had discovered where her daughter was? Even the suspicion she was close to finding Hope would have made Genevieve desperate. Maybe even reckless. So I'm not going to start with the murder and work it backward. I'm going to walk in Genevieve's steps as she tries to find Hope."

Miss Doris reached for the strawberry jam. "In other words, you are going to follow the same path that led to her murder."

Well, I hadn't thought of it exactly like that, but . . . "Yes."

"All right. So how can I help?"

I picked up a pastry. "Tell me everything you know about the Marshalls. And Nicholas Eaton."

The maid chose that moment to make a round, and Miss Doris looked up at her. "We're going to need more hot water." As the maid left, she picked up her cup and toasted me with it. "Prepare, dear Star. It's going to be a long afternoon."

*

I did not return to the Overlander until almost eight. Tea turned into a light supper of grilled chicken and salads, and when I left, my head swam with details. I had fourteen text messages from Mike, including one that let me know he'd done a drive-by at the Rankins' house to make sure the Carryall was still in the drive and then swung by my trailer to make sure all was sound and locked up. I sent him a quick text back to let him know I was at the trailer safely and that I would be packing up everything for the transfer to Birmingham tomorrow morning. He asked if we could meet for breakfast, and I agreed.

I turned on the heater in the trailer and sank into the recliner as it worked to break the light chill that had settled. I never left the heater running, for obvious reasons, and I'd found I enjoyed the brusqueness of the cold when I returned. It amplified the woody scent of the trailer, as well as that of the sandalwood candles I lit occasionally. After a few moments, I changed into my pajamas, took off my makeup, and went to the kitchen to make a cup of hot cocoa. I had consumed a lot of food and drink over the past twelve hours, but I needed a little something to soothe me before bed.

That was when I found the new bug.

I took a deep breath and reminded myself that Mike and I could have missed it in our original search. The culprit would have seen us discover the bugs, so we had to remove most of them. We had intentionally left two of the better-hidden ones with the goal of making our listener somewhat complacent, believing we had missed some of his devices, even as we tracked the others.

But had we overlooked one? Or was this one new? If it was, then there had been a return to the trailer . . . and a possible examination of my work area. I grimaced and straightened. As always with such things, working with the idea of a worst-case scenario made the safest course. So whoever was trying to hone in on my investigation knew where I was with information and where I wasn't. He would not have heard my discussions with Mike or Miss Doris, but he would know I had Genevieve's research and the approach I planned to take.

Which would, of course, put him on guard.

I finished making the cocoa and sat down in the recliner, staring at the ceiling. Mike had been right: the Overlander was no place to conduct this particular investigation. Right now all the intruder had gathered was information. If I made actual progress and he wanted to stop me, the Overlander was too vulnerable.

So why hadn't he already tried to stop me? Obviously he did not want to be discovered. And he had already killed once. So why the surreptitious moves but nothing more?

The obvious answer had to do with who I was. The investigation in the spring had brought national news coverage to Pineville. I had been interviewed on two major news programs, and my face had been in many of the local papers. Two national law enforcement agencies had been involved. Zebulon Rhone, on the other hand, had owned an auto collision repair shop in a community outside Birmingham. That investigation would be localized. But if anything happened to me while I was looking into a cold case that had been a high-profile case locally, all kinds of muck would go flying. It would be infinitely safer to stand back and watch until something significant broke.

In essence, I would probably be safe until I got close to a solution.

This was not as reassuring as I might have hoped.

So much for finding solace in my cocoa.

I drained the cup and stood. Tonight would not be conducive to sleep, since my illusion of safety had been tarnished beyond repair. I went to the workroom and made notes on the butcher paper about all I'd discovered today. Miss Doris's information, while not helpful in the actual investigation, began filling in the bare spots in my understanding of how the Marshall family worked.

Like a lot of supremely wealthy families, the Marshalls operated in the larger society around them with their own set of rules. They were generous to their employees and the community, so they were overall a beloved part of it. When a preteen Genevieve had disappeared, they had a small army of volunteers at their disposal. Authorities credited this blanket of volunteers for Genevieve being released so quickly by her captor. But it also meant that when the Marshalls locked out any subsequent investigation—including the press—the community supported them. What happened to Genevieve got a few vague mentions in the media, then . . . nothing.

Her brothers—Jack and Owen—who had been hot to track her abductor while she was missing, suddenly went quiet.

Something similar had happened when Hope had vanished. Lots of hullabaloo at first—dragging the lake, searching all the shore-side homes—then . . . nothing. The Marshall compound had shut down tighter than a snare drum.

Kinda like the Rhone family was doing now.

I stared at the paper in front of me, the realization hitting hard.

"They know. They all know." I squeezed my eyes shut. I had to talk to Margery. *If they know who is behind all this, why would she push me to—*

A stark yowl echoed under the trailer, matched by a high-pitched rattling screech of a raccoon. A thud hit the underside of the Overlander, and the whole thing rocked.

"Cletis!" My bellow had a snarl to it. The last thing I needed right now was to fetch that cat to the vet in the middle of the night. The closest emergency vet was an hour away. I grabbed a broom and flashlight out of the closet and was out the door in a heartbeat. The heavy odor of wood smoke hung in the air—the campground was littered with fire pits—and I sneezed as I peered under the Overlander. The yowling continued from the rear of the trailer, and I knelt in the dirt, turning the flashlight beam on that area.

A raccoon—a big boy that had to weigh twenty or thirty

pounds—hissed at me, blinking in the sudden shot of light. Shadows cast by various bits of plumbing and supports danced in the beam. He looked confused, then hissed again.

Cletis was in rare form. His arched back almost hit the bottom of the trailer, and fur stood out from every angle. His growl sounded deep in his throat, occasionally peaking into a screaming hiss.

"Cletis! Get away from him!"

The cat's hiss stopped, but his attack posture remained. He had heard me.

"I do not want to take you back to the *vet*, and you don't want to go back to the *vet*."

His tail whipped back and forth like a wind vane in a hurricane.

The raccoon hissed once more, then licked his snout and closed his mouth. His stance drooped. I turned the broom on its side and eased it between them. "Back away, cat, before you get both of us hurt."

The raccoon sank down on its haunches, apparently willing to give it up. Cletis's back relaxed, although his tail still snapped back and forth. I shoved the broom toward the raccoon, who gave a quick hiss, fled, and vanished into the dark. Cletis jumped, as if to make chase, but I swung the broom back in his direction. He backed up, swung his head at me, and hissed, distinctly unhappy I had interrupted his party.

"Oh, just be glad I didn't turn the hose on the both of you. You need more stitches like I need another—" A shuffling noise behind me got my attention, and I pulled the broom out, pushing to my feet. "Please don't tell me that raccoon circled—"

Pain exploded through my head, and I fell forward, my face hitting the side of the trailer as everything went black.

CHAPTER TWENTY-THREE

Sunday, February 11, 1996
Lake Martin, Alabama

"UNCLE WON'T LIKE it." Hope tugged on Lee's hand, urging him back toward the cabin.

Lee resisted. "Why not?" Chase had taken the boat and gone for supplies, leaving Lee to entertain Hope for the afternoon. They had explored the lakeshore, looking for signs of life near the winter-chilled waters. Sebastian had strolled along beside them, occasionally dashing into the woods after a squirrel or into the water after an imaginary fish. This time of year, the usual suspects in the lake—bass, bluegills, catfish—generally didn't hang out in the shallows except on exceptionally warm days—which this was not. But there were plenty of other flora and fauna to look for, and recent warm days had stirred a few critters out of their hibernation.

Chase had, in fact, started homeschooling Hope, including an elementary science book about animals and their habitats and basic information about plants. Lee had already flipped over a few dead logs to stir about some salamanders and a couple of toads. The little girl's curiosity seemed endless, and she'd asked him dozens of questions. They had seen chipmunks as well as squirrels, and even a turkey and a deer. An eagle had soared overhead, landing in a tree about a half mile away, and Lee had suggested a closer look.

For the first time, Hope had balked. "It's too far from home. Uncle doesn't like me to wander so far."

Yeah, I bet he doesn't. He let out a sigh. "I guess we don't want to make Uncle mad."

Hope dropped his hand and shook her head furiously. "No! He yells when he gets mad. It's scary."

Lee peered at her. "Does he get mad a lot?"

She glanced off into the tree line near the shore. "No. Not really." She paused. "Sometimes."

"What makes him mad?"

She shrugged. "Mostly when I walk too far into the woods. He says it's too dangerous. Too many big animals and nasty people." Another shrug. She crossed her arms. "He doesn't like questions."

Lee put his hand on her back. "Is that why you ask me so many?"

She relented and took his hand again. "Yes. You answer. You don't act like you're angry about them."

"I want you to learn. I'm sure he just wants to keep you safe."

"Is my mother really dead?"

Lee stopped in his tracks. No wonder Chase got angry at her questions. Lee's stomach tightened. He could repeat Chase's lie—or make Chase more enraged than a five-year-old could dream of.

"Hope, you know that when someone's dead, you never see them again, right?"

After a pause, she nodded. "That's what Uncle says. That they go up to be with Jesus in heaven. That even though they love us, they can't come back. God won't let them."

Lee wasn't about to tackle that scrambled bit of theology. "So the thing is, stuff happens to us that we can't do anything about. As much as we would like to change things, we can't. So we can be mad about it, or we can accept that we just can't change what's happened."

"Like being here with you and Uncle."

"You don't like being here?"

Another shrug. "I'd rather be with Mommy."

"I know. But you can't. I'm sorry."

"So even though I love her and she loves me, I'll never see Mommy again."

That much was definitely true. "Yes. I'm afraid so."

Hope fell silent, staring at the gentle waves that were brushing up against a grassy part of the shoreline. "Do you think," she said quietly, "you could get me a tea set? I used to have tea with Mommy."

She looked up at Lee, and his chest ached at the tears that clung to the corner of her eyes. He scooped her up and held her close, and she put her arms around him, leaning her head into his shoulder.

"I will, darlin', I promise," he whispered. "I'll get you anything you want."

CHAPTER TWENTY-FOUR

Present Day
Pineville, Alabama

DIRT. CENTRAL ALABAMA dirt had a particular odor to it, one of loose sand, thick clay, and acrid pinesap. As the campground where I lived had a lot of both sand and pine trees, those were the first scents that pushed through my awareness, shortly followed by sharp spikes of pain in my head, back, and sides. My entire body seemed to be on fire with pain. Then came the dancing lights—red, white, and blue—as I tried to open my eyes, which ached from the bright beams and the grit pressing into the skin around them.

I moaned.

"She's awake. Thank God." Not sure who said that, but it sounded like one of my campground neighbors. Mrs. Franny Davis fed Cletis as often as I did, which helped explain the girth that gave him the fortitude to face down raccoons.

A soft touch on my shoulder was followed by a Southern alto. "Lie still, hon. We want to get you into a cervical collar, then roll you onto a board."

EMTs. I hoped. I tried to speak, but my throat clenched with pain.

"No, hon. Don't move. We'll take care of you." Gentle but firm hands slid the collar around my neck, and I groaned again as a deep ache echoed down my spine, a pain that turned even more fiery as they rolled me onto a backboard. I pressed my lips together, trying not to cry out, but tears leaked from my eyes. Everything hurt, even my fingers, which tingled, as if they had been asleep. Yet when the EMTs were finished, the stability helped ease the agony. The fire lessened, although my hands and arms still stung with tiny prickles.

Sharp, booted footsteps approached, and this time the voice was a familiar Pennsylvania brogue. "What in the world happened here?" Mike demanded.

Franny stepped into the fray as the EMTs lifted me onto a gurney. "We heard that cat screaming like all get out, and we knew he'd been into it with that raccoon again. But Star came out and broke it up, and we thought all would be OK, but then we heard more noises, and that cat wouldn't shut up. So we came out and found it standing over her, screeching to the heavens."

Thank you, God, for angry felines.

"Why is there blood on her trailer?" Mike's voice held an edge of both anger and panic. Controlled but still there.

I swallowed hard and finally opened my eyes. Well, one eye. The other one seemed to be swollen shut. "Because I hit it with my face," I muttered, wincing as the EMTs—one female, one male—secured the straps on the gurney. "Someone hit me from behind."

Mike scrubbed his face with both hands, the anger and panic less controlled. "Star—"

"It was a man." A new voice. Another neighbor. "I saw him speed off in an old pickup. I didn't realize what had happened until Franny started yelling about 911."

"What kind of pickup?" Mike demanded.

"Ranger. Old. Maybe fifteen or twenty years. Shot outta here like a bat outta—"

The EMTs put the gurney in motion, and everyone moved back. Mike followed it toward the ambulance, stumbling as he moved alongside it. He grabbed my hand. "I'll meet you at the hospital in Gadsden."

"Check the trailer. He was inside."

"I will."

"Call Gran."

"Star—"

Everything paused for a second as the EMTs prepared to put the gurney into the ambulance. I squeezed his fingers. "I know."

I yelped as they lifted me.

"I'll be there as soon as I can."

His hand slid away as he backed up, and they closed the doors to the ambulance. The sirens fired up and it lurched forward. The female EMT rubbed my arm, then I felt a pressure and a sharp prick inside my elbow. I squeezed my eyes shut. I'd been in the back of an ambulance a few months ago, and I knew the feel of an IV being inserted.

The male EMT touched my arms and legs. A press on one side brought a new pain. "Do you remember anything after being hit from behind?"

I licked my lips and swallowed again. The tightness in my throat continued, but the ache eased. "No. I went out." I shifted my gaze to the female. "Did you put something in that IV?"

She patted my hand. "I keep telling you to be still. Don't move."

"I'm not moving." I looked at the man. "Broken rib?"

He glanced at his partner. "Possibly. Let's wait to see what the docs say."

Right. I couldn't blame them. We did live in a most litigious society. "Do you know what time the 911 call came in?"

"We got it about twenty-one hundred hours." The female EMT checked my IV, then lay the bag next to my head.

I had gone out to break up the catfight around 8:45. A sliver of hope blossomed that he would not have had time to do too much damage inside the trailer, if that had been his game. What unsettled me more was that my momentary illusion of safety—due to my relative high-profile local status—had been just that, an illusion. He had to have been in the area, probably watching me and either waiting for the right moment or planning on attacking me after I'd gone to bed. The catfight just provided an unexpected opportunity.

What he probably had not expected was a rather large and vocal protector in the form of a stray orange tabby.

Thank you, Lord. Again. For this thing with cats.

The ambulance hit a bump, and I winced, but the pain was not as bad as it had been. Either I was getting used to it . . . or whatever was in that bag was working. I closed my eyes again and tried to breathe evenly—deep breaths hurt—and I felt myself drifting.

"Star." That mellow alto again.

"Hmm."

"Stay awake. We're almost there."

The darkness, however, was far more comfortable. So comfortable. But the ambulance halted, jarring me just enough that I opened my eyes. "Ow."

"We're here."

The beeps of the backup alarm felt piercing, and the jostling began again as the back doors flew open and the gurney rolled out. Every sound felt extraordinarily loud, and the lights again blurred my vision with their glare. Time became a hazy stretch of sounds, tests, machines, questions, shifts, and prods. Controlled chaos reigned as the doctors circulated with rapid but efficient motions, determined to poke every inch of my flesh. Medications eased all the pain as the tests came back with mixed results. No concussion, but a severe case of "cervical acceleration-deceleration"—whiplash. This explained the lingering headache and tingles in my arms and hands, the soreness in my shoulders. "Ecchymosis"—my black eye—and a "cracked zygomatic bone," a result of my face being slammed into the Overlander. A substantial cut over the break.

I also had a broken rib and bruises around my throat. Although I had no memory of anything after the blow to the head, apparently my assailant had not stopped with knocking me out. Three hours later I was still in the emergency room, but able to sit with the head of the bed raised, my mind clearer, despite the medications. I was trying to absorb the details when Mike arrived, his face drawn and tense, day-old stubble lining his jaws with dark shading. He opened the door to the examination room and winced.

"Not too pretty right now, I'm afraid." My throat hurt less, but a grating noise still clouded my voice.

"You look like you need morphine and three weeks in Bermuda."

"Thanks."

He moved closer to the bed and slipped his hand into mine. "What have the doctors said?"

I gave him a rundown of my injuries. "They're waiting for one more test to come back, then they'll send me home. The doc is sending a foam collar for me to use a few hours each day. Otherwise, it's just meds and exercises."

He scowled. "You are not going back to that trailer."

"Mike—"

His hand tightened on mine. "No. You should never have gone back there after your afternoon with Miss Doris."

I flicked my gaze down at our hands, then met his eyes. "And where should I have gone? It was too late to go to Gran's. Would the motels out next to the interstate be any safer?"

"No, but you could have stayed—" He stopped, his cheeks shading red.

I smiled and tugged on his hand, leaning forward. The action made my chest hurt, but I didn't care. "Mike. Hold me."

His eyebrows arched. "Are you—are you sure? I don't want to hurt you."

"I'm sure." I pulled on his arm again.

With a long release of air, as if he'd been holding his breath for an hour, Mike wrapped his arms around me, as gentle as he might lift an infant. I leaned against him, resting my head on his chest. With my left arm encumbered by tubes, I put only my right around his shoulders. His warmth encircled me, and I closed my eyes.

Mike and I seldom embraced. With our relationship still finding its own path, open affection had been awkward and uncomfortable. We'd held hands. He'd put his arm around my waist. We'd kissed—rather chastely—a few times. But nothing like this nearness. And for the first time, it felt right. Perfect even.

"You don't have to protect me," I whispered.

"Facts to the contrary," he replied.

I snickered, which hurt only a little. "Please don't make me laugh."

He rubbed my back. "Please let me take care of you."

I stayed silent. What he wanted went against everything I'd worked for since my divorce. My determination not to be trapped again, to remain independent. I did not want to depend on anyone or have them depend on me. Yet the idea of having this man at my side, having my back, filled me with a sense of . . . what?

Relief.

As if I didn't have to carry a burden on my own.

Relief.

"OK."

He stilled a moment, then pulled back. He studied me, his gaze traveling over the bruises, the abrasions . . . my one good eye. "This really scared you, didn't it?"

I nodded once. "I found a new bug in the Overlander."

He stiffened and stepped away. "What?"

"Under the kitchen counter. I found it tonight when I was getting a pan out to make cocoa. I don't remember seeing it before."

He shook his head. "No. I looked under it. Nothing there."

"So he was inside again."

Mike looked toward the door, his mouth tense.

"Michael?"

"He was inside after too. After the attack." He looked back at me. "Star, it's all gone. All your research, all the butcher paper, all your printouts. And your computer. It's all gone."

CHAPTER TWENTY-FIVE

Sunday, March 17, 1996
Lake Martin, Alabama

LEE KNEW IT was a long game with short odds, but he had started the campaign with his uncle almost a month before, and he could finally see the results taking root. Murmurings that Lee repeated enough that Chase began making the statements as if they were his ideas. Fine with Lee. He wanted results, not credit.

"She cannot stay in the cabin forever. It's not healthy."

"Homeschooling only goes so far. She needs a real teacher, not someone pinch-hitting."

"She remembers phones and televisions and videos. Misses the *Little Mermaid* video tapes. Already begging for them when she's tired or whiny."

"She's almost six. What happens when she becomes more aware?"

"It's obvious her father cannot take over her care on a permanent basis." Lee now doubted the man even existed. Obviously Hope had a father, but whether he truly had an interest in his daughter by rape was another story.

"She needs a real family. She'll miss the old one less if she has a new mother and father." A lie, but Lee didn't care as long as Chase bought it. And he seemed to. Or maybe he was just tired of being tied to the cabin and separated from the rest of society.

Now, as they stood on the dock and watched Hope and Sebastian scour the shallows for the first spring tadpoles, Chase abruptly announced, "I'll talk to your mother."

Lee tried not to cheer—or to imagine his mother's reaction to the idea of adopting a little girl. It was a start. Maybe even progress. His folks lived up in Pineville, more than one hundred miles away from this side of Lake Martin. Although he had heard from Clarissa that the Marshalls still searched for Hope privately—and that Genevieve was particularly frantic about it—the girl's disappearance had vanished from the local news. After all the accusations thrown about by the rumor mill, the Marshalls had become uncooperative, and the county authorities had presumed the girl drowned, despite the tip to the contrary. Their efforts had stopped, although the case remained open.

Hope giggled as Sebastian suddenly splashed out from the shore, padding happily in the chilly water. Spring had erupted unexpectedly through the area the last two weeks, with temperatures bouncing up into the seventies every afternoon, although they still dropped into the low fifties at night. Daffodils had burst out, and the early spring wildflowers had perked up out of the ground. Hope had wanted to be outside more, explore farther from the cabin. Chase had tried to keep a rein on her, but he had lost his temper more than once, scaring her.

"Mother always said she wanted more kids."

Chase gave a harsh laugh. "Every time you fouled things up, right?"

Lee bit his tongue. He would not start this fight again.

Chase glanced sideways at Lee. "Why does Hope call you by your first name?"

Easy. Respond without being ugly. He's trying to trap you. It was Chase's way—wait for someone to be a little off guard, then blindside them with an unexpected question. Lee wondered if they taught that in cop school. "Because I asked her to. It's time I grew up and stopped answering to that baby name."

"Lee-lee."

"Yes. I've asked my parents to do the same thing."

Chase snorted. "And?"

Lee shrugged. "Mother's willing to try. My father says it would be disrespectful to the man I was named for. But he'll come around."

"The king?"

"Right. *His* king."

"It could be worse. Your first name could be Elvis."

Lee snorted. "Hey, now, don't be talking down my man."

With a short chuckle, Chase murmured, "You and your mother."

"Can I help it if we have great taste in music?"

Chase remained silent a moment. "You'll help me persuade her?"

"Like they'll listen to me? Seems to me you hold more on them than I do."

Chase smirked for a second. "So I do. Over your parents, yes. But I've seen you with Hope. I've been watching you two get all cozy together."

For a moment, Lee's gut tensed, as a touch of uncertainty sliced through him. Where was Chase going with this?

"So she's much more comfortable with you than with me."

"You scare her."

Another silence passed. "If this is to work, a lot will depend on you. If it doesn't, you know what will happen to you, to your family."

Yeah, we'll all go to prison for kidnapping, much less whatever else you have on them. "I do."

"You better be up to it."

"I will be."

"No room for error. You have to earn that first name. Understand?"

Lee watched as Hope scampered away from the shoreline, Sebastian in hot pursuit. The dog stopped and shook, spraying lake water all over the little girl. Hope squealed and danced in the spray. Stage one of his plan was about to get its tryout. As Chase indicated, failure was not an option. The consequences were too great.

But she was worth it. Hope Marshall was worth it.

We will get you back to her, little one. Back to your mother. I promise.

CHAPTER TWENTY-SIX

Present Day
Pineville, Alabama

ONE DISADVANTAGE OF living in a small town was that everyone knew everyone else's business. Of course, one advantage of living in a small town was that everyone knew everyone else's business.

As I signed the final papers for my release, gathered up medication and the foam collar, and let the nurse tuck me into a wheelchair, Mike's phone went nuts, chirping repeatedly with incoming messages. The first one made him scowl. His eyebrows arched at the next one. The third brought widened eyes, and the next four made him smile.

I handed the nurse back a tablet with the last of my required signatures. "What? Good news? Bad news? It's after midnight."

His grin broadened. "Time has no meaning for the ladies' network of Pine Grove Baptist Church." He held one arm wide. "Cinderella, your chariot awaits."

I stared at him, muttering, "Carriage. Cinderella rode in a carriage. What are you nattering about?"

"You'll see." Mike led the way to the exit as the nurse pushed me in the chair. The doors slid open, and we rolled out onto the drive outside the ER to find a burgundy Mercedes-Benz S-class sedan waiting there. A handsome young man in a suit and tie lounged against the front fender, his fingers flying over the screen of his phone. Mike cleared his throat, and the man looked up, then straightened up, pocketed his phone, and opened the rear passenger door. I recognized him immediately from the many times I'd seen him at church or waiting for the car's owner outside the drugstore in Pineville.

That owner? Miss Doris.

"Brett? What are you doing here?"

Brett pushed a lock of blond hair off his forehead. "Miss Doris sent me to fetch you."

Mike took over from the nurse and pushed the chair toward the big sedan. He leaned over, speaking into my ear. "Apparently your neighbor who called 911 also made some other calls."

"But if I'm not going back to the trailer—"

"Your trailer is a crime scene."

"Then where is Brett taking me?"

Mike locked the brakes on the wheelchair. "Can you stand, or do I need to pick you up?"

I glowered at him. "I can stand perfectly fine, thank you. I hurt. I'm not an invalid." But as I went to push up out of the chair, my rib protested mightily, and I winced.

"Seriously?" Mike muttered.

And with that he scooped me out of the wheelchair. I yelped and clutched his shoulders. "I said I am not—"

"Just hush a minute."

I did. As he settled me into the back seat, he explained. "Miss Doris has been texting me all night. A significant number of your personal belongings have been moved to her carriage house."

"I told you it was a carriage."

He laughed, then squatted next to me. "Her network of ladies went into action, and under the direction of my officers at the scene, they packed your bags. Miss Doris said that you are welcome to the carriage house as long as you need it, and she mumbled something about it keeping the grandkids out of her hair."

I grinned. "They use the carriage house instead of a hotel when they come to town. She's been inundated with them lately, and she'd like to have some time alone with Mr. George."

"Well, it's yours for now. Brett will take you, give you the keys if Miss Doris isn't there. I'll bring Belle over in the morning."

I reached out and touched his cheek. "And my cell phone?"

"Of course."

"Thank you. I can't . . . I can't believe he took everything, especially the computer. That had all my notes."

"Tell me you backed everything up to the cloud."

"Of course."

"I'll put the word out to all the area pawn shops. My guess is that he wants the info, not the computer, and will dump it as soon as he can." He took my hand and kissed my palm. "We'll get you back up and running."

I nodded. "Thank you."

He stood and stepped back. "I'll see you in the morning."

Brett shut the door, and I settled back against the soft comfort of the leather seats. The medications kept most of the pain at bay, but I ached all over, and moving my torso even a bit reminded me sharply that one of my left ribs had a crack in it. Breathing was uncomfortable, and my reluctance to take deep breaths left me feeling sleepy.

And yet I felt blessed. *Thank you, Lord, for these people.* For a community that had welcomed me even though I had torn their lives to shreds only a few months ago. For the friendship of a woman more than twice my age, who saw me as a confidante. Who had supported me almost since my arrival, as if I were her fourth daughter.

And then there was Michael Luinetti, a man whose patience, honor, and integrity were like nothing I had ever known. I knew much of his character had been built out of his faith, but with a past like mine, such qualities felt like a fairy tale. For months I had been waiting for Mike's "true" character to make an appearance, for the other shoe to drop. For whatever dark side he kept behind that to flair into the light.

But it never had, even when the opportunity arose for it to do so. Even when he was furious with me.

I felt as if I'd found my own personal unicorn.

Intellectually, I knew that truly good men did exist. My grandfather was one. But such men seldom crossed my path, much less were attracted to me. It just didn't happen.

So at first I'd assumed Mike's attraction to me was purely physical.

I was one of the few strangers in Pineville, a rare woman he had not met. I was tall and reasonably attractive. Men were drawn to my looks, without a doubt. But Mike's perseverance once all my weaknesses and flaws started showing up, once it became clear that my chosen profession would make me an unrooted nomad who would often be obsessed with a case for weeks on end, had astonished me. He simply had never stepped back or walked away.

It was just downright weird. But I was getting used to it.

I might even like it. I wasn't quite ready to drop the guard around my heart just yet, but realizing that I had felt such intense relief at having Mike want to protect me, to help me, had opened an unexpected door. I definitely had a lot to mull over. And pray about.

When Brett pulled up the long drive to the Italianate mansion off Pineville's square, I had almost fallen asleep. I jumped when he opened the door, blinking at both the inside car light and the floodlights that flamed around the carriage house. He held out his hand, and I took it, maneuvering myself out of the Benz with a series of scoots, rolls, and groans.

"Well, don't you just sound like a sad old woman." Miss Doris stood near the car, perfectly coiffed and dressed, even though it was after midnight. She wore a different outfit than she had earlier in the day, which told me she had probably been in bed when all this started. She leaned on a cane, however—the first time I'd seen her do that. When I glanced down at it, she scoffed. "It's after midnight, dearie. Better a cane than a broken hip from traipsing around in the yard after dark."

I smiled. "Thank you, Miss Doris."

She waved a hand. "Pshaw. It's nothing. Gives me some time with George without a bunch of children underfoot. Let me show you around." She thanked Brett, who moved the car toward the garage in the main house's basement as I followed Miss Doris into the carriage house.

All the lights inside were ablaze, and I paused inside the door as she moved toward a large fireplace in the main room.

"The fireplace is gas. Operates by that switch on the wall." She pointed, then gestured to the galley kitchen to my right. "Fully furnished. You shouldn't need anything. There's even food in the pantry, but I won't guarantee quality or expiration dates. Ellen did the last major shopping."

My sleep-addled mind turning slowly. Ellen . . . ah, one of Miss Doris's granddaughters. She had stayed here when she and her husband were having trouble. Got it.

Miss Doris went on. "It's just a small place. Two bedrooms that way"—another point—"and what you see here."

"Do I need to point out it's bigger than the Overlander?"

She grinned and wagged a finger at me. "You. You do not need to be staying in such a thing. A woman like you—"

"A woman like me?"

"—you need to be in a house—"

"I have a house in Nashville."

"In a house with Mike Luinetti."

Heat flooded my face. "Miss Doris—"

She cackled. "Got ya."

I forced a scowl onto my face. "It is too late and I'm too sore for you to be giving me a hard time."

She waved away my concern as she crossed to me, her face slowly turning serious. "You need a lot of sleep. You've taken on too much. It's not only that someone wants to hurt you. You are doing it again."

"You mean stirring the pot."

"Stirring up families. If Hope is alive, she has been hidden for more than twenty years. You do not do that without a family. Support. And if she knew she was Hope Marshall, part of a rich, powerful family like that? She would have gone home. If she is alive, then she does not know. You are about to disrupt a lot of people's lives."

"It seems to be what I do."

"You know why I wanted you here?"

I considered a dozen snarky answers, none of which fit the mood of the moment. "Why?"

She pointed at a keypad on the wall near the door. "This place is alarmed. I know you are armed, but so is Brett. Cameras all over the place. These grounds are more secure than any place in town aside from the jail. The Marshalls are my friends. Hope needs to come home. They, finally, need something good to come out of all this. I believe you are the one to do it. But we need to keep you safe so you can make that happen. Keep you safe. Mike and I."

Blessed indeed.

CHAPTER TWENTY-SEVEN

Sunday, May 5, 1996
Lake Martin, Alabama

BOTH LEE'S PARENTS declared the plan to be complete madness. The idea of moving one of the highest-profile kidnap victims in the state's history into their home terrified them. One false move and Hope would be recognized, and the plan would be blown apart. But—as Lee had suspected—they were more afraid of Chase than the authorities, although he did not know why. When Lee had first brought his parents to the cabin back in late March, his mother had hissed at him as he'd helped her from the boat to the dock.

"She's five! She won't forget her parents. What was he thinking?"

"It's not about her forgetting her family. It's about her believing they are either dead or don't want her anymore." Lee had stopped at the edge of the dock, facing her and lowering his voice. "Do you understand what Chase can do to us if this doesn't work?"

His mother had turned pale. His father turned to look out over the lake, muttering under his breath and clenching his fists at his side.

Lee grabbed his mother's elbow. "You have to become the most loving, caring, and devoted mother who ever lived. Nothing like you were with me. Got it?"

She yanked her arm away. "Yeah. I got it." She gestured toward the cabin. "Let's get this over with."

To her credit, his mother had complied, turning on the charm as they'd entered and met Hope, who at first cowered with Sebastian behind a chair. The gregarious puppy had even given a low growl of warning. They had taken it slow, however, and by the end of the visit, Hope had grudgingly emerged, allowed them to talk to her, and even answered a few questions. Chase had watched, wary and hyperalert to every movement, every word. Lee could tell from the anxious glances his mother shot Chase's way that she'd become determined to please her brother. She, more than anyone, knew how vicious he could be and had the scars to prove it.

But Chase had been pleased, and he made arrangement for Lee's parents to visit three times a week. Then every day. Lee had worried at first—them being there when he was in school—but it had worked out. Hope had accepted them first as part of his and Chase's family, soon to become hers. She'd adapted quicker than Lee had believed, but when he saw Hope leap from a chair into his father's arms, he realized that kids adapted quickly, just as Chase had told him. Hope had even agreed to letting Lee's mother dye her hair red so she could be just like Ariel, the Little Mermaid. With a promise of her own room with her own video player so she could watch Disney movies as many times as she wanted, Hope clearly looked forward to having more people for company than Lee and her grumpy "Uncle."

Today was moving day.

And Hope was excited. As soon as Lee eased the boat up against the dock, she darted out of the cabin, Sebastian on her heels, barking like mad. She skipped, bounced, and half ran to the dock, her now-red hair shining in the sun. She called Lee's name—his first name—as she ran, and he saw his parents exchange a quick glance. They didn't like his new insistence on using his first name. He no longer cared. His life. His name.

Lee paused and turned as Hope bounded onto the dock. He scooped her up and swung her around, and she giggled madly. "I have it! I picked it out!" Sebastian circled his legs, continuing to bark.

Lee stopped, then hugged and peered at her. "What we talked about last time?"

She nodded vigorously. "Yep!"

"Tell me."

She shook her head. "Uncle says we change my name when we're all together. A new start. New family, new name." She poked him in the shoulder.

"Ow!"

Hope giggled again. "That didn't hurt, silly. I'm a little girl."

"Did too hurt."

"I got my new name out of a book. It rhymes with yours."

"It does?"

A firm nod. "Yep."

"Then I can't wait." Lee tickled her side, and Hope squealed. "You have to tell me now!"

"No, no! I can't!" She giggled and poked him again. "You have to wait."

Lee pouted and set her down on the dock. He sat down beside her and crossed his arms. "Not fair."

Hope put her arms around his neck, and Sebastian tried to push his nose between them. "But you still love me?"

That he would never tease her about. He relented and hugged her back. "Always. Are you packed?"

She let go of him. "Yep!"

Lee looked up to see Chase on the cabin porch, arms crossed, a dark glower on his face. Chase had waffled about this plan the last couple of weeks, as if he'd finally realized it had not been his idea after all. Or maybe he had soured on the idea of his sister taking over Hope's care, of him not controlling every moment of Hope's day. "Well, let's not keep Uncle waiting." *Or give him a chance to change his mind.*

"Come on, Sebastian. Let's get our stuff." Hope turned and trotted back toward the cabin, Sebastian at her side.

"You might make a decent big brother after all," his father mumbled.

Not that I'll get much of a chance. Lee stood, brushed off his butt, then helped his father finish securing the boat. He didn't respond to his father, but glanced up to see Chase stroke the girl's hair and escort her into the cabin.

Two months. He had two months to get everything else in play. And he had to get it right—or everything in their world would go completely wrong.

"Come on," he said. "Let's get this show on the road."

CHAPTER TWENTY-EIGHT

Present Day
Pineville, Alabama

I HEARD BELLE when Mike turned into the Rankins' driveway the next morning. The big engine of a 1966 GMC Carryall made a distinct roar moving down the street . . . and I probably should get the mufflers replaced. But I learned a long time ago that subtlety and surreptitiousness were not my best tools in the skill set, so why sweat it. Use what you've got and make the best of the rest. And Belle did kinda make a statement.

I had slept. Fitfully but sufficiently. The main bedroom of the carriage house had been outfitted with a bedroom suite that had to be more than one hundred years old, although the mattress felt new. The whole house was a blend of antiques and modern comforts, and it smelled as if rose potpourri had been left in every room—although I never found solid evidence of that. I did sneeze several times until I got used to it—which did not make my rib happy at all.

Most of the pain—except for the rib—had eased into dull aches and annoyances. My neck and shoulders made sitting in one spot for more than a few moments difficult, and the rib made it hard to move around much. So I did a lot of fidgeting and quick moves from one spot to another. My hands tingled enough that I was prone to dropping things—so coffee that morning had been an interesting experiment. But over-the-counter painkillers were helping and cutting the edge on my foul mood. I hated being incapacitated. Physically or intellectually.

With my computer and all my notes gone, my brain had been a miasma overnight. There was a reason investigators kept a murder book or a murder board. The physical nature of photos, notes, connections, and timelines helped keep the puzzle together—there was simply too much information flying around in an investigation for most people to keep it all straight in their heads. One of my fellow investigators described it as a 3-D chess game with half the pieces turning invisible overnight. They would still be there, but you couldn't see them. Yet as a player, you would be expected to remember where all those pieces had been and not make any moves that would violate the game.

Not an exact analogy, but it was what I got for hanging out with a *Star Trek* fan.

I would have to re-create everything. But if my assailant's goal had been to delay or derail the investigation, he instead made me all the more determined to get to the bottom of this. I had already cleared off two walls in the second bedroom of the carriage house and tucked into drawers all the fragile tchotchkes decorating the dresser and bedside tables. I could get a little frenetic when I was working, and the last thing I wanted to see was a Meissen figurine go flying across the room. And I suspected my work would amplify from here on out.

Stubbornness was, in fact, in my skill set.

A light tap on the front door drew my attention, and I entered the code on the keypad to disarm the alarm. I snatched open the door, expecting to see Mike standing there. And he was . . . right behind Miss Doris, whose bright-red hair looked particularly fluffy.

She grinned. "I heard him drive up. Thought I would see how you were doing." She pressed by me into the living room.

Mike's expression was one of affectionate amusement, and I couldn't wait to hear what she'd said before I opened the door. I followed her in. "You mean you wanted an update on the case."

She headed straight for the fireplace and turned on the gas. Small flames erupted from beneath the fake logs and released a slight scent of natural gas into the air. She turned her back to it, holding her hands behind her. "Why, Star, are you assuming I'm nosy?"

"That's not an assumption. It's a well-known fact."

Mike entered and shut the door, hefting a tote bag off his shoulder. "Where do you want all this?"

"The back bedroom." I pointed, and he headed that way.

"What is all that?" Miss Doris left the fireplace and settled on one of the two sofas that sat perpendicular to it.

"Tools of my trade."

She perked up. "What kind of tools?"

"Mostly butcher paper and a laptop Mike is loaning me."

Miss Doris deflated, and I laughed. "I've told you before, there's nothing glamorous or particularly exciting about what I do. Forget what you see on television. It's mostly paperwork and conversations."

"Says the woman who got beat up last night."

"Sometimes those conversations irritate people."

"That's because people don't always want to hear the truth."

"That's a pretty major understatement." Mike emerged from the bedroom and handed me my phone. "Our jobs are primarily centered on people who lie."

Miss Doris nodded. "And you do an excellent job of ferreting out the truth and are one of the best chiefs we have ever had. We are glad to have you in Pineville."

Mike and I exchanged glances. "Did that sound like a political statement to you?" I asked him.

"It did."

We both looked at her, and Miss Doris sighed. "My son has decided to run for city council."

Mike made an odd choking noise in the back of his throat but kept silent.

"I take it not the one who's the megachurch pastor in Texas."

She shook her head. "No. The one here. Daniel. Number two."

"And he'd like an endorsement from Mike?"

She hesitated, then nodded.

"You know . . . he might want to wait until we actually solve this case? He might not be so eager if we mess this up."

"What do you mean 'we'?" Mike muttered under his breath.

Another hesitation, another shake of the head. Miss Doris looked up. "Do either of you know anything about something called TikTok? I mean, other than the sound a clock makes."

I chewed my lower lip, and Mike made that choking noise again. "I do. It's a social media app. I haven't explored it much—"

"You two are famous."

I glanced at Mike, then stared at Miss Doris. "What are you talking about?"

She took a deep breath. "Daniel sent me a text this morning. He said there are TikToks, whatever that means, with the two of you. One of you at the campground, being put in the ambulance and—"

Mike jerked his phone out and turned away from both of us.

"—one at the hospital. When he picked you up and put you in my car—"

A slight chill settled over me, despite the blazing fire. That parking area had been empty.

"—which to me sounded quite romantic, except for that part about you being hurt—"

He had been there. The man who had attacked me had been at the hospital. And he wanted me to look like a failure.

"—Daniel said it looked great for Michael, although not so much for you. He did ask if you were all right, and I told him you were fine, that you were here—"

"You what?" Mike swung back around.

She stopped and stared at us. "It was just Daniel. He would know sooner or later. He comes around here all the time."

I put a hand on Mike's arm. "It'll be all over Pineville by noon, if not before." I nodded at his phone. "And beyond. The whole county knows who Brett drives that burgundy Benz for."

His brow furrowed, and his hand tightened on the phone. "You know who had to post these."

I nodded, and Miss Doris perked up. "The man who attacked you posted those?"

Mike poked at his phone again. "The same user posted both, plus one of us in the parking lot at Local Joe's."

"We're surprised he's found new ways to follow me? I just wish I knew what I'd discovered that made him so nervous."

"Obviously you're on the right path in some form or fashion."

"Wonder what he'll do when I talk to Nicholas Eaton and Margery Marshall again?"

Miss Doris stood. "You want to bait him?"

I stepped closer to her. "No. I want to solve this. The fact that I've pulled a rat out of the closet means that someone has the answers and they don't want them to see the light of day. In terms of my investigation, this is a *good* thing. It's even an indication that Jill may be right—this has nothing to do with her family. They were just collateral damage in someone's attempt to cover up two, possibly three, crimes."

"So what's next?" Miss Doris rose up on her toes, her face alight.

I had to smile at her enthusiasm. "Mike will continue investigating from his side, including the attack at the trailer. I will pull down my notes and restart my puzzle making, and I'll reinterview Nick and Margery. From what I've discovered, they left a lot out the first time."

Behind me, Mike cleared his throat.

"And I need to talk to Mike about some things." I paused and lowered my gaze at her. "Without you here."

She scowled. "Hmph. Spoilsport."

"Thank you for letting me stay here. But . . ."

She gave a long, dramatic sigh. "Ingrate."

"You knew all too well what you were getting into."

Another sigh. "I know." She glanced from me to Mike to me. "But you will tell me all you can?"

"I promise."

"I'll just tell the girls you aren't sharing because you want to keep me out of danger."

"Good idea. And in essence, quite true."

Miss Doris headed for the door but paused before opening it. "Star?"

"Yes, ma'am?"

"Do be careful."

"I will." She left, and I muttered, "People keep telling me that."

"Because you keep getting beat up."

I turned to Mike. "Excuse me, but it's been at least six months since the last time."

He tilted his head, giving me his curious puppy look. "Do you *ever* listen to yourself?"

I headed for the back bedroom. "I'm sure I have no idea what you mean."

He followed me. "Most people go a lifetime—" He broke off as he entered the bedroom, looking at the bare walls and flat surfaces. "Did you sleep at all last night?"

I went to the bag, which he had placed on the bed, and pulled out my roll of butcher paper, scissors, markers, and tape. The laptop came next, which I brandished toward him. "Thank you for this, by the way. With Gen's original material in Gran's safe, I need to download everything I saved to the cloud. Is it yours or the department's?"

"Mine."

"Any secrets I need to look for?"

He grinned. "None you don't already know."

"Well, that's disappointing. I was hoping to discover your deepest and darkest."

He spread his arms wide. "All you have to do is ask."

I set the computer on the dresser and lined up the scissors, tape, and markers in a neat line. "Have you heard from your tech guys?"

"No. The manufacturer is in California. They aren't out of bed yet."

I hesitated, still facing the mirror on the dresser. "Anything on a Ford Ranger?"

Mike moved in behind me, his hand warm on my lower back. "My guys are pulling records on all the older Rangers in the area, but you and I both know who that Ranger belongs to."

I looked at him in the mirror, resisting the urge to lean back against him. I took a deep breath, ignoring the protest from my rib. "The same person who seems to have misplaced his high school jacket. But we shouldn't just assume—"

He placed his other hand on my elbow. "It gets worse."

Our gazes met in the mirror. "How could it get worse?"

"We got a call from Kevin Turney this morning. Ricky didn't go home last night. And he's not answering his phone. Kevin called, wondering if we had arrested him again."

I turned to Mike. He backed up a little, but not much. I didn't protest. His closeness brought a warm comfort with it. "But you hadn't."

He shook his head. "No. I called Clarissa. She said she'd seen him yesterday afternoon at the library. The library is only open from two to five on Sundays. He was there around three, but left to run some errands, so he told her. They were supposed to go to dinner, but Ricky never showed. She passed it off as Ricky being Ricky. It wasn't the first time he had stood her up."

"So someone wants us to believe that Ricky is the culprit."

"Are you so sure he's not?"

"Too many assumptions would have to be in play, and we can't do that. Is Ricky smart enough to borrow a car to follow me but dumb enough to use his own truck when I'm attacked? And why would he borrow a car from Zebulon Rhone? Why would he even bother?"

"Whoever did it wanted to divert suspicion—"

"And if Ricky were involved it should have been away from his family, not toward his cousin."

"Then I guess we both have work to do."

"Yes." I put my hand flat against his chest, and a sense of warm comfort spread through me. Standing this close to him reminded me exactly how strong and capable he was.

His pupils dilated, and his breath caught a hitch. "Star?"

"Yes?"

"I'll stop saying it, if you'll start doing it."

I smiled. "On one condition."

"Does it involve me kissing you?"

"As a matter of fact—"

And he did. A soft but firm brush of his lips on mine as he slid his arms around me. I held him as well, the firmness of his shoulders and back under my hands reminding me of the way he had scooped me up the night before, as if I weighed nothing. As the kiss broke, I leaned against him, and his hold tightened.

"I don't want to lose you," he whispered. "Not like this."

I didn't have to ask what he meant by "this." I'd seen it in his eyes at the campground and the hospital. Something I almost never saw in his face. Something I'd almost never seen in anyone's face, not where I was concerned.

Fear.

"Then let's make sure you don't have to." I released him. "Let's find Ricky."

CHAPTER TWENTY-NINE

Saturday, May 18, 1996
Pineville, Alabama

"SO . . . WHAT ABOUT it? Am I pretty enough for you?"

Lee posed for Hope, draped in his crimson gown and mortarboard. The tassel with the gold "1996" affixed dangled in front of his face, and he nodded his head to make it dance. His mother knelt beside Hope, showing her how to use the little disposable camera.

Hope wrinkled her nose. "You're a boy! You're not supposed to be pretty."

"Handsome?"

She nodded, aimed, and took the picture. She handed the camera back to "Mother" and ran to Lee's side. "Now one with me!"

Lee squatted beside her and gave Hope a quick tickle. She squealed and pushed at his shoulder. "Don't mess the dress!"

Grinning, Lee helped her straighten the gold-and-cream dress she wore, then smoothed her red hair. Lee's mother had been repeating that statement most of the morning, as they had prepared for the ceremony that afternoon. "Don't mess the dress."

Graduation day should have been Lee's big day. Instead, his whole family focused on Hope, whose two weeks in her new family had been filled with missteps and gaffes. She adored her new room but hated living on a farm in the middle of nowhere. One way Chase had been able to lure her away from the Marshall compound had not only been because he seemed oddly familiar to the little girl, but he had appealed to her sense of isolation and separation on the compound. Boat rides with two new friends were fun. But Hope had disliked the remote cabin for the same reason. The idea that this secluded farm was her "final" new home had resulted in a few meltdowns.

Hope had wanted to go back to a real school, to make friends. Only the idea of going to her new brother's graduation had soothed her restlessness. They had also promised to show her the new school she'd attend in the fall.

Lee's mother began to fear that Hope would run away, an action sure to bring the police—and Chase—down on their heads. Preventing that from happening had turned his parents into tense knots of irritability. As a result, Hope had relied more and more on Lee for comfort, reassurance, and entertainment.

Just as he had hoped.

Now he prayed that no one at the ceremony would recognize the new redheaded girl in their midst. That needed to happen on his own timeline. He and his parents had planted the news of their upcoming adoption with all their friends and their church. Lee had talked about her red hair, and his mother had told her Sunday school class all about the birth mother, the agency, the endless paperwork. They'd used her new name to plant the seeds.

At the same time, the news coverage about Hope's disappearance had evaporated months ago. Surely no one around Pineville knew the Marshalls personally—Lake Martin was a long way off, and the Marshalls' penchant for privacy had worked against them in the long run. Pictures of Hope were rare—and were now more than six months old. Hope had grown an inch over the spring, and she'd lost weight. She had turned six the week before, and seemed more trim and athletic, mostly from running around with Sebastian.

In fact, she smelled faintly of wet dog at that moment.

"Have you been playing with Sebastian?" he whispered after they'd posed for a picture.

She jerked back, surprised.

"Right," he whispered in her ear. "Go wash. Don't want you stinking like wet dog for my graduation."

She giggled. "OK."

He urged her toward the bathroom, then stood and helped his mother to her feet.

"I'm too old to be getting up and down like this," she grumbled. "I don't know what we'll do when you go off in the fall."

"I'll be here through the summer." He adjusted the gown across his shoulders. "Have you thought anymore about what I mentioned earlier? About the July Fourth fair?"

His mother dropped the camera into her purse and began inspecting her own dress for any "mess." "Let's just get through today first, OK? If she does well and no one says anything, we'll talk about it. Lot less control at a fair than a graduation ceremony." She looked up at him. "You sure Chase will be OK with it?"

"I'll talk to him. Should help if he's there. Watching out for her will give him something to do besides follow us around. He can play at being a cop again."

His mother snorted. "Not that he was that good at it in the first place. That's why he quit to start playing PI."

Lee had his own theories but kept them to himself. "I'm sure he misses his old friends." *One in particular.* One Lee had just found out about, thanks to Clarissa. With her help, a lot of the pieces had begun to fit together. A lot of things that had not made sense, that had kept Lee befuddled over the past six months, had started to become clear. Clarissa had helped him gather a lot of information, but it had also made her suspicious. She, too, was making sense of Lee's puzzling questions and research.

That was *not* a good thing. If she started sharing it with anyone else, Chase could find out. And the last person Lee wanted in Chase's crosshairs was Clarissa. But that's exactly what would happen if his July Fourth plans fell through. Chase was already suspicious of the time Lee spent with the pretty librarian and had started visiting the library himself. Hovering. Too close for comfort.

So this had to work. Had to. For all of them.

Failure would bring consequences too awful to consider.

CHAPTER THIRTY

Present Day
Pineville, Alabama

KEVIN TURNEY, FOR a man who had recently threatened to shoot his own son, seemed particularly frantic about Ricky being missing. As we pulled up to the farmhouse in Mike's cruiser, the big man paced the porch from one end to the other, muttering and flinging his hands in rhythm to whatever words spewed forth. Dressed only in overalls and a T-shirt, he seemed impervious to the brisk wind that stirred a scattering of leaves in the front yard. We climbed out of the cruiser, watching him a few moments before Mike called his name.

Kevin jerked, as if he'd just noticed us, which he quite possibly had. His muttering had been intense, his stare distant. "Chief! Any word?"

Mike shook his head. "Not yet. I've got officers searching all his usual haunts, but no one reports seeing him yet."

"This . . . this is just not like him!" Kevin threw his arms wide. "Yes, he gets drunk, gets arrested, but he never stays out all night without calling. Even in his blackouts he finds a way to let us know. Never. Not in twenty years."

"Since he came back after 9/11?" I asked.

Kevin froze, then his hands dropped to his side. "You know about that."

I stepped closer to the porch, pulling my jacket a little tighter around me. "Where did he go?"

The old man dropped onto one of the rocking chairs and leaned forward, resting his elbows on his knees. He stared down at the peeling blue paint on the porch floor. "We still don't know. Out West somewhere. Maybe. I came home one day, and Willa said they had a big blowup. But they did that a lot back then. Always getting into it about something. He stormed out and never came back. Called a couple of days later saying he was fine, just needed time. Didn't hear from him again for more than a year."

Mike moved in beside me. "Did he ever call collect?"

Kevin looked up, his eyes narrowing. "You mean did he call from a jail somewhere?"

"Pretty much."

His mouth tightened. "Couple of times."

"Maybe he's done that again?" I asked.

Kevin shook his head furiously. "Not this time. No fight, no nothing. Just . . . gone."

Mike gestured to the empty spot in the yard. "He left in the truck?"

Nodding, Kevin sniffed. "Yeah. Sometime after lunch. Said he was going to see that girl."

Girl? Ah. "You mean Clarissa?"

He waved a hand. "Yeah. That librarian. She's been a problem for him since high school."

"How so?" Mike asked.

"Cute thing back then. Had several of the boys sniffing around, stringing them along. New girl in town. No one cared she was a librarian. Prim and proper she was not. And not just the boys either. Some of the older men started acting like they'd never seen a girl before." He gestured toward the house. "Willa's brother took a liking to her, which put Ricky in a real bad way."

"Is that what the blowup with Willa was about?" I asked.

Kevin's gaze turned distant again. "Not sure."

"Who's her brother?"

Another shrug, then he huddled in on himself even more. "Chase. Chase Rhone."

Mike scowled. "The private investigator?"

Kevin nodded.

"Where does he live?"

Kevin's voice became hard to hear. "Down near Dadeville."

One of my red flags popped. "You mean near Lake Martin?"

Silence.

Mike stepped in front of him. "Kevin. Look at me. Where's Willa?"

Kevin gestured toward one of the fields. "She went out on the tractor this morning."

His answer surprised me. "With her son missing?" I asked.

Both Kevin and Mike glanced at me but said nothing for a few minutes. A small alarm went off in my head, but I waited, watching the two men.

Mike straightened his shoulders, his voice dropping in pitch. "A little late in the year for plowing, isn't it, Kevin?"

Kevin looked at his hands. "Said she wanted to plow under some of the late crops. We've gathered everything we can of the summer stuff."

Mike's words turned hard. "Does Willa usually do your plowing?"

Kevin looked up, and I was startled to see tears streaming down his cheeks. "She wants to put in some turnip greens, rotate them from last year's planting . . ." He wiped his eyes as his voice trailed off.

Mike did not move, but I didn't like the way his neck abruptly flushed red. His face remained calm, but his tongue put in that microsecond appearance, and I knew he had stifled what he really wanted to say. The red spread up his jawline and his voice turned somber and even. "Which field, Kevin?"

Another limp gesture to the west, another drop of his gaze to the ground. "There. You can take the field road a-ways in. That part of the farm slopes down toward the quarry on Langston Road. But she'll be back soon. She didn't take a lunch with her."

The red spread into Mike's cheeks as he pivoted toward the cruiser. I didn't know exactly what was going on, but my head sang with alarms, and I'm sure Mike's did too. I barely made it into the seat of the cruiser before he spun the car in reverse. Kevin stood, eyes wide, as he watched us do a 180. The cruiser lurched hard as it bounced into the twin ruts of the field road leading to the west side of the Turney farm, and I grabbed the dashboard and held on. Mike fought the wheel, then activated his communication system. The dispatcher came on, and I stared at Mike as he ordered both the department's drones into the air and a request for the sheriff's department to put their bird up—one of the few helicopters in the area. He gave the location and asked that the helicopter focus on the Langston Road quarry. As he ended the call, the cruiser surged again, the bottom dragging as Mike pressed harder on the accelerator.

"You want to tell me what's going on?"

"Just pray that I'm wrong."

I did. And for both of us as we spotted a large tractor in the distance, a dark-haired figure in the cab, the big round blades behind it churning the soil.

Churning the soil.

I snapped a look at Mike as my stomach flipped. "She wouldn't—"

He didn't even look my way. He jerked the wheel to the left, plunging the cruiser off the road and directly toward the tractor's front end.

"Her own son?" I wanted to scream it.

The red had claimed Mike's face. "He's not her son. He's Kevin's."

"Dear God, no." I whispered the prayer, now begging that Mike was wrong, horribly, excruciatingly wrong. But as we closed in, I could see red smears on those big round blades, smears that would have been obliterated with a few more rows of plowing. And my morning coffee threatened to make a return visit.

I swallowed hard, my voice barely audible over the roar of the cruiser. "If she's not his mother, who is?"

Mike didn't respond, his face a hard mask. As the cruiser charged for the front of the tractor, I could see Willa gear down, increasing the speed on the tractor, her pale face set in a determined frown. Mike did not let up, and as he set us on a collision course, I saw a dark flash overhead. Willa saw it too, her eyes darting upward as the drone circled and dropped toward the tractor. With a snarl, she finally braked, the tractor slowing to a halt mere feet from the front of the cruiser.

Mike was out like a shot, gun drawn, screaming for her to cut the engine and get out. He assumed a firm stance, feet planted wide and both hands on his gun, and repeated the command.

Willa remained where she was, the scowl on her face deepening.

Then she cut the motor, and the giant engine ground into silence. She still did not move, then reached behind her, as if to pick up something.

"Don't!" Mike bellowed. "Willa, get down!"

Overhead, the drone dropped even lower, almost level with the cab of the big tractor. Willa glared at it, her face tight and hard.

"Get out, Willa. Slowly! Hands where I can see them."

I finally emerged from the cruiser, watching Willa carefully as she opened the door of the cab and descended to the ground. She kept her hands up as the wind whipped dark strands of her hair around her face.

"I can cuff her." I raised my voice above the buzz of the drone.

Mike nodded. With his gun still trained on her, he used one hand to toss me his cuffs. I motioned for Willa to turn around, and she did, facing the tractor. I brought one arm down, then the other, securing the cuffs to her wrists. I frisked her and pulled her cell phone from her back pocket, tucking it into my jacket pocket. Then I turned her to face Mike and stepped away.

Mike gestured for the drone to make a larger circle, and it rose and scudded away to the east. At the far edge of the field, it made slow circles from the outer edges toward the center.

Mike approached Willa, holstered his gun, and recited her rights. Her only response was a terse "I want a lawyer." She said nothing else as he marched her to the cruiser and put her in the back seat. I followed them but waited until she was shut inside.

He turned toward me, but his eyes focused on the blades behind me. He swallowed hard. "I want to be wrong."

"I know."

His gaze still went beyond my shoulder, but his eyes lost their focus, developing a thousand-yard stare. "I should have known."

What? "How could you?"

"We both knew Ricky was not your attacker. Knew that someone wanted to make us think he was, if nothing else, to keep the focus on the Turney family. But the minute it was clear we knew about the deception, Ricky would be in danger."

"But there was no way you could have known Willa—"

He finally looked at me. "Think about it. For more than twenty years, the Turneys have protested their innocence, even as they kept their own dark secrets. Ricky was born after they married, but they never let on that Ricky was from an affair Kevin had. This came out in the original investigation, but it seemed irrelevant to the case. It explains why Willa and Ricky didn't get along, but what would that have to do with Gen's murder? And after all twenty years of claiming innocence, maybe they were right. Gen was just in the wrong place at the wrong time and the Turneys's barn was just a convenient dumping ground. But we didn't know that Ricky disappeared immediately after Genevieve's body was found. Why would he do that unless it was to extract himself from the investigation? My guess is that he was either involved in the murder or knew who was. Clarissa was trying to warn us. He's been the key to this thing all along. That's why they've tried to make him look guilty."

"And when they couldn't, he became a liability. Why wouldn't Ricky have just gone to the police?"

Mike glanced back at the car. "I'm not sure. But would you turn in the only mother you'd ever had if you knew she was involved in a murder?"

"Me? Yes. But I didn't exactly have a normal childhood."

The corner of his mouth jerked, then his face returned to its scowl.

"Mike, who is Ricky's mother? His birth mother."

Mike shook his head. "I'm not sure. Rumors I've heard."

Suddenly a flash of words appeared in my mind. *"We wound up in the same gardening club. Nice man. Good man. I liked him—he was fun to talk to and really listened to me, liked my ideas."* Was it possible? "Margery Marshall."

Mike's eyes widened a bit. "How did you—"

"Something she said when I interviewed her. The way she talked about meeting and knowing Kevin Turney."

He looked beyond me then, and his eyes narrowed. "We'll have to finish this later."

I turned.

The drone had stopped its search pattern, hovering over a recently plowed section of the field. With a long sigh, Mike trudged in that direction. I followed, watching him—not the drone—as his shoulders hunched and his strides became long and heavy. My heart ached for him, knowing his tendency to take on responsibility for anything that went wrong in his community.

But he could *not* have known this would happen. Too many moving parts were in play in a twenty-year-old murder, complicated by a previous rape and two abductions in other jurisdictions. Too many unknowns.

As we closed in on the area where the drone hovered, Mike slowed, studying the ground. He stopped, staring, and motioned for me to hang back, which I did. He pulled his flashlight from his belt, squatted, and turned the beam on something in the dirt. After a moment, he clicked it off and stood, turning back to me. He headed my way but passed me without stopping.

"Mike?"

He kept going, heading for the cruiser. "I wasn't wrong."

Three hours later, I leaned against the cruiser's fender and watched as a swarm of officers and techs mapped out a search grid in the field, centered on the first spot the drone had found. The wind had stopped and the sun had warmed the morning, and I dropped my jacket back into the cruiser. I had begun to ache as the painkillers wore off, and I hugged myself, trying to give the rib some support.

A slight breeze stirred up as noon approached, bringing with it the scent of freshly plowed earth and approaching rain. Clouds clustered on the western horizon, the puffy tops stretching and billowing higher in the sky. Thin sticks with evidence flags on them flitted in the wind. A lot of evidence flags. Yellow crime scene tape surrounded the tractor, and short poles stuck into the ground allowed for a perimeter to be set around the gridded section of field. Not that many spectators were expected, but it also established the scene for the photographers.

Willa had been transported to the police station, and the drone sent home. The helicopter had flown over the flooded Langston Road quarry and the stream that fed it, and the helo team had found an outline of a small pickup in the water near the edge of the quarry. Another team had been sent there, along with a diver, to make sure the truck was the right one—and empty—before they brought it up.

Kevin Turney, alerted when an entire convoy of official vehicles headed down his field road, had gotten in his old Buick and followed them. Seeing what was going on, he'd screamed and tried to get to the scene, only to have several officers block his path. Mike had talked to him, and I had watched as the older man collapsed into Mike's arms. When he'd been able to stand, two officers drove him back to his house, while another followed in the Buick. According to what I'd overheard from the team processing the tractor, they had stayed with him until his pastor showed up.

That team's chatter had been the closest I could get to the investigation. I had been ordered to stay away from the grid—I was a civilian, after all—and I was content to do that. I wanted to stay, instead of being sent home if I interfered, but graphic crime scenes had never been my cup of tea. And watching the teams work helped ease an unsettling sadness that had enfolded me without warning or reason. I had met Ricky Turney exactly twice. He had seemed to be an extremely complicated man—happy-go-lucky until he'd turned on his father with an unexpected rage—who had been dealt a hard-luck life.

No one—*no one*—should have this kind of business thrust upon them, especially in death. Or maybe it was a residual emotion from knowing Jill. Despite all his problems, Jill *adored* her brother. With the age difference, he was almost as much a father to her as Kevin. She would get mad at Ricky's alcoholism, furious at the way the community had treated him after Genevieve's murder. But Jill never failed to bail him out and try to get him into rehab. She begged and pleaded for their parents to get him help. In one of our first meetings, she told me that she had tried to get him to join her in Chicago, but that he'd given up trying to improve his lot, that he had had one shot at turning things around and he'd blown it. Afterward, he'd settled into a bottle and refused to come out.

I did not relish telling Jill that Ricky had been murdered and her mother was involved, much less that his death could have resulted from the investigation she'd insisted I reopen. I did not want her to carry that guilt. Because I knew she would.

Why is it that the people least responsible for such tragedies are always quick to claim their part in it, while the truly guilty deny their roles?

Mike conferred with one of the Tyvek-suited techs, then checked his cell before heading my way. I straightened as he slid behind the wheel of the cruiser, and I scooted onto the passenger seat as he started the car and backed away from the tractor. I had a million questions, but the hard set to his face did not encourage speech. We rode in silence down the field road, past the Turney farmhouse, and out to the main road.

When he finally spoke, his words clipped hard. "I'm taking you back to Miss Doris's."

"OK." There was no way I was going to get into his business at the moment.

"I need you to stay away from this investigation."

"I will."

He glanced my way once. "I'm serious."

"I know."

"Since this relates to Zeb Rhone's murder, I'll be coordinating with Trussville. It's also tied to your attack. So you are a victim as well. This has to be done strictly by standard protocol."

"I understand."

And I did. Whatever happened in Pineville at this point had to be at Mike's lead. Which was fine with me for now. I had other fish to fry, but I didn't want to bring that up. What I hoped was that once he slept on this, worked out a few of his own misgivings, he would confide in me again.

After a few more moments of silence, some of the tension seemed to ease, and his hammerlock grip on the steering wheel lessened. He cleared his throat. "It wasn't the tractor."

An odd sense of relief settled between us, which made no sense, really. The man was still dead. Then again, maybe it did.

"How–"

"We found"–his hands tightened again on the wheel–"he had been shot in the back of the head."

Why was he telling me this? "So it would have been quick."

A single nod. "Will you call Jill?"

Ah. "I will. But I suspect Kevin will have already done so."

"I'm not so sure he could handle that. He was pretty wrecked."

"Understandable. I'll talk to her anyway."

"Let me know . . ."

He went quiet again, remaining so until he turned into the drive and pulled up to the carriage house. He put the car in park but stared straight ahead.

I kept my voice low and even. "Mike, I will stay out of the way on this. But when you can let me know something, please do." I hesitated. "And if you just want to come over and sit, I'll make hot cocoa and we can stare at the fire."

He blinked, hard, squeezing his eyes shut. When he spoke, a touch of gravel darkened his words. "I may do that." He finally looked at me and reached for my hand, his eyes glistening. "Thank you." He squeezed my fingers.

I squeezed back. "I'm here." I pulled away and opened the door, knowing if I stayed any longer, the moment would turn awkward. I grabbed my jacket and got out. I waited till he backed away, then went inside, checking the alarm and locking the door. It was just after noon. With luck, I could grab a bit of lunch before heading out for my appointment with Pastor Harris at one.

Heading for the kitchen, I slung my jacket over one of the dining room chairs. It hit with an odd thunk, and I stopped, staring down at it. "Why did you thunk?" I hefted it, realizing one side hung heavier than the other. I ran my hand into that pocket, and my stomach clenched.

I had Willa Turney's cell phone.

CHAPTER THIRTY-ONE

Wednesday, July 3, 1996
Pineville, Alabama

THE BRIGHT LIGHTS of the fair showered them with glittering colors as the sun's last rays illuminated the countryside. The midway of rides, games, and food trucks covered most of the city's municipal park, with the fireworks display set up on the far side of the sports fields. The spectacular event would begin at 9:00 p.m., which was why Lee's anonymous note to Genevieve Marshall had given her 8:30 p.m. as the time to meet her daughter at the Ferris wheel.

Lee knew exactly what risk he'd taken in contacting Hope's mother, but he kept reminding himself of the vow he'd made months ago—this was all about Hope. What was best for her. And he believed with every fiber of his being that being returned to the Marshalls was best. The last thing he wanted was for this bright spirit to have the same crushing childhood he'd had.

Hope tugged at his arm for the fiftieth time that afternoon, this time toward a ride that went up and down as well as round and round, and Lee was glad he'd avoided the corndog stand. His father had consumed anything fried or stuck on a stick, and after three hours had retreated to their car with a pale face and roiling gut. His mother had wandered away to the sideshows and games. Chase, who had come in his own car, lurked but refused to eat or ride anything. He glowered behind silvered sunglasses, rendering Lee's spine stiff and his mood wary.

Lee scooped up Hope, making her giggle. "I cannot believe you want to ride yet another bucket that turns you upside down."

She clutched at his shirt. “Please! Please, please, please, please!”

He relented. “All right. But I want to be on the Ferris wheel by 8:30. With luck, we’ll get stuck at the top when the fireworks go off.” This had been his excuse for refusing her access to the big ride all afternoon.

“OK!” she shouted in his ear.

He groaned with a broad exaggeration. “Stop yelling.”

She giggled again. “Put me down.”

He did, holding tight to her hand as she tugged him toward the ride. Lee went with feigned reluctance, inwardly thrilled at her glee. Ten minutes later, staggering as if he were truly drunk, he let her lead him toward the Ferris wheel.

While 8:30 remained a few minutes away, Lee began his search of the crowd for Genevieve Marshall. He’d scoured the papers at the library for pictures of her as well as recalling as much as possible of his and Chase’s surveillance in the weeks before Hope’s kidnapping. An extraordinary number of blonds peppered the crowd, most of them with dark roots, and none—so far—with the reddish tint that identified Genevieve. He spotted one blond paired with a tall black man—but no, not her either.

Maybe his note never reached her. Or she dismissed it as just a dark joke. Lee did not hold much to religion—his entire childhood had been a discouragement to it—but in those few moments, he prayed. For Hope. For rescue.

He finally turned over the tokens for the Ferris wheel, and they got on. As it started up, their seat going backward, Hope’s enthusiasm bubbled over, and Lee wrapped an arm around her to keep her from bouncing in the seat. They topped the wheel three times, and she squealed her delight as she pointed out the rides they had been on, the distant parking lot, the small corral where the pony rides were.

“The ponies!” She clutched his arm. “We haven’t done the ponies!”

He tugged her closer. “Sit still! You’re rocking us.”

She did. “Can we do the ponies?”

“If they are still going when we get down.” *If you’re still here.* “If you will sit still.” Maybe having a six-year-old on a Ferris wheel wasn’t such a good idea after all.

"OK!" She quieted for almost fifteen seconds, until their seat reached the peak again, this time stopping. "Why did we stop?" she demanded.

"Probably to let some people on."

Hope settled again. "OK." She twisted to look behind them. "The ponies are still going."

Lee, scanning the crowd below, finally saw the face he'd been searching for. Genevieve Marshall hovered by the entrance to the ride, looking around, frantically scanning the crowd.

No! Go to the exit! Lee willed it as if he could move her by telepathy. The exit, a simple gate on the opposite side from the multiline entrance, would make for an easier transfer. In Lee's mind, he merely wanted Hope and Genevieve to spot each other and be reunited as he slipped away in the crowd. If she didn't go to the exit, there were too many people around, too much confusion. He had specified the exit in his letter. *What is wrong with her?*

Lee's stomach clinched as he spotted Chase standing only a few paces away from Genevieve, his jaw tight and his mouth a fine line. His silvered glasses looked ominous as they reflected a thousand colored lights. Chase looked from Genevieve up toward the top of the Ferris wheel, and Lee watched his uncle's mouth form the words, "I will kill you."

Genevieve kept searching, and Chase headed for the exit.

A harsh chill slid over Lee, despite the heat of the day, and he pulled Hope closer. "Listen, pumpkin. Listen to me."

She looked up at him, her eyes bright. "What?"

"No matter what happens in the next few minutes, please remember that I love you. I will always love you. You're my little sister, and the best of us all. Got it?"

She stilled, apparently recognizing the somber tone in his voice. "Is something wrong?"

He shook his head. "No. Everything will be fine. Just remember what I said. OK?"

She nodded. "OK. I love you too. And you're the bestest."

Lee smiled and hugged her again. *If only . . .*

The Ferris wheel started downward with a lurch that startled them both, and they hung on as it slowly descended and stopped. The operator helped them out, and Lee took Hope's hand as they moved toward the exit and into a nightmare.

Chase reached them first. In one motion he scooped Hope up and out of Lee's grasp and landed a right cross on Lee's jaw that snapped his head back. Sparks blinded Lee as the pain speared through his head and down his spine, and he dropped to the ground. Hope screamed Lee's name as Chase turned, wrapped his arms around her, and plowed a path through the crowd.

Lee fought to his feet, trying to clear his vision as he stumbled after them, circling toward the ride's entrance. He saw Genevieve spot the squirming Hope. She released an eerie, high-pitched screech that was partly Hope's name and partly panicked mother. Lee tried to get to her, pushing aside people who barely took note of the drama. Genevieve darted in and around people, rushing after Chase, when another body collided with hers, throwing both of them to the ground. Lee stared in horror as his mother lay on top of Genevieve, apologizing furiously but not releasing her. She clung to Genevieve, begging forgiveness, even as Hope's mother struggled to extract herself.

Finally shouting, "Get off me!" Genevieve pulled herself up and turned once again in the direction she had last seen Chase's broad back. But within seconds she had obviously lost sight of her daughter's kidnapper. Dissolving into tears, she turned to the crowd around her, begging for help. A security guard approached her, and after listening a moment to her pleas, escorted her away, even as she begged him to go after her child.

Lee sagged against the side of a food truck and slid to the ground. He needed a drink. He had not touched the bourbon in months, since Hope had moved in. Now, he needed it more than water.

His mother kicked his knee, and he flinched, pulling back from the pain. He peered up at her.

"Get up."

Lee rose to all fours, then used the truck to brace himself as he stood. His head spun, and he squinted as he looked at her. His head ached almost as much as his jaw.

"We're going home. You know you deserve anything he dishes out. I just hope he doesn't take it out on us."

Lee cradled his jaw in one hand, realizing he could taste blood. "I didn't do anything."

"Oh, and I suppose Ms. Genevieve Marshall Eaton just happened to show up at the Pineville fair for no reason whatsoever."

"Maybe she was in the neighborhood."

His mother slapped his chest, and he staggered. "That's your problem, you know that? You and your smart mouth. You think you're better than the rest of us."

"I don't—"

She hit him again.

"Stop that!"

"Wimp. Ain't nothing like what he'll do to you. Now let's go before the guards circle back around and wonder why you're bleeding from the mouth."

Lee followed her. They had to wake his father up, but he took one look at Lee and said nothing. The journey home, silent except for the blasting rattle of the car's air conditioner, felt shorter than it should have, even as Lee began his descent, his separation from himself, something he'd learned to do back in childhood, a remoteness that let him deal with the pain of punishment that had always come at the hand of his mother. His purple vortex of silence, where pain had no effect.

Another prayer for Hope hovered in his mind. Against his mother. That Hope would never have to learn this skill, this way of coping with pain.

Chase waited on the front porch of their farmhouse. As they approached the steps, he announced that Hope was in her room. Lee's father hesitated, but his mother pushed her husband from behind, urging him inside. Lee started to follow, but Chase blocked his path.

"What did you do?"

Lee tried to face him but could not. "Nothing."

"Liar."

"I'm not."

Chase exploded into action, shoving Lee backward. Lee lost his balance, falling headlong down the porch steps. He tried to catch himself, but his wrist and knee hyperextended, and his head hit the bottom step with a thunk. The pain blinded him, and he cried out and rolled to a halt, clutching his wrist, drawing his legs up into a fetal position.

He heard Chase's boots on the wood, then shards of pain pierced through his body as one of those boots connected with his ribs. Lee fought to get his breath as Chase grabbed his shirt and hauled him to his feet, throwing him backward across the hot hood of the car.

"You don't get it, boy. They should have told you!"

Chase slapped the side of Lee's head, which made him bite the inside of his mouth. Lee groaned and tried to roll away, but Chase pinned him to the hood, leaning over him, his words a hoarse growl.

"I own them! They will do whatever I say because I own them. I own this place. Your father couldn't manage a farm if he had a million dollars. I pay their debts. I keep their secrets. I change my mind, and you'll all be out on the streets."

Lee blinked at him, trying to absorb the words, the threats within them. "What secrets?"

Chase barked a harsh laugh. "You want to know why your father puts up with it? Because he cheated on my sister with a Jezebel who didn't want you any more than Willa did. You get it? You are nobody. You belong nowhere. You're nothing. We let you stay here, but one word and you'll go packing, along with your father. I own you."

Lee turned his head and spit, blood spraying over the car. "But you don't own Hope."

Chase laughed, a sound so evil that Lee cringed. "I own her just as much as I own my sister," Chase whispered, "and there isn't anything you can do about it."

The next blow came from a fist, which, blissfully and thankfully, brought the darkness.

Lee was not so thankful, however, the next morning. Chase had left him lying in the yard, and it was well after midnight before Lee regained consciousness and dragged himself up on the porch, where he spent the rest of the night. His father, horrified to find him there the next morning, helped Lee into one of the rockers and tried to convince him to go to the hospital. He refused. That would raise too many questions. Lee watched from within his remoteness as his father seemed to process this.

"You could file assault charges."

Lee shook his head once, shuddering. "You want him coming after all of us?" He swallowed, still tasting blood. "He told me. He told me what he could do to us. To you."

His father looked away into the distance. "We can't live like this."

"We already do. We already have."

"I can't stand what he's doing to you. Taking in Hope—this was supposed to keep you safe."

Lee squinted at his father. "You did this for me?"

His father looked down. "It was all for you. To keep you safe from him. It was our bargain—I let the girl stay, and he and Willa leave you alone. Now it's all gone south."

Lee tried to take his father's words in, but that would have to wait. They needed one focus. "Now we have to figure out how to keep doing it, keep him off us." Lee tried to raise his head but groaned and let it fall back.

"I want to keep her safe."

There was no need to explain who "her" was.

They went silent as a car approached, tires crunching on the gravel. Lee fought a surge of fear—Chase might be returning. Then his father stood slowly, and they both watched a sheriff's patrol car ease into the yard. Neither spoke as the oversized figure of Sheriff JoeLee Wilkes rolled from behind the wheel and sauntered up to the porch.

"Mornin', fellas."

His father nodded. "Sheriff. What can we do you for?"

The sheriff squinted at Lee. "Boy, what in the world happened to you?"

"He fell down the stairs," his mother called from behind the screen door. "He oughta be more careful."

Sheriff Wilkes studied Lee from head to toe. "I didn't realize stairs came with fists these days."

His mother stepped out onto the porch, letting the door slam behind her. "What do you want, Wilkes?"

Wilkes looked from Lee to his father, then his mother. "We had a report come out of the fair last night. Genevieve Marshall. You know her?"

"We heard of her. Why?" His mother moved closer to the edge of the porch. "What's it have to do with us?"

Apparently his father was going to let his wife take all the questions. He stepped back and took up a position behind Lee's rocker. Lee closed his eyes a moment, unmoving, sliding deeper into his distancing vortex. He felt as if he were watching the whole scene from somewhere in the trees. It wasn't him who hurt.

Wilkes leaned back and stuck both thumbs into his belt. "She claims she spotted her daughter there last night. The one who was kidnapped."

"I heard that girl was dead."

"Presumed to be, yes."

"So the woman's crazy."

"Maybe. But the man she described as taking her sounded a lot like your brother. He around?"

"He don't live here. You try his place?"

Wilkes nodded. "I did. Not there. Thought he might have been visiting his lovely sister."

"Well, he ain't. And we don't know where he is. So you can go now."

Wilkes didn't move. "I hear y'all adopted a little girl."

Lee's mother froze. "What of it?"

"I'd like to meet her. Welcome her to Pine County."

"She's upstairs in her room. Playing."

Lee watched as Wilkes's entire demeanor changed, reminding Lee why everyone in the county feared getting on the sheriff's bad side. His good-old-boy attitude vanished. His stance stiffened. He dropped his hands to his side. His eyes narrowed, and his tone left no room for argument. "Bring. Her. Down. Here. Now."

His mother pivoted on one toe and went back inside. A few moments later, Hope emerged slowly, her eyes wide as she spotted the big man near the steps.

Wilkes changed again, his body seeming to soften as he bent forward and smiled. "Well, hello, little lady."

Hope looked at Lee. He nodded, and she looked back at the sheriff. "Hi."

"You're a pretty little thing."

"Thank you. You're huge!"

The sheriff laughed, Santa Claus without the red suit. "I am, ain't I? But I'm just a big teddy bear." He held out his hand. "I'm JoeLee. Can you tell me your name?"

Ricky's breath stopped, and he dared not look at either of his parents. Instead, he waited, watching Hope.

She straightened and gave the sheriff a wide smile as she walked over and took his hand, shaking it firmly, despite the fact that hers almost disappeared within his. She spoke clearly, with no hesitation, as she declared, "Hi, JoeLee. Your name is almost like mine. I'm Jilly. Jilly Turney. It rhymes, like my brother's. Get it?"

Wilkes smiled, an expression oddly close to that of a viper. "I do. You are very pretty. I bet you have lots of friends. Do you know a little girl named Hope?"

Jilly blinked. Then slowly shook her head. "Nope. But I can ask my new friends."

Wilkes released her hand. "Promise?"

Jilly nodded vigorously. "Yes, sir. And I always keep my promises." She looked up at Willa again. "Can I go play now?"

Willa nodded and Jilly flew back inside, the screen door slamming behind her.

And Richard Lee Turney let out the breath he'd been holding, suddenly back in his body, stifling a groan. His Hope. No . . . his *Jilly*. Pride surged through him as he had watched her face the big sheriff, declaring herself to be his sister. He had to protect her from whatever Chase had in mind. Getting her back to the Marshalls might be a lost cause, but he could make sure she stayed safe. That they *all* stayed safe . . . whatever was to come. He would be there for her. And maybe, just maybe, they would get through this.

CHAPTER THIRTY-TWO

Present Day
Pineville, Alabama

I STARED AT the phone on the table, well aware that I should call Mike and have him come get it. I also knew that whatever damage had been done regarding the chain of evidence had been broken when I'd gotten out of his car. Plus, he was headed back to the crime scene. No further harm to be had by my taking it to the station later.

This debate went on in my head for almost a full minute before I went to the bedroom for Mike's laptop. I set it up on the dining room table and began downloading everything I had saved to the cloud, including all reports from the first investigation and the photos of my butcher paper layout, testing my memory, but this time looking for something more specific. Sure enough, the original documentation included statements made by Willa Turney, several of them, in fact, dating back to the county fair incident in 1996. Scanning them, I found most of her basic information, including her birth date.

I pressed the home button on her phone and entered it as the passcode. Her screen lit up and I was in. People should know by now not to use birth dates or anniversaries as passwords, but they still do. I checked her recently made calls and scrolled through seventeen calls to the same number, starting at noon the previous day. The name on the number was merely "Brother," and I took a picture of her screen with my own phone. The next two calls were to unknowns—although I recognized one as the main number for the Pine Grove Baptist Church. Then there was a three-day gap before previous calls to a few people . . .

including Miss Doris. A phone call that had not been mentioned in any of our recent conversations.

I made another note.

Willa's recent texts were similar. A dozen or so to "Brother" with the same two words: "Call me."

So who, exactly, was Willa's brother? Kevin had said "Chase Rhone," but I didn't have a clue who that was. Mike obviously did, but we had not talked about it further. Did Rhone help Willa with Ricky's murder? Ricky had to have weighed a good two hundred pounds—years of whiskey and barbecue had not been kind to the man. I couldn't see the gaunt, sixty-something Willa, no matter how strong she was, moving his body alone. It made sense that she would have had help getting the body to that field.

I scrolled through her contacts, but she had surprisingly few in her list. Jill. Brother. Miss Doris. A pharmacy and several doctors. That was it.

But the ones missing intrigued me. Nothing for Ricky or her husband. No calls, no texts, no contact numbers. I knew women who regularly texted their husbands within their own homes. Here . . . nothing. No church members. No neighbors. No local businesses, not even the local vet or co-op.

Obviously a woman who had kept to herself.

I made a few notes, then sent Mike a text that I had the phone and I would bring it by the station later that afternoon. He responded with one letter—"K"—which told me he was more than busy. I then texted Nick and Margery and asked to meet with them again. Nick agreed to an appointment the next day, but Margery's was a terse "Let me check my calendar," which raised my eyebrows. I wondered if I were about to get as shut out as the investigators in the past had been. Not a good sign. I decided to skip lunch, and I grabbed my keys, jacket, and Willa's phone, and headed out the door. I would have to follow up on Rhone later, although I doubted Mike would be open, given his recent orders to me. But the internet could be useful. Once I got back to the carriage house, where I hoped to spend most of my afternoon—after meeting with Pastor Harris—I'd look Rhone up and re-create my butcher paper display and check in with Miss Doris. Perhaps one more night's sleep would keep my rib from pinching me each time I moved. Maybe.

I arrived at the church a few seconds before one, astonished that I had made it on time. I sent Mike a quick text that I had arrived safely, as well as the information on meeting Nick the next day. I figured the meeting with the pastor would not take long, and I included in the text an approximate time I'd be at the station. I received no response, but I hadn't expected it.

The church secretary sat in a small office outside the pastor's study. An elegant and ancient woman, Mrs. Ellis—so her nameplate announced—stood almost as tall as I did when she rose to greet me. A closely tailored and classic business suit encased her trim frame, and her silver hair gleamed in a short, stylish cut.

"Ms. Cavanaugh, the pastor will be with you in a few moments. Would you like a beverage? We have bottled water and soft drinks."

Since I'd skipped breakfast and lunch, I said yes to a Mountain Dew, then sat in an oversized wingback chair near her desk. She tilted her head, curiosity widening her eyes as she handed the soda to me. *Ah.* I pointed to the side of my face, swollen from the previous night's attack. "It's been an eventful twenty-four hours."

I had gotten so used to Mike paying it no mind that I'd almost forgotten I must look a fright.

"So we've heard."

It was my turn to appear curious.

She smiled. "Small town and all."

"Miss Doris?"

She sat back behind the desk, easing into the chair as if she were portraying the queen on an intimate stage. "A number of people have called to add you to the prayer list for this week."

"Word spread fast."

"I am sure no one meant to violate your privacy. They are just concerned."

"I know. And to be honest, if I wanted to keep my life private, I would have stayed in Nashville."

Her smile held a hint of glee. "You have been an open book since arriving in Pineville. It's been intriguing to have you in our church."

"Pine Grove has been quite welcoming."

"Have you considered joining the choir?"

The non sequitur startled me, and I blinked, my chin dropping. "I beg your pardon?"

"I sit on the other side of the church from you. You have a beautiful voice on the hymns. You would make a lovely addition to the alto section."

"I couldn—" I stopped and cleared my throat. "It is not something I have ever considered."

"Perhaps you should." She smiled, but her gaze shifted to the study door, which opened to reveal Pastor Harris.

Unlike Mrs. Ellis, who looked as if she'd stepped out of a corporate law firm, the pastor's Monday attire consisted of a sweater, jeans, and running shoes. He took one long stride toward me, his hand out for a shake as he greeted me with Baptist preacher tones. "Ms. Cavanaugh! Welcome!"

I stood and shook his hand, which was firm and dry. He backed away instead of turning away from me as he ushered me into the study. I had not been in many pastors' offices, but this one seemed logical, with bookshelves filled with theology tomes and a moderately neat desk. A calendar blotter held center stage on the desk, littered with dates, circles, and notes. He pushed the door almost closed as I settled in a chair in front of his desk, leaving a foot-wide gap. As he returned to his chair, he gestured toward the outer office. "Mrs. Ellis. She was a paralegal. Completely trustworthy."

"I would expect no less."

He leaned forward, resting his forearms on the edge of his desk. "I'm going to ask the same of you, if you don't mind."

"Confidentiality is a key part of my business, Pastor."

"Good. We understand each other." He took a deep breath. "You see, on my side of the desk, I'm usually the one keeping secrets, not sharing them. Even the police respect that. And what I was told was done so with that sense of confidentiality. But I cannot in good conscience keep this to myself, and I can't quite bring myself to share it with Mike. I mean, the information is important and may involve a crime being committed. Maybe. Maybe not. But it involves your case—I mean your investigation into Genevieve Marshall Eaton's murder."

"I see." I waited. I had heard this kind of speech before, when someone was on the fence about sharing details. Encouraging them usually had the opposite results—they withdrew, as if probing questions reinforced the need for silence. Leaving open air, with no words, pushed them to fill that dead space. Human nature. The longer I waited, the more they talked.

It also worked with friends and ex-husbands.

Pastor Harris leaned back in his chair. "I decided bringing you up to date, but knowing you will keep my confidence is a necessary step."

"I am honored you trust me."

"I also trust your professional ethics."

I wasn't sure my profession's ethics should be on the table, but I kept quiet. Too many people get their impressions of private investigators from television. The reality is far different. A point for another discussion at another time. "I appreciate that."

"I know you have had an . . . eventful . . . weekend. I wasn't even sure we would make this appointment. I . . . I heard about Ricky. I did not want to add to that, but what I have to say is perhaps related."

Yes, as a matter of fact, it did take some people quite a long time to get to the point. I waited.

He paused, then leaned forward, tapping his fingers on the desk. "Please forgive me if this is too invasive, but it is another vital reason I wanted to talk to you. Specifically you."

"As I told Mrs. Ellis, my life is pretty much an open book these days."

"I understand your first husband was an abuser."

OK, well, *that* came out of the blue. I refused to squirm. "Yes. He was."

"And it took you a long time to find a way out."

How in the world . . . Ah. Miss Doris. But why would she . . . An image flashed in my mind then, of Willa's phone. That call to Miss Doris. An ever-growing circle of information.

"Eleven years."

He nodded, glancing down at the blotter and running his fingertip along the bottom edge of it. "Clarissa Newton called me Saturday afternoon. She used to be a member here, in her twenties. Almost succeeded in getting Ricky Turney to join. She was on a campaign to get him to stop drinking, but never made much headway." He picked up a pencil and began to twist it between his fingers. "You know Ricky disappeared for a while after the murder."

"I had heard." I was intrigued to find out what he would fidget with next.

"I thought, maybe if Clarissa had married him . . . but it was not to be. He left, and she married someone else." He put the pencil back in a cup of pencils and plucked a staple remover off a tray near the cup. This definitely added a sense of danger to his fidgeting. He tapped it on the desk, then turned it over and over in his fingers, deftly avoiding the sharp points. Obviously not his first fidgeting rodeo. "So when Clarissa called Saturday, I wondered if she might be considering coming back to church. She had left because her husband—now ex-husband—did not want her out of his sight, much less around people who would support her in times of trouble. Their divorce was final earlier this year, and I knew that Ricky had started paying attention to her, so"—he shrugged and set the remover aside—"no matter how much I know about these situations, I always believe there's hope."

"That's your faith."

"Exactly!" He placed his hands flat on the blotter, a sign he knew he was fidgeting. He tried to stop. "But I'm sure you know as well as I do that . . ."

I kept my voice as soft and level as possible, even while a slow rage began coiling inside. I knew all too well how these things could go. "Why did she call?"

He took a deep breath. "Have you met Clarissa?"

"I have."

"One of the calmest people on the planet. But she was frantic. Unsure where to turn. She said her ex had found out about Ricky coming around to see her again, and he had started ranting about how dangerous Ricky was."

Ricky? Dangerous?

"Said he was too much of a risk, that he knew too much."

I squinted. "Knew too much about what?"

"I couldn't get it out of her. I tried. She said her ex threatened Ricky, threatened you, said everything was coming apart, that it had to be stopped, that if she didn't stay away from him, he'd kill her too. The ex, that is. That he would kill Clarissa if she didn't stay away from Ricky."

"Why didn't she call the police? A serious threat on someone's life *is* illegal."

"She said . . . she said she didn't want to get Ricky in trouble. She was terrified that if she went to the police, he might kill Ricky anyway, but also that he—Ricky—had done something awful in the past he could still go to jail for."

"But she didn't tell you what that was?"

Pastor Harris shook his head. "She was confused and scared and desperate to talk to someone. She'd been threatened, as had people she cared about. Too scared to call the police and too afraid to tell anyone." He paused a mere second. "If you were her, what would you do?"

Full circle. "You mean as a former abused wife?"

He nodded.

"I'd go into hiding." Which was exactly what I had done ten years ago. I was a cop and the divorce was final, but Tony O'Connell terrified me. He'd found out I was dating a friend who worked for the Nashville field office of the Secret Service and let me know what a bad idea that was. He knew just how to skirt the law with his threats. My friend and I were two highly trained law enforcement officials, but eleven years with Tony's gaslighting had done a number on my head. I just knew he could kill me and my friend and get away with it.

Therapy helped me regain my common sense as well as my courage, but I'd looked over my shoulder for a long time. At times, I still do.

Just ask Mike.

"And I would stay hidden. At least until I could get my head on straight."

The pastor sat a little straighter. "Maybe she did. Maybe that's why I can't get in touch with her."

One of my red flags popped in my head. "What do you mean?"

"After I heard about Ricky . . . I've been trying to get in touch with Clarissa all morning. She's not answering her phone."

"Did you try the library?" He nodded, and I sat forward. "Please give me her phone number and address."

"Now?" His eyes widened. "You don't think–"

"Yes. I'm going there now. Give them to me. Also her ex-husband's information–name, phone, anything you have. You keep trying to reach her."

He pulled a pad over and began writing on it. "Her ex-husband is Chase Rhone."

I froze. "What did you say?"

"Chase Rhone. Her ex-husband is Chase Rhone."

I stood. "I have to go. Now." I held out my hand, and he slapped the paper into it.

"Let me know what you find out."

"I will."

Belle left skid marks as I spun out of the church parking lot. Once I had her straight on the road, I called Mike, not bothering to use the earbuds–I just clutched the phone in my right hand. He answered on the second ring, not happy to hear from me.

"Star, I cannot–"

"Mike, you have to listen to me. It's urgent." He did, and I went through the short conversation I'd had with the pastor as well as what I'd seen on Willa's phone. I braced my knee against the steering wheel and smoothed out the now-crumpled paper clutched in my left hand. I read off Clarissa's address and phone number. "I'm on my way there now."

"Star, don't–"

Belle lurched forward, slammed from behind, and I screamed, dropping the phone and scrambling for the wheel, which had jerked from my grip. The Carryall veered sharply to the left, then to the right again as I caught the wheel and tried to brake and pull it straight. I fought it but overshot the correction, sending the passenger-side tires off the pavement and into the rutted gravel of the shoulder.

My attacker hit me again, on the rear left fender, sending me into a skid, the back end of the Carryall sliding farther off the road. I turned into it and might have pulled out of it, except that my attacker pressed the advantage and slammed into the front left fender, shoving the metal deep into that tire. I got a glimpse of an oversized pickup as he gunned the motor, shoving the Carryall off the road.

I felt a momentary sense of weightlessness as Belle began to roll, and my last thoughts before I hit the roof were the words: "seat belt"—which I had neglected to fasten in my rush—and "Mike"—who I could hear screaming my name from the phone, which bounced off the dash and hit the top of the Carryall about the same time my head did. My vision faded, but I heard one final scream—my own—and the deafening sound of crushing metal.

CHAPTER THIRTY-THREE

Monday, August 26, 1996
Pineville, Alabama

RICKY AND CLARISSA watched Jilly and April, Clarissa's daughter, hold hands as they skipped their way toward the front of Pineville Elementary, two peas in a pod. "Think they'll be all right without us?"

Clarissa smiled and slipped her hand in his. "They'll be fine. Independent little critters. Why? Are you worried?"

"No. It's just that I"—his mouth jerked into a scowl—"I don't like being away from her."

She patted his arm and leaned against his shoulder. "You sound like a fussy old grandma instead of a big brother."

"Hmph. You young whippersnapper." Their running joke with each other, born out of her being a few years older.

Clarissa laughed, which lightened his mood, then tugged him back toward his pickup.

Ricky had done the math about Clarissa, and it did not add up. At least, not in the usual way. But he didn't care. The one bright spot besides Jilly in this miserable summer had been Clarissa Newton. She had helped him, encouraged him, comforted him. At twenty-two and less than a year out of college, she was almost four years his senior—too much in some people's eyes, even though it would be different if she were thirty and he twenty-six.

Then there was her daughter, April. Same age as Jilly, which—again—made his head ache when he did the math. Although he had begun to feel as much like a father as a brother to Jilly, he couldn't imagine becoming a father two years sooner. At sixteen, which was when Clarissa had become a mother. He felt weak in comparison, barely able to cope with all that had happened in the last two years, whereas Clarissa had had a child, finished high school, and made it through college in four years using scholarships, student loans, and a part-time job. The strength it took to achieve all of that astonished him.

They had finally introduced the two girls two weeks ago, as both prepared to start the same school, Pineville Elementary, and the girls had become fast friends. They had spent a long, hot Saturday in the park, with the girls playing assorted games of the imagination on the playground, as Ricky and Clarissa watched from under a giant oak, his head in her lap. She had wanted to move slow physically—she obviously knew the consequences of moving too fast—and she kept inviting him to her church. But Ricky wasn't ready for that. Getting to know her faith was more intimacy than he could handle.

Clarissa did not know Jilly's full story—or maybe she knew enough not to be too inquisitive. But they had entered into a quiet peacefulness in their friendship, and Ricky had begun having a sweet fantasy about the four of them becoming a family, far and away from Pineville and all that had happened.

After all, his own family had withdrawn from him, as if he were a leper who was suddenly untouchable. Willa had enrolled Jilly in school the week before, but she had made it clear that the girl was primarily Ricky's responsibility. She'd play Mom enough to keep her brother happy but not much else. She had barely done that much when Ricky had been younger—although now he knew why.

Chase came to the house often, several times a week, which made Willa cross and Kevin nervous, but he and Ricky had reached a stage of détente with each other, now that all the secrets were out in the open. Chase acknowledged the bond between Jilly and Ricky, seemingly content to play the doting uncle. They all ignored the obvious: the fact that Jilly's "father" never put in an appearance. There was no contact from Chase's supposed client, and since the fiasco of the Fourth, even Chase had dropped the fiction. Acknowledging, finally, that the man had assaulted a twelve-year-old and left her with a child horrified Ricky, and the idea that Chase might be grooming Jilly for the same eventuality electrified his determination to protect her.

But it took Clarissa to put the topic into words on that pleasant Saturday afternoon, after Ricky mentioned how much April and Jilly looked alike.

"Possibly," she had responded softly, "because they have the same father."

Ricky did the math. He didn't like the answer. The very idea made his gut churn, but it made too much sense. He didn't dare confront Chase about it, but it was the piece that made the puzzle look a bit more whole. He had not responded to Clarissa about it then, and she had allowed his silence, as she usually did. It was one of the things he liked about her—a willingness to just be with him in silence.

But now, as they walked back to his pickup, he knew the time had come. He helped her in the passenger side, then got behind the wheel but didn't start it.

"Clarissa?"

"Hmm?"

"Is Chase Rhone really April's father?"

She nodded. "Yes."

"Was it"—he swallowed hard—"was it . . . forced?"

Her eyebrows arched. "No. That's not how he works." She twisted in her seat to face him. "He is what some people call a groomer, a seducer. Patient. In it for the long term. He first approached me when I was twelve. The brother of a friend introduced us. He only turns violent if something goes truly wrong."

"How did you . . . get away?"

She shrugged. "I got old. He got bored."

Ricky stared at her. "You are *not* old!"

She smiled and reached for his hand. "You are sweet. I'm not old in my mind, or yours, or even the world's. But I am to him. At least for now, he has no use for me."

"Would he want you again?"

Another shrug. "I gave up second-guessing him a long time ago."

"Is that how he meets . . . girls? A friend's introduction?"

She nodded. "Usually. A friend of a friend. An older brother." She paused. "You know he used to be a cop, right?"

"Yeah. He got booted off his last force, so I heard."

"Apparently he tried to seduce the younger sister of one of his fellow cops. It didn't go over too well. The guy found out, stopped it." She shifted uneasily. "Which is odd. He usually is a better judge. I heard rumors that everything went south in a hurry, but I never heard any of the names involved."

A nagging thought tugged at the back of Ricky's mind. Something . . . an earlier conversation . . . The source hit, and his eyes shot wide. He straightened in the seat and started the truck. "I need to get home."

Clarissa fastened her seat belt. "What's wrong?"

"I don't know for sure, but I need to call Colorado."

"Colorado? Whyever for?"

He shook his head. "I'll tell you later. It's just that a couple things are suddenly making more sense, and I need to check on some things."

Clarissa fell silent, watching Ricky as he swung the truck through the turns leading to the library. "You . . . you aren't going to stir him up again, are you?"

Ricky pulled into a parking space. "Not if I can help it. I'm still recovering from the last time." He turned toward her to realize Clarissa's face had gone stark white. Alarmed, he reached for her, but she drew back against the door. "Clarissa?"

Her eyes glistened. "Listen to me, Ricky. You do not know how bad this can get."

"After the Fourth–"

"That was nothing!" Her shout silenced Ricky, and he leaned away from her. She licked her lips. "That was nothing. Nothing compared to what he could have done. If he comes back around, he could make me–" She stopped and looked away a moment. When she turned back, her eyes glistened as she pleaded with him. "Please. For all of us. Let this go."

"Clarissa–"

"No!" She opened the door, gathered her backpack off the floor, and got out. "Let it go. Please." She slammed the door and headed to the front door of the library, where she used her keys to get in, locking the door behind her.

Ricky watched her for a few moments, accepting the fact that she was as terrified of his uncle as the rest of them. But somebody should stop him. Stop this. Stop all of this.

"We deserve better," he whispered, as the lights came on in the library and Clarissa moved behind the front desk. "You deserve better."

CHAPTER THIRTY-FOUR

Present Day
Pineville, Alabama

THE FAMILIAR SCREECH of a red-tailed hawk. The gentle brush of water lapping against a hull. The scents of oil, tar, and dead fish. A rocking sensation that both soothed and irritated, as every motion caused a new line of pain somewhere in my body. All indications that I was on a boat.

A boat? What about the wreck?

As consciousness dawned over me, specific injuries let themselves be known—my right wrist and left knee ached as if they'd been sprained, the blood flow to each joint making them throb in a painful rhythm. I lay on my side, my head tilted down toward the hard surface beneath me, and my neck and shoulders told me the whiplash damage had been renewed. That rib pinched and probed, making me wonder if the crack had become a break. Everything else just hurt like crazy, and I knew my bruises would have bruises.

Yet I could not see.

I groaned and tried to push up, but a hand gripped my upper arm and pushed down. "Don't move."

I relented, confused. That dark male voice was not Mike—nor did it sound like any EMT I'd ever met. Who was he?

Images from the crash flooded back through me in a rush, and I gasped. The whole incident had taken mere seconds, yet imprinted on my brain were flashes of the big truck, the rammed front fender, and the sense of falling as Belle had slid off the road and rolled.

Belle!

My beloved Carryall—left to me by my father. I had a quick hope that she wasn't totaled before my mind went back to that voice. *The driver?*

I swallowed and cleared my throat. "Who are you?" The words emerged like boots on gravel.

"I suppose it would be too clichéd to say that I was your greatest dream and your worst nightmare. The one you've been looking for."

"You don't sound like Ben Affleck."

"Funny girl. They told me you had a mouth on you."

They? "Nice to know someone's been talking about me. You should probably only believe about half of it." I tried to open my eyes again—this time I realized I was blindfolded. An oily rag, by the smell of it, but the tight grip it had on my head could explain that discomfort.

He moved, revealed by the sounds of creaking leather, sloshing water, and boots on something solid. "Oh, I believe most of it, which is why I should shoot you before doing this. But I've always liked a challenge. A game." His mouth hovered above my ear. "A risk."

He jerked my feet together, and I yelped. I tried to kick, but the pain that showered over me left me breathless. "I love the risks," he continued, pinning my feet down with his knee as he tied my ankles together. "The adrenaline rush." He pulled my hands together behind my back, and I screamed as my right wrist sparked with fire. "I almost wish this weren't going to be over as fast as it will be."

The realization of what he was about to do blindsided me, and I fought a sense of panic with deep breaths, repeated as often and as deeply as I could, trying to ignore the agony that would make me gasp with shock.

Calm, Star. You have to be calm. Calm. Breathe. Calm. Remember.

"You survived a blow to the head that would have killed a normal person. Now a wreck that should have sent you to hell. It's almost a challenge to try to kill you at this point. I want to see how much you can survive."

And with that, he lifted me up and hefted me away from him with a toss that left me falling free. I took a deep breath and held it. *Calm. Stay calm.*

The water of Alabama lakes this time of year was roughly twenty degrees below body temperature, about that of an average lap swimming pool. Not frigid by any measure, but still a shock to the system. I hit the water on my back and rear, which stung but kept me from sinking too far. But as my clothes became soaked, I knew I would not have much time to get my head in gear.

I could hear my assailant's laughter floating over the water, and I forced myself to stretch out flat in the water. With a little effort, I got my mouth above water and inhaled as deeply and rapidly as I could before my weight carried me down again.

Calm. Don't struggle. Remember.

I held my breath, but as my lungs ached, I let out tiny, tight streams of air, which made me drop even lower in the water, bringing back a spike of panic and the urge to fight.

Calm. Don't struggle. You can do this. Remember.

Remember your skills.

Skills. More than ten years ago, in an attempt to spend even less time with my husband, I enrolled in scuba diving classes. Tony accepted it, as I told him that I wanted to apply for a position on the police department's diving team. Rescue and recovery. I took every class I could, one right after the other. Open water. Advanced open water. Wreck. Rescue. Divemaster. Dive instructor. As the certifications had piled up, I'd fallen more in love with the idea of joining the team.

Overhead, my assailant called out, taunting me. "Oh, this is too easy." He then gunned the motor, and the boat sped away, swamping me in its wash.

Calm. Don't struggle. Remember.

Part of my dive training was staying afloat for extended periods of time without swimming. Rescue divers often must tow people to safety using only their legs—so I learned a variety of kicking styles.

Calm. Don't struggle. Remember.

Pressing my knees together, I executed a hard mermaid kick, which shoved my head above water just long enough for me to gasp another deep breath before dropping under again.

Divers in training sometimes panicked, and instructors had to get them above water—so I learned how to get under them and push up. Divers learned a great number of skills that went beyond the ability to stay down and look at pretty fish.

Most of all, I learned to stay calm. Panic underwater kills faster and more often than any other problem, even lack of air.

Calm. Don't struggle. Remember.

During that time, I discovered my body was "positively buoyant"—a term that meant I floated easily. Because of the way we were designed, women often float more easily than hard-bodied men, who tend to sink like they were weighted due to the lack of body fat. Air—deep breaths—also helped me float.

I forced my body to stretch out on my back, trying to ignore the stabs of pain that begged me to panic, to flail, to fight the water.

Calm. Remember. Kick. Breathe. Slow release.

I focused on the sounds around me. Distant motors that moved along, some coming closer before they moved away again. If I could just stay afloat long enough, maybe one of them would see me. I clung to that slim hope, a dying woman's last grasp of sanity.

Calm. Remember. Kick. Breathe. Slow release.

The chill of the lake water leeched into my muscles, yet another reason to panic. Lap pools were set cooler because the swimmers worked so hard, the exertion kept them warm. But I could barely do the mermaid kick, and I knew the danger the cold represented. A cramp would be deadly. Again the urge to flail swept over me.

No! Calm. Remember. Kick. Breathe. Slow release. The cold will help ease the pain.

And it did. Even the rib hurt less as I repeated the routine over and over. My hands and arms went numb, and time seemed to slow, then stop.

Focus on something else, Star. Anything. Your routine. There is only the routine. Calm. Remember. Kick. Breathe. Slow release.

An image of Gran materialized behind my eyelids. *Please, Lord, take care of her. If this is my time, please see her through it. And Mike. Please.* I saw his somber face, the way he looked standing at the back of Pine Grove Baptist Church, keeping watch over the flock. A sheepdog keeping the wolves away. Handsome, those blue eyes taking in every minute detail. A wave of love swept through me. *My* sheepdog. *Lord, him too.*

Calm. Remember. Kick. Breathe. Slow release.

The kick wasn't as strong this time, allowing for a shallower breath. It would not be long now.

And an odd sense of peace settled over me. Almost inexplicable. A letting go of all the things of this world. A realization that only one thing mattered, and after years of fighting my relationship with God, it'd been Mike and Gran—the two people I thought of last, the two people I loved—who had brought me around. I was ready.

One more time. *Calm. Remember. Kick. Breathe. Slow release.*

As I dropped below the water, the top of my head hit something solid. The water swirled around me, lifting my face above the water for a second, and I grabbed my last breath, a harsh gasp before going under—again, my head hitting something solid.

"What in the world—dear God in heaven!" The shouted prayer came from above me, and for a second my pain-numbed brain wondered if angels shouted. Then hands were pulling at me with an unexpected strength, hauling me out of the water. Pain rushed back into every fiber, and I screeched as I shivered violently.

"Hon, what in the world happened to you?"

I tried to answer but couldn't, as I shook so hard my teeth clattered. Abruptly my hands and ankles were freed, and a blanket was cast over me and tucked in tightly as the blindfold slid off my head. I squinted in the late afternoon sunlight, my vision slowly focusing on my angels—two fishermen who looked as if they were straight off the *Deliverance* movie set. Another blanket was draped over me as one of them turned away, sat down next to the outboard, and geared it up.

Bass boats, apparently, could run at speeds more than sixty-five miles an hour with the right motor. Which this one had.

I tried to speak, but the other man patted my shoulder and started shouting into his phone.

I thanked God for fishermen. This was twice such people had been vital in saving my life. Later I would find out that they had been drifting, just lazing the afternoon away in silence, casting occasionally and pulling in a few fish. My kicks and the lake's current had carried me into their cove, and I had bumped headfirst into their boat. They'd both been facing the other direction and had not noticed my approach. They had assumed I was a log. Until I'd gasped.

An ambulance waited on the boat ramp as they pulled in. I knew that on television and the movies, the hero or heroine usually leaped up and got on with life, refusing medical aid, no matter how badly they were hurt. Yeah . . . reality was a little different. I literally had nothing left. No stamina, no fortitude, no wherewithal to even talk, much less move. I couldn't even tell the EMTs what had happened. And as I had warmed, the spikes of pain held at bay by the cold water returned in full flair. I was more than happy to have strong hands and arms lift me, strap me to a gurney, and plug an IV into me.

My attacker, who had to have been Chase Rhone, had transported me all the way to Lake Martin to dump me in the water, probably to put some distance between my body and Mike's jurisdiction. But by the time we reached the hospital in Dadeville, I had managed to mutter my name, Mike's name, and that I had been abducted. The jostling of the next half hour—the drive, the transfer onto an examination bed, the taking of vitals, being sent for tests, the peppering questions—kept me awake but barely. Every time I was left alone for more than two minutes, I drifted off. I lost track of time as well as the number of tests. Concerned about the repeated blows to my head—they had contacted the hospital in Gadsden for records—they admitted me for observation, slipped a number of painkillers into my system, and finally left me alone for a few hours.

Sometime after midnight, a nurse came in to check my vitals. I woke, but my mouth—as well as my brain—felt as if they were filled with cotton. I licked my lips, and she offered me a few ice chips, which I greedily sucked on. As she left, I realized another presence remained in the room with me, in a chair near the window. A strong, masculine, and quiet presence.

I wet my lips again, finding a coarse version of my voice. "You should be home in bed."

"So should you."

"I took a detour."

"Looks like the detour took you."

"Belle?"

"She's been towed to Troy's garage. He said he'll look for parts. He wasn't hopeful."

"I didn't mean to—"

"I know."

"It was him. Chase Rhone."

"I know. He's gone off-grid. Phone's off. Willa's not talking."

"Clarissa?"

Silence.

"Mike?"

"She's gone too. But her house has been ransacked." He paused. "There's blood."

I had no words. Tears flooded my eyes, and I wiped them away.

Mike stood and drew closer to the bed, but he was far enough away for his face to be hidden by the shadows. His voice remained low and even, his words adding to the pain that gripped my core.

"Star, I cannot do this. I cannot lose another"—he paused and straightened his shoulders—"I cannot deal with the danger you keep putting yourself in."

It wasn't my fault this time! But instead of screaming it, I waited. That was what I did. I waited.

And, if I were truthful with myself, it *was* my fault. Mike had told me to stay put. Instead, I had gone to see Pastor Harris.

"It's hard, even when you are equal partners. Partners have each other's backs. They stay together. They tackle things together. They don't go off—" His voice broke and he stopped.

I knew what was coming, and I did not want to hear it. But I heard the deep fear in his voice as he took a shaky breath. "We aren't partners. You won't let me in, and when you know I'll object, you keep it from me. I realize this time you had just gone to talk to Pastor Harris, that you thought this a quick and relatively safe side trip, but we knew your attacker was still out there. Still following you. That's why you were encased in the carriage house. So you could work and stay safe.

But you didn't. You knew the danger, and you went anyway. You could have postponed. Should have postponed. And before you mention it, I already called Nicholas Eaton to let him know you will not be seeing him tomorrow. Today."

"Someone needs to tell Jill."

"I went to see Kevin. She's flying in today to make arrangements for her brother."

He returned to silence then, a chasm between us growing until it felt all-consuming. My chest ached, and not from just the rib. For him to do this now . . . I knew he must have been devastated, but I wanted to stop him. Promise him . . . "I will go to Miss Doris's when they release me and wait until Jill and I can conclude our business. It's clearly your case from here."

"I'll let them know. I'm sure Miss Doris will send Brett to pick you up."

"Mike–"

He held up his hand to stop me. I waited.

"I can't–" He stopped and remained quiet several more seconds, as if gaining his nerve. "You don't trust me, Star. And I cannot trust you. It's time you returned to Nashville. For good."

A muddy fog consumed me, crushing me heart and soul. My mind spun, scrambled–again, no words came. I licked my lips one more time. "OK."

He stilled, watching me, then did an abrupt and precise about-face and left.

CHAPTER THIRTY-FIVE

Wednesday, August 28, 1996
Pineville, Alabama

TWO DAYS LATER, Scott Ketsler finally answered his phone, with an almost breathless, "Ketsler. Speak to me."

Ricky took a deep breath and added more coins into the pay phone. "Listen, you may not remember me, but we talked last December."

After several deep breaths, Ketsler asked, "You the one who called me about Hope Marshall's kidnapping?"

"Yeah. That's me." Ricky heard what sounded like pages flipping and a couple of odd beeps. "Can I ask you a few more questions?"

"I thought you didn't want to hear from me anymore." More background rustling.

"I . . . I didn't want you to call that number anymore. I . . . I didn't live there. I didn't want them in trouble."

"Right."

Obviously Scott Ketsler didn't believe him. Ricky didn't care as long as he would answer some more questions. "I wanted to follow up on something you said."

"OK. But this time it's going to be quid pro quo, my friend."

"What?"

"A trade off. I'll answer your questions, but you have to answer mine. Deal?"

Ricky hesitated. He was on a pay phone. No way to be traced. Ketsler had no idea who he was. "OK."

"Good. Me first. Tell me how you knew Hope Marshall had been kidnapped."

"Because I was there when she was taken. I saw it happen."

Ketsler's voice rose in pitch. "Are you serious? You were at the Marshall compound?"

"Yes."

"A witness? Why didn't you call the police?"

"I . . . I didn't want anyone in trouble."

"Wait. Are you the kidnapper?"

Ricky closed his eyes. He did not want to admit it. It was Chase. It was all Chase. "An accomplice."

"Man, why didn't you go to the police instead of calling me? Come to think of it, why *did* you call me instead of the cops?"

"It's complicated. Look, I wanted—no, I *want*—to get Hope back to her family, but just calling the police would put a lot of people in danger. You even suggested that yourself."

"I did?"

"You said the cops shut you down when you were trying to find out more about Genevieve's kidnapping. That they knew what was going on. That they might even be involved."

More silence, except for the rustling noise. Then, finally, "They might have known what was going on behind the scenes. I'm not convinced they were involved."

"Could they have been?"

Ketsler's voice turned sharp. "What do you know?"

Ricky closed his eyes a moment. He could help Hope—Jilly—or not. "The man who kidnapped Hope used to be a cop. And he was involved with what happened to Genevieve too. I recently found out he has a habit of seducing young girls. Really young. Genevieve wasn't the first."

"Genevieve wasn't seduced. She was—"

"Listen to me!" In the following silence, Ricky went on. "It's a habit! He grooms and seduces, and if that doesn't work, he attacks. Genevieve wasn't the first. She won't be the last."

"Is he grooming Hope?"

"No. I hope not. Hope is his daughter."

"Well, it wouldn't be the first time one of these predators—"

"No! I won't let that happen! But I need to know who I can trust. I can't trust the cops if they're going to protect a former cop."

"They won't protect him if you have proof. Get proof, and they'll put him away. They'll only protect him if it's conjecture."

"But I was there!"

"Legally, you would be an uncorroborated accomplice. Not proof."

Ricky felt his chest tighten as his mind flipped through all the encounters, all the times he had been with Chase and Hope. Nothing. Even now, "Jilly" lived with his parents. It would be their word against his as to how she got there.

"In other words, my best bet is to try to get her back to her family without anyone finding out."

"Either that or gather the proof. Listen, let me make some calls, see what I can find out. Can you call me Friday? About this time or a little later?"

Ricky slid down the wall of the phone booth and rested his head against one knee. "Yeah."

"Good. Talk to you then."

Ketsler ended the call, and Ricky sat there, the receiver dangling from his fingers, until its hang-up signal sounded, the raucous beeps hammering against his growing headache. He stood, hung up the phone, and returned to his pickup. Staring out the windshield, he had an urge to wrap Jilly in silk and deliver her to the Marshall compound, hoping not to be seen. He might get away with it.

But everyone involved would know who had done it. Chase's fury would start with him and move on to his parents. Possibly even Clarissa, if he knew they were involved.

"No," he whispered to himself. "There has to be another way."

The fair gambit had not worked because Chase had been too close, too suspicious. But maybe the premise had not been faulty, just the execution. If he could not take Jilly to her mother, maybe there was a way to get her mother to come to Jilly. Through no fault of his own.

Perhaps Scott Ketsler would be interested in writing a follow-up story.

CHAPTER THIRTY-SIX

Present Day
Pineville, Alabama

FROM THE MOMENT Mike left, Tuesday became a blur of doctors, paperwork, pain, and tears. I lost track of the number of times I was asked, "Are you all right, dear?"

No. I was *not* all right. Everything hurt.

Everything.

In a bit of pure shame, I felt grateful I could blame the tears, the desire to curl in on myself and hide, on my physical injuries. Of which there were plenty. The rib, which had been merely cracked after the first assault, had indeed separated, and my torso had been tightly wrapped to support it. This time I did have a concussion, which only added to the pain in my head, neck, and shoulders. The whiplash injury had been amplified, and I could barely feel my fingers. My wrist and knee were sprained. Bruises littered my body as if I'd walked between a wall and a graffiti artist.

But by God's blessing, I supposed, there were no internal injuries. The major organs had escaped damage.

Unless, that was, I wanted to put my heart on that list. It hurt too. A lot.

The sense that Mike was right hurt even more. Because of my own issues, I had kept him at bay for so long that even our tentative moves toward each other had come with reservations. And I had hid details from him when I knew he would object—or when my actions could hurt his job or his responsibilities. The very fact that as a PI I worked without the boundaries to which the police had to adhere had become a barrier between us. We had tried, but the time had come when that barrier could no longer be ignored . . . or eradicated. Our fragile trust in each other had been shattered.

Time to go back to Nashville.

As before, Miss Doris waited inside the carriage house for my return. Seated on one of the sofas, with a full tea service on the table in front of her, she looked as if she were about to host a society tea, with black slacks, a red shell, and a rose-patterned jacket. I didn't speak as I deposited all the paperwork, medicines, and other hospital detritus on the dining room table, but as I unloaded, Miss Doris poured tea, cleared her throat, and pointed to the shortbread cookies on a tray next to the teapot.

I gave her a half-hearted smile, limped over, and eased down on the sofa next to her. She handed me a cup, and I sighed as I sipped the caramel-colored brew, its heat steaming my face. It did have a soothing effect, spreading warmth throughout my chest. "Thank you."

"Well, you do look like the dregs of the pit, my dear. I figured you could use some renewal."

I managed a grin. "I appreciate that. I'm pretty scrambled." I reached for a cookie, nibbling one corner. *Scrambled* was an understatement. My mind dodged and weaved, jumping topics and derailing so often, I found myself amazed that my sentences made any sense.

"So I understand you will be staying here for a few days. Not going anywhere."

I put down the cookie. "You've talked to Mike?"

She set her cup down and pulled my cell phone out of her jacket pocket. "He brought this over earlier today. He said there was another one in the truck, but he kept it."

I nodded, taking the phone from her with a sigh of relief. "That one is evidence. I was on the way to deliver it to him when the accident happened."

She picked up her cup again but peered at me over the rim as she sipped. "Accident?"

"You know what I mean."

"I do. I also know that explains why our sweet Michael was in such a foul mood. He barely spoke when he dropped that off."

I looked at the phone, a question forming in the back of my foggy brain. *Why had he brought it here? Today? Why hadn't he given it to me last night?* The obvious answer annoyed me more than it should have, given the last twenty-four hours.

Because his tech guys weren't through with it.

Almost every police department, even the smaller ones, had the ability to dump contents of a cell phone into the evidence system—or they had access to someone who could. It didn't take long, and most systems these days could access everything on a phone, even deleted materials—which weren't really gone until they were overwritten by new data. *But why would he want my phone?* He knew I didn't keep research or evidence on it—cell phones are far too vulnerable to keep important information stored.

"Are you in pain, dear? You are scowling."

I placed the phone on the table. "My thoughts are flying all over. Hard to keep anything focused, especially with the pain. But since I'm to stay here and do nothing, I'm sure I'll rest and rely on the meds."

"Didn't you have an interview today?"

"Mike put the kibosh on it. He doesn't want me going anywhere."

"Could you call them?"

"Interviews are more revealing in person. But Mike wants me to drop the case entirely. It's intermingled with current crimes to the point he's taking over. Or rather, the Pineville PD is taking over."

"Without your help?"

"I . . . I can't. I'm part of the crimes now. A victim." The word came out with more bitterness than I intended, but then I'd never been great at controlling my emotions. I looked at the phone again. Victim . . . and apparently also a suspect.

"Hmm. Was that his intent?"

I looked up at her, my brain fog muddling things again. "Him who?"

"Your attacker. Did he intend to get you off the case by either killing you or involving you in it? I mean he probably just wanted you dead, but he could have just shot you instead of giving you a chance to live."

I blinked, trying to absorb her words, which made more sense than they should and no sense at all. "I . . . I don't know."

She peeked into her cup, then pour herself another. "More?"

I nodded.

She spoke as she filled the cup and added more milk. "You know, I had a friend in high school. Bah. Such a pest! She made us all crazy, following us around, talking nonstop. When a mutual friend of ours ran for class president, I suggested he put her to work, that her outgoing nature would spread the word. She loved it. Dove into it like a fly to honey. Made flyers, passed them out during football games, picked up the tossed ones afterward. She made him sound like the next coming of FDR. She made him sound so good, he started believing all she said. Built up his confidence."

"Did he win?"

"Yes, but barely. Turns out she annoyed so many people, they almost did *not* vote for him."

I snickered. "Please do not make me laugh."

She smiled. "My point is that she stopped pestering all of us because she was involved in something else."

"A distraction."

"Precisely."

"So what happened to her?"

"Oh, she married the guy. He became a lawyer. She took him as far as mayor of Gadsden. Served two terms, then retired and chased ambulances the rest of his career." She reached for a cookie. "Think about it. Now that you are out of the game, he's only facing one front instead of two. You are no longer nipping at his heels from the past."

I got it. "And without that, he can focus on evading the police regarding the current crimes."

"It's a theory."

"Not a bad one." I let out a long sigh. "But doesn't help my other pains."

"Ah. I cannot help you there, although I may be able to explain it."

"He told you that—"

She shook her head. "No, but it was not hard to guess, given the way he marched around here, barking and getting out as quick as he could. As if he had forgotten every manner he ever learned. And you, looking like someone shot your cat."

"Don't even say such a thing."

A wry smile crossed her face. "These past four days scared the life out of him, Star."

"I know—"

"Did you know he's been to see Pastor Harris?"

I really wish she would give my brain a chance to catch up. "I'm sorry?"

She straightened and paid attention to her tea for a few moments. "Did you know I was on the city council when we hired Mike?"

I closed my eyes. "Miss Doris, I'm not up to this."

"Then just listen. You can work it out later."

I wrapped my hands around my cup and sipped more warmth into my system. Maybe it would help. And I waited.

"Your Michael—"

"He's not my—"

"Hush."

"Yes, ma'am."

"There was a sergeant's position open here on the police force. Normally, the chief hires new officers, but the chief at the time was a little"—she paused and waggled one hand back and forth—"a little fond of the entertainment down at Dewey's Tavern. So the city council stepped in to, um, help him review the applicants. Michael Luinetti's stood out. He was already a sergeant. So why in the world would this Yankee boy with a good career want to up and move to a small Southern town? We asked him. He told us. Turns out things had taken an unexpected turn in his current position, and he wanted to get as far away from it as he could."

"An unexpected turn."

"His partner had been shot."

I felt the blow clear through to my spine.

"While it was not Michael's fault, he felt the guilt, knew the way other officers looked at him. Like a growing spiderweb that closed in around him. We gave him a chance to start over, and within a year, the whole council wanted him as chief. It was the renewal he needed."

"Until I came along."

"Something like that."

"A guess. His partner was killed because he took too many risks."

"She."

I closed my eyes, a dark sadness settling over me. "She."

Miss Doris replaced her cup and draped a linen napkin over the cookies. "I am going to send over supper around six. I will ask them to gather the tray at that time."

"Miss Doris—"

"Hush. Yes, I know you can get your own dinner, you independent cuss. But sometimes it is nice to have help. You need to learn that now, before it bites you in the rear again. Piece of advice you need to take to heart and never forget. Never turn down free food or free help."

I bit my lower lip. "Yes, ma'am." I pushed myself up and followed her to the door.

She paused, then reached up and touched my cheek . . . the one without the bruise. "I know I complain about my family a lot, and they do get on my nerves. But I have never, ever wished they weren't around. Independence is not all it's made out to be. Try to keep that in mind as you make your next decision. What you do affects other people. And vice versa." She opened the door. "Now. Set the alarm and go to sleep."

I did . . . eventually. But first I had a great deal to think about.

CHAPTER THIRTY-SEVEN

Sunday, January 5, 1997
Pineville, Alabama

RICKY SAT WITH Jilly on the floor as she watched *Touched by an Angel.* The show fascinated her, especially Andrew, the character played by John Dye, and she insisted on watching it each week. Ricky didn't understand the draw until the week she whispered, "Does he know my mommy?"

Andrew was the Angel of Death.

"Possibly," he had whispered back. "How about if we talk to Clarissa tomorrow?" This was definitely not a conversation he'd wanted to have with a six-year-old. She had asked other questions about the show, which he also could not answer, and the result was an ongoing Monday after-school trip to the library to see Clarissa and April and do a little research.

Tonight, however, Jilly was motionless and quiet, and he wondered why. He asked, but she only shook her head. It worried him, but he did not pursue it.

After all, it had been an eventful few weeks for all of them.

He and Scott Ketsler had talked several times. Ketsler had been interested in doing follow-up articles, and the Birmingham paper he had once worked for jumped on his proposal to write them. Using the one-year anniversary of Hope Marshall's disappearance as the excuse, the articles had appeared on December 10 and 11 of the previous year. Ketsler had managed to interview Genevieve, Owen, and Margery Marshall, as well as the county sheriff who had overseen both abduction cases. Genevieve had been more open about what had happened to her, even mentioning details that had not appeared in the press before.

Ketsler told Ricky this had not been happy news for the sheriff, who demanded those details not be published. He also demanded to know who Ketsler's tipster had been, which Ketsler refused to divulge. Much to Ricky's relief.

The articles had not gone over well in the Turney household either. Knowing the storm that would come, Ricky had taken Clarissa for a vacation to Gulf Shores. He'd left his parents a note that he would be out of town for a few days but had not left a location or a phone number. While he knew Chase's fury would burn bright and deep for a long time, they could avoid the initial blast.

When they returned, however, Jilly wouldn't speak to him and mostly locked herself in her room over the Christmas holidays—except for Sunday nights. Even Christmas Eve and Day had been somber, with a few presents for Jilly and none for the rest of the family. He only hoped that nothing traumatic had happened while he was gone, that her sudden sullenness had another cause.

As *Touched by an Angel* ended, his mother turned off the television. "Time for bed," she announced. "School starts again tomorrow."

Ricky helped Jilly up. "Do you want to go to the library after school?"

She shrugged and started a slow trudge up the stairs to her room. He followed, his chest aching at this withdrawal of his happy, gregarious little sister. As she headed into her room, he tried again. "Are you ready for school tomorrow? I know you'll enjoy seeing April again."

Jilly turned, glaring at him. "Andrew does *not* know my mommy." The pronouncement came with anger and the first tears down her cheeks. "Because my mommy is not dead! You lied! You and Uncle lied! She just doesn't want me anymore!" She slammed her bedroom door with a force that shook the wall.

Ricky stumbled backward, his chest burning with pain. *What had happened?*

At the end of the hall, his mother stood in her own doorway, a smug look on her face. "I told you she was too smart for her own good. Too smart for you and that brother of mine. She's going to be trouble. You watch and see. She'll bring this house down around all of us."

CHAPTER THIRTY-EIGHT

Present Day
Pineville, Alabama

THE KNOCK I had been dreading came at just after nine Wednesday morning. A firm and even knock, without insistence or demands. Just four thunks on the wood. With a long sigh, I disabled the alarm and opened the door.

Jill Turney stood there, almost looking every bit the Chicago defense attorney, with her tailored suit, Kate Spade accessories, and professionally styled makeup. But no amount of concealer on the planet could hide those dark blotches on her cheeks or the red rims of her eyes. Her right eye even boasted a broken blood vessel, the red spot covering most of the outside corner of the sclera.

She gave me a half smile. "Well, don't you just look like something the cat hacked up."

Chicago had not yet filed off her Southern edges.

"Rough few days, as you well know."

"Yep." She brushed by me and paused in the living room, looking around. "This looks like a soft landing."

I followed her and gestured for her to sit. "It's temporary."

"As are most things." She sat, setting her briefcase on the floor and leaning it against the sofa.

I eased down on the one opposite. "I'm sorry about Ricky. Neither of us—"

"We knew the risks." Her eyes were bright with tears, but her face had a determined set to it.

OK. So no soft pedals. "We did."

She crossed her arms and her legs, huddling in on herself. "Don't get me wrong, Star. I loved my brother with all my heart. He was my one champion in a tumultuous life. I hated some of the things he did and was doing. I despised his alcoholism. But I adored him, and I am going to miss him more than I can say. But we"—she pointed quickly to both of us, then tucked her hand away again—"we are women of a much larger planet than Pineville, Alabama. We both work in professions that deal with ruined lives. And I, especially, knew the dangers of stirring all this up. No, I did not expect anyone to get killed, but I did know it was dangerous." She paused. "Even if I didn't want to admit what it might cost me."

"So why did you do it? Why not let the sleeping dogs lie? Ricky would probably have been dead in a couple of years from his drinking anyway. Your last tie here."

"Honestly? Because I make a living getting unrepentent dirtbags off, and I had just gotten fed up with that happening in my own family. I didn't know for sure who killed Genevieve Marshall, but I had my suspicions."

"About whom?"

Her lips pursed a moment, but her eyes never left my face. "From what I have learned from my profession, along with a few memories, I have come to believe that one person could not have done this. The events were too complex. Too much knowledge about the Marshall family would be required."

"So someone inside their circle helped."

She sat a bit straighter. "The Marshall family deserves closure as well, after all these years, don't they?"

A woman of conscience? No, I did not quite believe it. "Even if you know they are not completely innocent in this?"

That half smile returned. "As I said, you and I are from a bigger planet. And we know the wealthy operate on a different plane from the rest of us. But what we sow, we also reap. Yes?"

"So a touch of vengeance as well?"

"When you cover up a crime, for whatever reason, you set up an infection that can poison the entire system. But nothing stays secret forever."

"When did you know?"

She straightened and dropped her hands into her lap. "You mean, when did I know that I was Hope Marshall, or when did I know that Hope Marshall was supposed to be dead?"

"Both."

She gazed down at her hands, but her focus seemed to be far in the past. "I actually remember being Hope Marshall. There are glimpses in the back of my head, barely even there, impressions really, of the compound on Lake Martin. Running down that lawn to the lake. Swimming. But there is some bad stuff mixed in. Screams."

"Abuse?"

She shook her head, her gaze distant. "I don't remember anything like that. But there's an overall sense that I was a stranger in a strange land. Unwanted. Damaged somehow." She looked up at me. "Only as an adult did I begin to put things together. That I was a child of rape. Loved, sort of, but never accepted. An outsider. If that makes sense."

"It does, actually. A lot of things from our childhoods only make sense as adults."

"That's why I stayed with the Turneys, even after I found out I was supposed to be dead. That was about a year after the abduction. Some reporter had done an anniversary story on the abduction. He had gone back and interviewed people, even about Genevieve's early assault, my birth, then my abduction. Ricky took me to the library almost every Monday, and he didn't know until later that I had found the articles and read them. They shocked me. I couldn't believe them. But my childish interpretation of the reporter's slant—which did *not* put the Marshalls in a good light and all but accused them of covering up what they knew about Genevieve's attacker—was that they had given me up for dead. That they didn't want me. That they were, in fact, glad I was gone."

"Which could not have been further from the truth."

"So they say now."

"So Genevieve said then."

Jill's eyes narrowed. "What are you talking about?"

"I met with Nicholas Eaton, who would have been your stepfather. Genevieve had become obsessed with finding you. I've seen much of her own research. No one believed that Hope was still alive, except for her. Especially after she saw you at a county fair."

Jill's face paled under her makeup, the dark blotches standing out in stark relief. "July Fourth. Only it was July Third."

"So not to compete with the Birmingham fireworks."

Her lips parted, her gaze distant again. "The Ferris wheel. Ricky took me on the Ferris wheel."

"Someone had contacted Genevieve. Sent her a note that you would be there at the Ferris wheel. The note was in her documentation."

Jill chewed her lower lip. "It had to be Ricky. He kept insisting we be on the Ferris wheel at 8:30. He said he hoped we'd get caught at the top for the fireworks." Her voice dropped to a whisper. "Ricky!"

But Ricky's name had never appeared in any of Genevieve's notes. There were other names, some mentioned only in passing, but one stood out. "Did Ricky ever go by another name, by any chance?"

She nodded, focusing on me again. "When he was a kid, everyone called him Lee-lee. Or Lee. His middle name. He switched to his first name when they renamed me, so we could do it together." Her mouth twisted. "Also because he hated it. Thought it sounded babyish."

I fought a surge of excitement. I was off this case. I needed to let all this go. "So his full name was . . ."

"Richard Lee Turney. Named for Richard Petty, the NASCAR driver. My father's—Kevin's—idol. Ricky even has—had—the number forty-three tattooed on his ankle. The number Petty drove under."

A tattoo.

Something Mike had said nagged at the back of my brain. I did not want to stir up anything more, especially not a sense of hope. But I had to ask. "Jill, have they positively identified Ricky's remains?"

Her face contorted. "No. But I—"

I held up my hand. "I do not want to give you any sense of false hope. None."

"But—"

"You need to talk to Mike about body parts. Tell him about the tattoo. Ask for dental records and two DNA tests."

"Against whom?"

"Kevin. And you."

Her brows furrowed. "But Ricky wasn't related to me."

"Supposedly. But Ricky also wasn't related to Willa."

Jill's hand went to her mouth. She stared at me, eyes wide. "But if that's not Ricky, then who is it?"

"An even better question. Where is Ricky?"

CHAPTER THIRTY-NINE

Monday, June 9, 1997
Pineville, Alabama

A SHARP POKE hit his shoulder, jarring Ricky to consciousness. The childlike voice in his ear turned insistent.

"C'mon, Ricky! Wake up. We're leaving. Chase and Clarissa are here to pick me up. I want a goodbye hug."

He struggled to peel his eyes open, peering at Jill through sleep-encrusted lashes. "What?"

She poked him again. "Get up. We're leaving."

"That's today?"

"Yes!" Her patience was evaporating. "You know it is. They got married Saturday. Remember? We're leaving today for the summer. Please get up!"

Married. Right. Ricky's head—and heart—felt leaden. Like the events of the last few months had surrounded him in wet canvas, weighing him down mind and soul. After Jill announced she knew Genevieve was not dead, Willa had told her brother, who started coming around even more to the farmhouse—and the library. Chase had showered the librarian with praise and gifts and promises to be the perfect doting father to April. He insisted he had made a mistake in abandoning her and April.

Ricky had known they were all lies, but Clarissa had been swayed, especially the part about being a father. April's father.

After all, he *was* April's father, and the same charm that had seduced a sixteen-year-old worked again. Chase's silver tongue helped him worm his way back into their lives, a betrayal that pierced hard and deep into

Ricky's soul. Clarissa turned away from him, lured by Chase's promises of a happy family. Worse, they were taking Jilly away as well. Just for the summer, so they said. A companion for April, her best friend. But Ricky knew it would be a turning point from which his relationship with Jilly would never recover.

He wanted to say goodbye like he wanted to chop off his foot.

But he did.

He rubbed his face and sat up, careful not to peel back the covers too far.

Jilly gave the long exasperated sigh of an impatient seven-year-old. "Did you give away your clothes again?"

"Apparently." He pointed to the closet door, which stood ajar. "Hand me the jeans on that hook." She did, and he made a shooing motion. "Wait outside."

"One minute," she declared. "And I'm coming back in."

He grinned as she closed the door. His independent little cuss of a sister. Six months had made all the difference in the world. Something had changed after her realization about her mother. She'd moped for a bit, then emerged with a new determination to make her own way. She'd regained her confidence and wedged a firm place for herself in the Turney family. She stood up for herself against Willa and Kevin in a way he had never been able to. Firm, but not so sassy she'd get punished. She quickly learned where the boundaries were and how far she could press them.

Jilly had started to shine at school as well. Her circle of friends expanded beyond April, and the teachers adored her. Willa had been right—she was smarter than anyone realized. Reading above her grade and asking questions that sent the teachers scrambling for answers—which they loved. She had won a chemistry fair prize in her age group for an experiment dealing with water density—seawater versus lake water—and had put in a request to join the school band a year early. When told she'd have to provide her own instrument, she had picked out a used student flute at a music store in Gadsden and started fund-raising by doing chores for housewives in Pineville. By the end of the school year, she'd raised enough to put the flute on hold until the fall.

Ricky fully expected her to finagle the balance out of Chase by the end of the summer. For all his cruelty and Machiavellian nature, Chase seemed to dote on both his girls.

And they were *his* girls. In his own unsubtle way, Chase had finally confirmed to Ricky that Jilly was his. No innuendo this time, nor oblique statements about his mystery client. He'd shown up at the Turney farmhouse one afternoon, just lubricated enough to admit it, claiming pride for all Jilly had accomplished. As if he were responsible for her achievements.

Typical. But it did leave one fact hanging in the back of Ricky's mind: there was no statute of limitations on child rape.

He opened the door to see Jilly leaning against the wall, arms crossed. "You had five more seconds."

"I'm going to get you a job as a timer at the drag races."

She stood up straight, head tilted back, eyes defiant. "And I'd be good at it too."

He grinned. "That you would." He bent, scooping her up, groaning as his head pounded.

"Serves you right. Drinking like that. Now put me down. I'm not a baby."

"Hug me first, you demon child. I'm going to miss you."

She relented and put both arms around his shoulders, nuzzling against his neck. "Miss you too."

Ricky squeezed her until she squirmed and giggled, then set her down. He held out his arm, as if offering her a dance. "Your carriage awaits, Princess Ariel. Shall we go?"

She grinned and took his arm. "We shall!"

They marched down the stairs and onto the porch, where everyone else awaited. Chase glowered at him, but Clarissa grinned, looking sheepish as she put her arm around April's shoulders. Ricky kissed the top of Jilly's head, then urged her toward the waiting SUV. "I do hope you have a good time."

As Jilly pranced toward the SUV, Willa muttered, "I can't believe you dragged yourself out of bed for this."

He gave the girls a final wave. "What? And miss my only friend leaving for three months?"

She made a scoffing noise. "Your only friend is a seven-year-old? That's pathetic."

"What makes you think I was talking about Jilly?"

He gave one more wave as Chase turned away and headed for the driver's side. He winked at Clarissa, who returned the gesture. Willa slapped his arm. "She's married."

"Doesn't mean she can't have friends."

"Boy, you stir in that mess at your own peril."

The SUV turned and headed out, the tires digging into the gravel. Ricky finally looked down at his mother. "I know exactly how dangerous that man is, after all we've been through. He'd kill me if he could get away with it."

Willa snorted. "Chase? He ain't got that in him. May make you wish you was dead. He likes to put the hurt on folks. Enjoys watching people in pain. It makes him happy to be that mean. But kill? That's one of the reasons the cops fired him. He couldn't pull the trigger when the time came. He couldn't even help me hunt for food when we were kids. He ain't got the guts to kill a squirrel." She turned, yanked open the screen door, and disappeared inside.

Ricky stared after her, his words faltering. "That's . . . but I thought . . ."

At the end of the porch, his father pushed out of the rocker, one strap of his overalls slipping off his shoulder. He shrugged it back up and headed for the steps. "I got plowing to do." At the bottom, he turned and looked back at Ricky. "Be careful who you listen to, son. Lots of folks lie around here. Got their own reasons. But it makes it hard to know what's true." He paused and shot a quick glance toward the screen door. "Just remember that Chase ain't the only mean one in that family. Not by a long shot." He turned and loped toward the barn.

Ricky watched him go, the slow, steady drumbeat in his head fading, but the ache continued, making it hard to put all the pieces together. He did know one thing—it was time to start mailing the letters he'd been writing. Genevieve Marshall might just be interested in where her daughter would be this summer.

CHAPTER FORTY

Present Day
Pineville, Alabama

THE KNOCK THAT came just after noon hit the door with far more insistence and demand than Jill's had. I opened the door, and Mike stormed in several paces before unleashing on me, his face heatstroke red.

"I told you to stay out of this!"

"I am! I did! I sent her to you! Should I have let her sit on that information given how it could affect the case?"

"You should have done exactly what you planned. Close your books with Jill and stay out of it."

"So if vital information rolls over my feet, I'm to ignore it? Let your case go south for no other reason than you want me out of your sight?"

"I don't—" Mike glanced away, scrubbing his hand over his mouth.

He had once told me that he'd given up spewing profanity long before he had arrived in Pineville, a gift to his mother. Right now he looked as if he were ready to take up the habit again.

"Mike, I'm here. I'm safe. I'm not going anywhere. But I opened a lot of doors, and some of them are still producing results. I won't act on anything, but do you want me to stay silent as well as safe?"

His shoulders dropped, as did the tone of his voice. "Of course not." He continued to look away from me. "We both know information is dangerous. It's especially dangerous in this case—knowing details about the crime has gotten people hurt. Killed. And yes, this place is safe, but it's not invincible."

"So I put a sock in their mouths?"

He finally turned around. "Send them to me before they talk to you. Yes."

"But Jill didn't even know her information was important until she talked to me. She had not considered ways to identify the body since we'd all said it was Ricky. She just wanted—"

"There's no tattoo."

I stared at him. "What?"

He crossed his arms. "There's no tattoo."

"Are you sure?"

He looked away again. "Willa had just started her . . . work. Top to bottom . . . so to speak. We have legs. Feet."

"But you said—"

"I said he was shot in the back of the head. The face was close but not—it was mangled. And there's something else that made me—" He scrubbed his face again. "The . . . body . . . had on the varsity jacket everyone has been looking for. It's definitely Ricky's jacket."

"But Ricky said he gave it away."

"Did you believe him?"

My lips pursed. "No."

"Neither did I. Sounded too much like an excuse."

"But you're sure it's not—"

"The fingerprints don't match. It's not Ricky."

I moved to the sofa and dropped down on it, not able to stand. "If it's not Ricky . . ."

"We're not positive yet who it really is. We have a supposition, but no confirmations—and no, don't ask."

I closed my mouth because I was about to do just that.

Mike went on, his voice slightly calmer. "We checked the prints against Ricky's in our files. When there was no match, we put them into the larger databases, but that will take time. Whoever it is has no criminal record we can find." He sat on the sofa next to me. "There's something else. The bullet was still in the skull. We ran ballistics."

"And?"

"It's the same gun that killed Zeb Rhone. And Genevieve Marshall. That bullet had remained in her skull as well."

I stared at him. "So if you solve this murder—"

"—it'll bring us closer to solving Genevieve's as well."

I could not help but study him. This information had brought excitement back to his eyes—those remarkable blue eyes—but confusion to me. "Mike, why are you telling me this?"

He stilled, and those eyes clouded. He looked down, and his tongue made that signature appearance, a microsecond between his lips.

"Just say it," I whispered.

"Because I can't seem to help myself." He looked up. "Your brain takes in information, turns it around, and spits it out in ways no one else even considers. The messier a case gets, the more convoluted the information, the more likely you are the one to make sense of it. I don't know how you do it, but quite frankly, it's a little addicting to give you raw details and see what kind of cake you bake."

Without a doubt, the strangest—and most exhilarating—compliment I'd ever received. "I . . . um, wow. I—"

Then he kissed me. He moved much faster than I expected, cupping my face between his hands, his lips warm and insistent. My yelp of surprise stalled in my throat, especially as our lips parted and the kiss became exploratory, deepening and sending a spike of desire for this man straight down my spine. I closed my eyes and returned each move, feeling as if something cold inside me suddenly cracked.

I kept my eyes closed as he ended the kiss with one last brush of his lips against mine.

"Star?" he whispered.

My eyes remained closed. "Does this mean I'm not going back to Nashville?"

"Probably. But I am still mad at you."

"If this is what happens when you're mad, do I dare risk making you enraged?"

He chuckled. "And *that* is what I'm talking about."

I opened my eyes. "What do you mean?"

"The way you turn things on an angle. You shift an approach to a crime one iota, and all this new stuff starts raining out. Like this case. No one, and I mean *no one*, has ever been attacked before when investigating Genevieve's murder. People have looked at it six ways to Sunday, with no results, no headway, and no assaults. As if her killer knew it was a waste of time. You turn it slightly sideways—going after Hope and following Genevieve's investigation—and suddenly people are getting killed and the investigator gets attacked."

"And are we still convinced Chase Rhone is our killer?"

"I am. He's certainly the one who went after you. But I'm open to ideas. Why?"

"Something he said just before he tossed me overboard." I stood and went to the laptop on the dining room table. I booted it up and scrolled through several files before finding what I wanted. I pointed to the screen. "There."

He pulled up a chair and sat down next to me as I went on. "Right before he threw me into the water, he said that he should have just shot me before putting me in the water."

Mike muttered something that I didn't hear and promptly ignored. "He said it was too much of a challenge to see what I could survive. That he liked the challenge, the risk of it." I looked at Mike. "But I didn't believe him then, and I don't now. It sounded like bravado, like a cover for something else."

I pointed at the computer. "Then there's this. Genevieve kept meticulous notes. During the summer of 1997, she got a series of handwritten notes, all signed with the initial 'L,' that kept dropping hints about where Hope was. As if they were goading her, trying to get her to go after Hope. They were all in the same handwriting as the note that had sent her to the Pineville July Fourth celebration, where she insists she saw Hope for the last time."

Mike scowled. "So that encounter wasn't happenstance?"

I shook my head. "In Gen's notes, she indicated that she and her family made their stonewalling look like it was to protect whoever her informant was. Anyway, in one of those notes, the writer mentioned that she didn't have to worry about Hope's safety. That the man who had taken her adored Hope and would keep her safe. That he would never kill her because"—I glanced at the screen again—"he didn't have the guts to kill a squirrel."

"Did she follow up on any of these notes?"

"She tried but quickly figured out that her kidnapper had Hope on a tour of the US. By the time she got to the first couple of locations, they had moved on. So she quit, frustrated with the futility of it. She decided she was being teased."

"Any idea who her informant was?"

"Later in her notes, the name Lee came up."

"Lee?"

I nodded. "That's why I sent Jill to you with the details about the tattoo. Ricky's full name was—is—Richard Lee Turney."

Mike bobbed his head, as if the obvious had just occurred to him. "Thus the forty-three tattoo."

"You've been in the South too long if you immediately associate Richard Lee with forty-three."

"It's systemic."

I looked at the screen again. "Y'know, if Chase really isn't able to kill me but thinks I'm a challenge—"

Mike jerked out of his chair, shoving it backward. "No! Absolutely not! We will not use you as bait. I can't believe you would even—"

I stood and went to him, placed my hand on his chest. "No! No, Mike! That's not what I'm saying. Not at all. I'm not going anywhere. I'm safe!"

"Because I am still mad at you."

I grinned, and he shook his finger at me. "That does not mean I'm going to kiss you again."

"A girl can hope."

His steam level dropped a notch. "Don't even consider such a scheme."

"I wouldn't do that to you."

Mike looked incredulous, eyes wide and mouth set, and I shrugged. "At least, not again."

"Hmm." He definitely did not look convinced. "So what *did* you have in mind?"

I sat down and glanced at the computer. "Well, what we know right now is that Ricky, Clarissa, and Chase are all missing. What would it take to bring Ricky and Chase out into the open?"

"Jill."

"Yep."

"Would she be up for it?"

"She would do just about anything to get all of this behind her. But would any of the media outlets be interested?"

Mike gave me one of his curious-dog head tilts. "You haven't been keeping up with the news, have you?"

CHAPTER FORTY-ONE

Monday, August 25, 1997
Pineville, Alabama

RICKY STOOD NEXT to Jilly, his hand on her shoulder, as they stared at the entrance to Pineville Elementary. "You sure you're ready for second grade?"

She grinned up at him. "You mean are *you* ready for me to go to second grade? You haven't let me out of your sight since we got back."

For good reason. Jilly had returned from the summer-long trip taller, tanned, and toned—and with a closer bond to April, Clarissa, and Chase. Ricky was, quite frankly, still worried about his relationship with his sister as well as her relationship with Chase. Even though she knew her real mother was alive, Jilly had made no attempt to run away. And Genevieve had apparently made no attempts to retrieve her daughter. There had been no contact. Clarissa would have let him know if anything like the July Fourth incident had happened.

Now that Genevieve and Nicholas Eaton had been married for a while, it was as if she had forgotten about her missing daughter. He'd seen her in the paper, doing this or that with her husband's family. Not even that much with the Marshalls anymore. Like she'd moved on.

Maybe he should too.

"I just missed you, that's all."

"Yeah, me and Clarissa."

Ricky put his hand on his chest, his mouth open to protest, and she giggled. She nudged him. "Maybe you'll find someone new on that job of yours. That's why you can't pick me up in the afternoon, right?"

"Right. Second shift at the pipe plant. I have to be there by three." He wrinkled his nose. "I'll only get to see you in the mornings."

She nudged him again. "Maybe it'll keep you sober."

Yeah, good luck with that. "Maybe. Gotta make money somehow."

"Or you could be rich like Chase."

His brows furrowed at the joke but paused. She was serious. "Chase is rich?"

"Gotta be. Paid for everything all summer. And he doesn't work. So he must be."

"Right." Ricky shook off the confusion and gestured toward the school. "Now. Go be brilliant."

"My golden plan!" She pulled away, skipping toward the door.

He grinned. She had told him about her "golden plan" the night before, during *Touched by an Angel.* Smart people, she informed him bluntly, were more successful. If she wanted to be successful, she needed to get as smart as she could as fast as she could. He couldn't argue with that.

But as he watched her skip toward her goal, he knew where she had gotten her ideas about success. Whatever Chase was grooming her for, it wasn't what most people would suspect. "Oh, Jilly, you are about to have one twisted childhood."

Ricky headed back to his truck, turning it toward the library. He had known the Rhone family his entire life. They did not have money. And the last job he knew Chase to hold had been as an officer on a nearby police force . . . one he couldn't hold on to because of his own perversions. So how did he pay for a cross-country trip? He really wanted to know how Chase Rhone made his money. And who would know better than that new wife of his?

An hour later Ricky left the library with a handprint on his cheek but a grin on his lips. His dear uncle was about to take the fall of a lifetime.

CHAPTER FORTY-TWO

Present Day
Pineville, Alabama

I HAD NOT, in fact, paid any attention to the news since being whacked in the head on Sunday night. I'd been a little busy. But apparently having the man who'd assaulted me post videos on TikTok had triggered some kind of local news tsunami. The murder of Genevieve Marshall Eaton was one of the great unsolved cases of the entire area. Because of her family and high-profile husband, the case held a minor celebrity status, along the lines of Marcia Trimble or Janet March in Nashville. The fact that the same PI who had broken open the Pineville corruption scandal had taken on Genevieve's case had put my picture on the local news for three consecutive cycles.

Mike's office had been fielding a dozen calls a day, which he had not told me about. One of the stations had even tracked down the reporter who had done the original newspaper stories on the cases, prompting him to take a sudden camping vacation in the High Sierras. Jill had dodged calls by blocking any unknown number, but when Mike called her to suggest using the media to our advantage, she was on it like lightning. Mike called the Marshalls, but they refused to cooperate and called it a "circus for the media sharks." A formal statement from their lawyer arrived in Mike's inbox late Wednesday night, with instructions that all communication would need to go through their legal team and they were not to contact either Margery or her son Owen.

So much for me speaking with Margery again.

Owen's name raised my eyebrows, but Mike asked me to be

patient—Owen's fingerprints had come to light in two locations, but he wanted me to wait until he knew more. That the oldest Marshall son might be involved shed light on Genevieve's notes about a "heart-crushing betrayal."

Secrets upon secrets.

Mike called a press conference for Thursday morning at the Pineville Police Department, and Jill and I spent Wednesday evening going over her prepared statement. It would be carried live on two local stations and livestreamed over Facebook and YouTube. Most people would have anxiety about such exposure, but Jill went over her statement with me like a pro, almost eager to push this to the next level.

When the time came, Miss Doris and I lit the gas logs and piled up on one of the sofas, drinking tea and watching the drama play out. Mike, looking far too handsome in his dress uniform, came to the microphone first.

Miss Doris poked me. "Right smart-looking, that Yankee boy."

I shushed her. "Behave."

After introducing everyone behind him, he briefly explained the background on the case, giving the basic details of Hope's disappearance, Genevieve's search for her missing daughter, and her eventual death. That in reopening the case, the new investigation had begun with the premise that Hope had not drowned, as previously assumed, but had survived to adulthood. The course of the investigation was to follow in Genevieve's search for her daughter, with the idea that what Genevieve had discovered had led to her death.

He spoke of the progress we'd made, without giving too many specifics, but that the perpetrator—or perpetrators—who had engineered the original crimes were still in the area and active. While headway had been made, the investigation had also led to the murder of two other people and assaults on one of the investigators.

The media peppered him with questions, and I smiled as I watched him handle them with grace and a poise I had not seen in him before. "He's really good at this."

"He is. One reason we moved him from sergeant to chief so quickly."

I looked at her. "You've seen this side of him before?"

"Oh yes. Although it's not been your experience since showing up in town, murder is relatively rare in Pineville. He was the lead on a murder not long after he came on as a sergeant. He was pretty poised then as well. And much younger. He's where he's meant to be."

"That's your faith talking again."

She grinned at me. "Yep. God sometimes drops you into some odd places. You may not understand at the time, but he does not make mistakes."

I skipped the fact that she had said those words to a woman who had been tied up and dropped over the side of a boat. I let it go and focused on the conference.

Mike concluded his initial remarks, answered a few more questions, then introduced Jill. She stepped to the mike, placed her statement on the lectern, and faced the camera head-on. I braced myself.

"Good morning, and thank you, Chief Luinetti. I am here today because other than the Marshall and Eaton families, the Turneys have been impacted by this case more than anyone else. Over the years we have been blamed for everything from Ms. Eaton's death to the drought a few years ago. We were considered a cursed family, and the attitudes of some people in this community have driven our family to the point of desperation. My father and mother can no longer work. My brother is an alcoholic."

I noted the verb tense, and from the looks of some of the officers arrayed behind Jill and Mike, so did they. She continued.

"I, on the other hand, got out of the state, pursued my degrees, and found success in Chicago, where I am a defense attorney." She paused and took a sip of water. "But the truth is that this murder haunted me in more ways than you can imagine. Most of you know me as Jill Turney, daughter of Kevin and Willa Turney, adopted by them when I was five years old. But the truth is my birth name was Hope Marshall."

"What?" Miss Doris sat straight up, glaring at me. "You knew and you didn't tell me?"

I shook my head. "We only confirmed it yesterday. Jill herself wanted it withheld until today. She didn't even tell Mike until last evening."

Miss Doris leaned back, muttering, "All this time."

The press corps came unglued. People shot to their feet, shouting questions at her. She stood in silence until Mike stepped up beside her and put his rather commanding baritone into the microphone. "Ladies and gentlemen, we will answer all questions, later and one at a time. Please allow Ms. Turney to finish."

"You mean Marshall!" one of them shouted.

"No. My legal name is Jillian Turney." Jill recentered herself on the mike. "If I may." The room settled, but a buzzing undercurrent remained. "As I said, I have been Jillian Turney since 1996. I did not realize it was not my legal name until I was in my teens, and when I was eighteen, I had it legally changed."

"Why didn't you go back to Marshall?"

Jill ignored the shout. "A few months ago, my need to help my Turney family here had caused severe complications to my work in Chicago, and I decided the time had come to bring an end to this. I approached Star Cavanaugh about investigating my birth mother's death, hoping she might be able to resolve it. We set everything in motion, and I returned to Chicago. When she told me the approach the investigation would take, I knew I would have to tell her who I was. Before I could return, however, the investigation heated up, and it's been rather a roller coaster ever since."

"Ya think?" Miss Doris asked the television.

I shushed her again. I had to admit that Jill's poise had held together well, just as Mike's had. Plus, she had lost most of her Southern accent. Her Chicago persona had arrived.

"We now have three persons of interest in this case, and I will address them directly now."

"Is it true your mother, Willa Turney, has been arrested?"

Jill remained focused, talking to the camera. Now for the bombshell.

"Richard Lee Turney. Chase Rhone. Owen Marshall. Please listen to me. We know. We know all of it. You need to come forward now. Give your story. Your side of this long, tragic tale. Talk to us. Continuing to dodge the police when they have this much evidence will be all the worse for you when they do finally track you down. And they will. They are on the move now and closing in. I beg you. As men who were always kind to me, always said you loved me, do this now. Let us resolve this."

Jill closed her eyes, then looked up and reached for the water again. As she set the water down, she faced the reporters and called on one to her left before the rabble-rousing could begin again.

"Oh, she's good." I looked at Miss Doris, who would probably give me the same reaction most of Pineville would.

Her face had gone stark pale beneath her makeup. Her mouth hung open, and she stared at the television, her eyes wide with shock. Finally she faced me. "Owen?"

"Gen's brother."

"I know who Owen Marshall is! Are you serious? He's a pillar of the entire Lake Martin community!"

"His fingerprints were also found at two of the crime scenes—places he had no business being. He was on the same police force for a while with Chase Rhone. They were friends, according to some of the cops Mike has talked to. There's also a possibility that he knows more about Genevieve's assault than he's ever made public. There's even a possibility he withheld information on purpose. He probably won't be charged, but the cops want to talk to him to get his side of the story, fill in some gaps."

"And Rhone?"

"He's Willa's brother. He's also wanted in the disappearance of Clarissa Newton, so there will be that to answer for as well."

"Is he the killer?"

"We don't know. There's a lot of evidence but also some doubt."

"And you don't know where Ricky or Owen is?"

"Not a clue."

We turned our attention back to the television, where the questions were still bounding about the room.

Where's Star?—Recovering.

Why didn't you go home?—I liked being Jill Turney.

Are these three your murder suspects?—They are persons of interest. Nothing more at this time.

Do you have evidence connecting all three crimes?—For the first time in twenty-five years, yes. We can now prove all three are connected.

Have you been in touch with the Marshalls?—I have not.

Do they know you are Hope Marshall?—Obviously, they do now.

How do you feel about your mother's death?

That one brought the room to a halt. Jill paused for a moment. "My mother was ripped from me when I was five. I was told she was dead. I grieved her then. I did not know when she was killed, as I was on a school trip to a national science fair. I was also out of town when they found her. It barely registered, except in that way that a child who loses a parent never really stops grieving for them. Knowing where she was buried did not really change that journey."

"So you still grieve for her?"

"Yes." And with that one word, Jill left the podium and exited through a side door, where a limo was set to take her to a hotel in Birmingham. She would stay there until she was no longer needed on the case, then return to Chicago, which was her home now. As she told me the night before, when this was over, she did not plan to return to Pineville. Ever.

I turned off the television. Miss Doris sat, staring, her mouth slightly open.

"Are you all right?"

She shook her head slowly. "It's like before." She waved her hand in the general direction of downtown Pineville. "Like back in the spring. These people, they've just been living and working right here beside us. Like it was nothing. Evil all around, like it was nothing."

"Unfortunately, that's usually the way it works. They are here with us, and we never know. Buying groceries, having yard sales, even going to church with us. You never know the true hearts of most people."

"God does, though. Even if y'all don't get them this time, he knows their hearts."

"Thankfully," I said softly, "God is more merciful than human law."

"True," she said, "but he still holds us accountable." She stood. "Come over to the house for lunch today. You should be relatively safe just crossing the courtyard."

"I will. Thank you. What time?"

"Noon."

My cell phone rang and I picked it up, despite the unknown number. "Star Cavanaugh." In the background there was a burst of laughter, music, and the distinctive sound of a slot machine. "Hello?"

"Star!" The voice was low and obviously inebriated. "This is Ricky Turney. I hear"—he belched—"that rumors of my death have been greatly exaggerated. Can we talk?"

CHAPTER FORTY-THREE

Monday, January 12, 1998
Pineville, Alabama

RICKY WENT OVER the two notes one more time. Carefully printed. No mistakes. One friendly, which gave him hope. One anonymous, written so that nothing would give away who he was or how he had gotten the information. He signed the first one, its message short and to the point.

Dear Scott,

Thanks for your last call. Looking forward to meeting you next month for the camping trip to the mountains. Much needed, given all that's happened here. Another week at work and I'll have the money I need. I'm buying a cell phone for the trip. Will call when I leave. Here's hoping the old Ranger makes it to the Rockies!

Ricky

He folded the note and slid it into the envelope he had already addressed and stamped. The second note deserved one final read-through. This one he did not hold out much hope for. He had written Genevieve Marshall at least twice a month since August, but he had seen no sign that she had ever received them. No visits from her or her family. No police. No questions. No news reports. Scott Ketsler had even called his old friends at the Birmingham paper, but they had heard nothing either.

Maybe they had been right all along. Maybe the Marshalls didn't want Jilly back as much as they'd indicated in the news. Maybe that had all been an act.

Ricky sorta hated himself for how much he wanted that to be true. But he also couldn't imagine anyone giving up on the vibrant child who had become such a part of his life. He never would have dreamed a little girl could turn his life around, but he had also been startled by how much he liked being with her, seeing her grow and learn and explore. During their weeks at the cabin, she had been ever inquisitive about life in and around the lake. Now she was doing science experiments she'd found in the library books about water temperature, pollution, and the life cycles of fish. She'd taken second place in her age group at the school spelling bee—which he'd thought was marvelous and she'd thought a failure. She'd insisted he quiz her each week on new words.

All of it told him she needed to be with a better family. She needed to be with the Marshalls. Thus, he was going to try one more time.

Dear Mrs. Eaton,

I have seen no indication you received my letters, but I must try one more time. I am sending this to your husband's company, as the only other address I have for you is the Marshall compound, which may be why you have not seen my other letters.

Your daughter Hope lives in Pineville. She attends Pineville Elementary and is quite happy. She is not being abused or taken advantage of. She now goes by Jillian Turney.

She was kidnapped by her biological father. Since he has never been arrested or charged, I assume that is because of the other people involved in your attack and the circumstances of Hope's birth. If you are unaware how that came to happen, you should talk to your brother Owen, who arranged for you to meet Chase.

"Meet." Ricky had a bitter taste in his mouth when he thought about the acts hidden in that innocent word. But it was the one Clarissa had used in describing what had happened. Owen, who had been Chase's fellow police officer at the time, had brought Chase to a family party. Had introduced Chase to his young sister. Whether Owen knew his friend's perversions at the time was unclear, but Owen's involvement had set all of this in motion. It was also the reason Chase had been blackmailing Owen since it had happened.

Owen might not be guilty of anything but bringing a friend to a party, but his silence over what he knew about the assault and his guilt over bringing Chase into the Marshalls' lives had been the wedge that had kept Owen under Chase's thumb for years.

Chase had no need to work. He lived on Marshall guilt. Owen had gone on to be a lawyer and a pillar of the community. The money he sent Chase was nothing to his family, and Chase knew not to get too greedy. Everyone's secrets stayed in the dark.

> *Jillian is doing well at school. She is smart and vibrant. On January 19 she leaves for a week, a school trip to a science fair in Washington, DC. She won regional in her age group here, and her experiment is being displayed there. She will be back the next Saturday. The bus will arrive at 2 p.m., which would be a good time to approach her in public.*
>
> *I recommend a public approach because her father has worked for more than a year to turn her against the Marshalls. She believes your family abandoned her, and this has built in a deep anger. She has forgotten a great deal about your family, and it will not be a happy reunion. But I believe she is too smart and has too bright a future to stay where she is.*
>
> *This will be my last attempt to contact you.*

There was, of course, no signature. Ricky's hope was that the letter would seem to come from a teacher or other school worker. He folded the letter and slipped it in its envelope and sealed both. He inserted them into a book he had to return to the library.

A light tap on his bedroom door preceded it being pushed open slowly. "Hey, bro. You ready?" Jilly stood there, her now half-red and half-brown hair pulled back in a ponytail. She had passed through her obsession with *The Little Mermaid* and had moved on to *Free Willy*.

Posters of Ariel still wallpapered her room, and the *Little Mermaid* comforter covered her bed, only because she had not found the equivalent *Free Willy* accessories. But she had announced at Christmas that she wanted an aquarium for her birthday.

Ricky intended to make that happen. If she were still here. If he was.

He stood and tucked the book under his arm. "As always. Lead on." He gestured toward the stairway, and they headed down. But she was uncharacteristically quiet on the way to school. As they neared the drop-off line, he asked, "Are you OK?"

She nodded. "Yeah. Just thinking."

"About?"

"You know I want to be a marine biologist."

"Yeah. Although six months ago you wanted to be a mermaid."

She giggled. "I know. But girls can't be mermaids, silly."

"Well, boys definitely can't be mermaids."

She poked him, still giggling. "I'm serious!"

"So I see." He edged the truck into the long line of cars easing up toward the school.

Jilly gathered her backpack off the floor and clutched it to her chest, preparing to leap out. "Clarissa said that it takes college. And college takes a lot of money."

"It does."

"Is that why you didn't go?"

Ricky braked and looked at her. "Is that what's on your mind? Why your doofus of an older brother didn't go off to college?"

She shrugged, then took a deep breath. "It's not because of me, is it? And you're not a doofus."

His eyes widened as he stared at her. She was, in fact, why Ricky had not followed up on any of his applications. Or acceptances. But he was not about to tell her that. "No. I wasn't ready for it. Wanted to make some of that money first. There's time." He pushed at her shoulder lightly. "Y'know, kiddo, you don't have to do everything the way 'they say' it has to be done. You can set your own way."

"Is that what you're doing?"

"Let's just say I'm considering all my options."

She stared at him a moment. "You're falling behind."

"What?" A horn honked behind him, and he jumped, realizing he was holding up the line. He eased off the brake as Jilly snickered.

"I guess the drop-off line is not a great place for heavy conversations," he muttered.

"Guess not. See you in the morning?"

"As always."

She opened the door and was out and gone in a second, slamming it behind her. As Ricky pulled out and turned toward the post office, he realized, like a blow to his chest, how much he would miss these mornings with her. He had never dreamed of having children, but Jilly had sparked that desire in his gut, and for the first time in his life, his dreams had turned not toward college and getting out of Pineville but toward having a family.

Ricky had never understood why his father stayed with the bitterness that had become Willa Turney. He had witnessed how being with her had changed his outgoing, gregarious father. But now he did. Perhaps, for some men, being with a family, no matter how small or chaotic, was worth the sacrifice.

And still, he pulled up to the box in front of the post office and dropped both letters in. Because Ricky had also realized that loving a family also meant wanting the best for them. And Jilly deserved a better life than the Turneys could give her. As he pulled away from the post office, he whispered a quick hope that Jilly would find that better life—and soon.

CHAPTER FORTY-FOUR

Present Day
Pineville, Alabama

"RICKY?" I PUT my finger in my other ear and pressed the phone hard against my head. "Where are you? I can barely hear you."

"Is that Ricky?" Miss Doris asked, and I waved at her to hush.

"Hiding in plain sight."

"You sound like you're at a casino." I shuffled through the paperwork on the dining room table, looking for my earbuds.

"You know a better place for a man to get lost in a crowd?"

I found the earbuds and mouthed at Miss Doris, *Call Mike*, then gestured for her to leave. She nodded and headed out.

"I have to admit it sounds like a good one. Why are you hiding out?" I plugged the earbuds in as he answered.

"Y'all found a body, right?"

"Yeah."

"Thought it was me?"

"Yes."

"What if I told you it was supposed to be me?"

I hit the recording feature on my phone. "I'd say that was a pretty good reason for you to be hiding out." He cackled, and I could almost smell the booze through the phone. "How drunk are you?"

"Drunk enough to call you despite all wisdom to the contrary."

"Who wants you dead, Ricky?"

"All of them."

"Them who?"

He belched again. "All of them. The Marshalls, my sweet old mama. The Rhones. Everyone but my daddy wants me out of the picture. Have for years."

"Why do they want you dead?"

"Because I know too much. Know it all, in fact. Took me awhile to put it together, but yep, I know it."

"Know what?"

I heard ice rattling in a glass. "Let's see." I heard him drink something, the glass banging against the phone. "I know, for instance, that Chase Rhone, my sweet mother's evil brother, has been preying on young girls for thirty years or more. Somebody shoulda killed that man long ago, but nope, he's still walking around being evil. Just ask Clarissa."

Clarissa. "Um, Ricky–"

"He's the one who raped Genevieve Marshall. Seduced her, they kept telling me because she was so sexy, but she was twelve. Twelve, Star. She was *twelve*. Evil."

"Ricky–"

"And I know that Ms. Eaton's brother helped."

I froze. This was new. I also found it interesting that he switched from Marshall to Eaton as if this happened yesterday. Maybe for him, it did. "Which brother?"

"Owen. He was friends with Chase when they were younger. Oh, and dollars to doughnuts that body y'all found is Owen."

"Why would you think that?"

"Because my sweet mama and her evil brother have been blackmailing Owen for more than twenty-five years. All kept quiet until you started stirring things up. You got too close, so Owen had enough. Mama told me that Owen was on his way to confront Chase, so that's when I knew I needed to get outta town."

"Chase killed him?"

Ricky took another drink and his voice held a scoff in it. "Nah. Chase? That man is evil, pure evil, but he can't kill. Can't bring himself to do it. Actually pull the trigger, so to speak. He can get close. Like he did with you, but he can't go through with it. You know it was him, right?"

"I didn't see him, but we're assuming it was."

"Few other people in this county that evil, I can guarantee that. But I'll bet that when he dumped you in the lake, he left before you went under."

I thought back over the last things my attacker had said to me. "He said he liked the challenge of how much it would take to kill me."

"Then he left."

"Yes."

Ricky cackled again. "Evil coward. Evil *and* a coward. One of the most dangerous men on the planet, and still a coward."

"I've met a lot of evil men who were also cowards."

"Maybe that's why they turn evil?"

"I have not spent a lot of time wondering about it."

"Hmph. Maybe you should. Maybe we all should."

"Ricky, you're implying that Chase didn't kill Genevieve."

Another thud of the glass on the phone. "Not implying. Saying outright. He didn't kill Genevieve."

"Then who did?"

A long pause followed, and only the background noise let me know the call had not ended. Then he took a deep breath. "Star, my dear, why do you think I've been drunk for twenty-five years?"

*

By the time Ricky had finished his sordid tale, Mike had arrived, escorted in by Miss Doris, both of them entering silently, watching me as I took the final notes. In the last moments of the call, Ricky's inebriation had taken full hold of his senses, and his last words were barely more than a mumble. I heard someone—with a commanding cop-like voice—telling him to give back the phone and go to his room. The call went dead.

Mike and Miss Doris looked over my shoulder at the scrambled notes I had taken, and Mike grimaced. "Tell me you recorded it."

"What? Don't like my chicken scratches?"

"I could get more sense out of the chickens."

"Thanks. Yes, I recorded it." I handed him my phone.

"Is that it?" Miss Doris asked. "You can arrest someone now?"

I shook my head. "No. We may have Ricky's story, but he was horribly drunk, and his statement is uncorroborated and I'm not a cop. So nothing's official. Even with the recording, he could change his mind when he sobers up."

She glanced at Mike. "You really need to make her a cop." When we both stared at her, she said, "What? You're trained. It's not like you haven't done the job before."

I ignored her and pointed to a section of my notes as I spoke to Mike. "If he's right about this, it could be the evidence you need." I then pointed to another part of the scribbles. "Then there's this."

He nodded, pocketed my phone, then took his own out. He headed for the back bedroom. Miss Doris watched him, then looked back at me.

"Have y'all made up completely?"

"Mm . . . I'm not sure I'd say completely. But we are on speaking terms again." I didn't want to mention the kiss, even though it lived prominently in my mind.

"So why did y'all look at me so funny when I mentioned you becoming a cop?"

I motioned for her to sit, which she did. "Because I haven't been on the job in almost a decade. Even then I was a rough fit. Being a PI has suited me well. Being nomadic has suited me well. And you don't just hop back into a force because you change your mind. There would be some hoops."

"You seem to be quite adept at jumping through hoops."

I laughed. "I appreciate that. But . . ."

She glanced at the notes. "Ricky's in a lot of trouble, isn't he?"

"Yes, but his crimes are twenty-five years old. I'm sure the DA will take some things into consideration."

"If he turns himself in."

"Yes. Right now we're not even sure where he is."

She pointed to where I'd circled the word "casino." "Probably Wetumpka. That's the closest. He could take 231 out of Pell City and be there in a couple of hours."

Miss Doris looked over my notes again, her lips pursed. "You know, when you brought down so many of Pineville's so-called stalwart citizens back in the spring, I believed it was an isolated thing. That so many people I had known and admired all these years were caught up in something like that had been a shock. I suppose I told myself that it really couldn't happen again."

I took her hand. "Miss Doris, we don't know everything for certain. But I can tell you that in my experience, very few people are as clean and upstanding—as stalwart—as they appear to be. The longer people live, the richer they get, the more entrenched into a community they are, the more likely they are to have some truly ugly secrets. Those who are clean actually have to work at it, because the darkness will tug at them from all directions."

"I have certainly seen that for myself." She stood. "I know you and Mike have things to do. But you will keep me posted."

"I will always give you the inside scoop, Miss Doris."

She grinned and left, and I followed Mike into my workroom, where he was just ending a conversation. "Well?"

He pocketed his phone. "The evidence team has finished at Clarissa's, and I'm meeting them at the Turneys' house. I've asked a judge for material witness warrants for Clarissa and Ricky, so that if we do find them, we can hold them for their safety. I have a detective looking into property records for anything on Chase Rhone, and I've asked the sheriff's department to have their bird standing by."

"Ricky said his uncle's lake property was only accessible by boat."

"The marine team is standing by as well. You wouldn't believe the spots I've seen those helo guys land that thing. They are really good. But we want to confirm first that we have the right place. If he's even there."

He paused, and a beat of silence settled between us.

"Mike?"

"No."

"I want to go with you."

"No." But he remained standing at the end of the bed.

"Let me rephrase. I want to be with *you*."

He looked down, then at the butcher paper on the walls, which I had spent much of the morning, before the press conference, re-creating. The timeline stood out in bright red. Notes from Gen in blue and green. Sketchy descriptions of the men we now knew were Chase Rhone and Ricky Turney. An even sketchier one of a man involved on the periphery, impressions that Gen remembered from a party.

Thinking over the notes I had taken from her information, I realized now that she knew her brother Owen had been involved—she just could not admit it to herself. It had been a family conspiracy, one meant not to harm her but to protect him, no matter what the cost. But in the end, what a cost it had taken.

"I know the work you've put into this—"

"It's evidence gathering. I'll be with all of you. Safe. Like in the Turneys' field. I'll even stay outside the perimeter."

He looked back at me then, a slight gleam in his eye.

"I will! I promise."

"Right."

"Mike—"

"Get your coat. Let's see what kind of cake you can bake this time."

CHAPTER FORTY-FIVE

Monday, January 19, 1998
Pineville, Alabama

THE SUN HAD barely peeked above the horizon as Ricky turned into the driveway. He had delivered Jilly to school just in time to catch the charter bus taking the science fair winners to DC. He had forgotten about the 5:00 a.m. departure time until his father had roused him at 4:30. Getting up and to the school in thirty minutes had to be some kind of record, but they had done it, and he now looked forward to dropping back into bed. His father had left at the same time, heading for a livestock sale in another county.

Ricky's plans for the day had been simple—extra sleep, then packing to leave tomorrow for Colorado. He and Jilly had talked one more time about his trip. With her love of nature, she had been a bit jealous but understood his need to get away.

He didn't want to explain that he did not want to be anywhere in the county when Genevieve Marshall showed up. Or that the trip would help him adjust to her absence. He was going to miss Jilly more than he could put into words.

When he rounded the curve in the driveway, his headlights fell on the back end of a strange car, and Ricky braked, staring. He'd seen that car before—the dark Mercedes with the vanity plate of EATONCO2—and suddenly Ricky could not breathe. He sped up to the farmhouse and threw the gearshift into park. He left the truck running, the headlights casting dark shadows across the porch, as he heard the screams from inside the house. He almost fell getting out and bounding up the stairs, tripping twice, scrambling to get to Jilly's bedroom. His heart pounded as he recognized his mother's piercing shrieks, but the other was a stranger, a woman that he recognized the minute he got to the top of the stairs and saw the strawberry-blond hair and the wide blue eyes.

"Get out of my house! You have no right here!" Willa's words echoed off the walls with a deafening staccato.

"Where is she? Where is my daughter?" Genevieve Eaton's demands matched Willa's in volume and anger. She pointed at the room's decor. "This is her. This is all her. Where is she?" She lunged for Willa.

Willa shoved her backward. "You're crazy! There's no girl here!"

Genevieve stumbled but caught herself against the bedpost. "I know she's here! She's supposed to leave on a field trip today. She has to be here!"

Ricky pushed by Willa into the room, facing Genevieve, a huge presence between the two women. He towered over both as he stood between them. "What are you doing here? I told you to go to the school!"

Both women hushed, the sudden silence stark and terrifying. Genevieve stared up at him. "You? It was you?"

He heard Willa stalk from the room as he stepped toward Genevieve, his voice low, his shoulders hunched. How could she do this to him? "Shut up! I told you to go to the school when they got back. They've already left!"

He heard Willa stomp back into the room, growling, "Both of you! Get out of my house!"

Genevieve gasped, staring past Ricky. "What are you doing?"

Ricky pivoted, and his breath stopped. His mother held a pistol in both hands, her arms outstretched and her finger on the trigger. "Get out!" She waved the pistol from Genevieve to Ricky. "Traitor! Both of you. Out!" The barrel shifted to Genevieve again.

"Mother, don't do—"

"I'm not your mother!" Willa's scream reverberated through the house as she pointed the pistol at him again. "Traitor. Traitor!"

Standing behind him and to his left, Genevieve began digging through the purse hanging on her shoulder. "You're insane. I'm calling the police." She pulled out a cell phone.

"No!" Willa swung the pistol toward Genevieve and raised it a fraction higher.

Ricky knew in that instant she was about to fire. He stepped in front of Genevieve, his hand reaching out toward Willa.

The gunshot sounded like a cannon from hell, searing and deafening in the tiny room. Liquid fire pierced Ricky's left arm. He bellowed from the pain and grabbed his bicep. Behind him Genevieve collapsed, a marionette with severed strings. As blood seeped through his fingers, he stared down.

The bullet had passed through his arm and embedded in Genevieve's skull, leaving a small jagged hole. A small bit of blood had pooled in the wound, but she had obviously died instantly.

His vision blurry from the pain, Ricky swung toward Willa, who stared at both of them, her eyes wide with shock.

"What have you done?" Ricky's voice rasped, and he felt the strength in his legs waning. He staggered backward and sat down on Jilly's bed, watching Willa, waiting for her to fire again, to kill him as well.

Instead, the gun slipped from her hands and thudded to the floor. She put both hands over her mouth and panted, sucking in air through her fingers. "I didn't mean—" The panting picked up speed. "I didn't—" Her words choked off, her eyes rolled upward, and Willa dropped to the floor.

Ricky sat, still numb. The pain in his arm had lessened slightly but still felt very much like a hot poker had been shoved through his bicep. Blood leeched down the sleeve of his varsity jacket, which soaked up a lot of it. Finally, he stood, stepped over Willa, and picked up the gun. He threw the gun onto his bed as he headed for the bathroom. He peeled off his jacket and shirt and dropped them into the tub, then did his best to stanch the bleeding with a towel. The bullet had sheared through the outside of his muscle, opening a trench almost three inches long but not deep.

As he sat on the toilet, tending to the wound, Ricky realized that something deep inside had snapped. Broken. He had tried to fix this, but it had all gone wrong. He had wanted to keep everyone safe, everyone out of trouble. No cops, no press, no shame, no pain. Everyone safe and living their lives. Jill, Genevieve, his parents. Even Chase.

But he'd been riding a wobbly fence. He had wanted to force all the good into place and hold it there and face none of the bad. But now all of the bad had landed on them, and Genevieve Marshall Eaton had paid the price.

The price of his lack of guts to face all that had gone wrong. All the bad.

The numbness in his chest spread, consuming him, splitting him from himself. His emotions vanished, the purple vortex descended again, and he felt nothing except the need to survive the next few hours.

He wanted to stay that way. He hoped that he would never feel anything again. It was just too hard.

Having wrapped his wound with a bandage, he returned to Jilly's room. Willa stirred, and as she opened her eyes and struggled to sit up, he nudged her leg with his boot.

"Get up, you witch. You got a choice to make. We can call the police and go to prison until Jesus returns, or we can get rid of her body. You killed her. You choose."

Willa blinked, staring at Genevieve's corpse, then up at Ricky.

His eyes narrowed. "I am done with you, woman. We get through this day and I am leaving. You got a day to get most of this cleaned up. You want my help, or do I just leave now?"

She stared at the corpse again, blinking.

"You killed a woman." He wondered if he looked and sounded as cold as he felt.

Shaking, Willa pushed to her feet. "I don't . . . We can't–"

He turned away from her. "I'm going to the barn for a tarp." Even as Ricky headed down the stairs, his arm on fire, he knew he was still riding that fence, trying to make everything all right for everyone. Make the sin go away. *I just want to get through this day. Then forget. Forget forever.*

When he got back to Jilly's bedroom with the tarp, Willa had curled up into a fetal position, rocking, a slow keening moan echoing out of her. Ricky stared at her for a long time, then picked her up as if she were a child and carried her to the bed she shared with his father. He closed the blinds, shut the door, and left her there.

He found some of Willa's pain pills in the bathroom and took two. He changed his bandage, wrapping the new one tighter around his arm. Then he wrapped Genevieve in the tarp and carried her to the barn. Three hours later, he had managed to bury her in one of the stalls, pat down the dirt over the shallow grave, and cover it with fresh hay. He drove her Mercedes to the quarry on Langston Road and let it roll off the edge into some of the deepest water. Then he walked home.

By the time he got there, Willa had emerged. She sat at the kitchen table drinking coffee and smoking a cigarette, her hands trembling so wildly, ashes had been strewn all over the table. Silently, he walked by her and headed to the stairs.

"Where's the gun?"

He paused in the kitchen doorway. "Hidden. I'm taking it with me when I head west. I'll dump it in a river out there."

"And her?"

"Don't ask. You don't know, you can't tell."

"It was an accident."

"Yeah, you meant to kill me."

"I want you out."

"As soon as I'm packed. And I won't be back."

"You shouldn't have contacted her. This is on you."

He walked back to the table, his voice so low and tense he sounded like a stranger. "You ever try to put this on me again, you will regret it. I'm not a boy anymore. You need to remember that. And I know your secrets."

She glared up at him. "It should have been you."

"And I will remember that. Goodbye . . . Willa."

CHAPTER FORTY-SIX

Present Day
Pineville, Alabama

WITH RICKY'S INFORMATION, the pieces of the puzzle that stretched from 1989 to the present fell into place. So it turned out that the one person Jill had most wanted to save was the one person who could provide the solution to all the missing parts. If Ricky's curiosity about his uncle's Machiavellian maneuverings had not kicked in, the crimes might not ever have been solved.

I kicked myself a few times for not pushing harder to interview Ricky alone, but Mike reminded me that I had been working on this case—officially—less than two weeks. I had been gathering information and forming a picture in my head of the people and circumstances involved when everything suddenly unraveled.

"Remember," he said, his words tempered with patience, "you talked to Margery and Nick just over a week ago. Have you ever had a case come together this fast?"

I hesitated as he turned into the Turneys' driveway. The yard already swarmed with official vehicles. Kevin Turney sat in his rocking chair on the porch, an officer standing watch nearby. Kevin struggled to stand as he spotted Mike's car, using the arms of the rocker to push himself up.

"Not a cold case, no. And not most regular cases either."

Mike eased his cruiser in between two other vehicles. "Maybe I'm crazy, but I believe Genevieve wanted this case to be solved just as much as we did."

"And Ricky is ready for this to be over."

Mike glanced at me as he shut off the engine. "Why now?"

"Clarissa's divorced. She has put Chase Rhone behind her."

Mike grimaced. "Now let's hope she's still alive."

Right. So many pieces of the puzzle remained in play.

We got out, and Kevin stepped to the edge of the porch, focusing on me. "You are sure it was my Ricky you talked to. You aren't joshing about this."

"I promise you it was Ricky."

His chin jutted forward. "Prove it."

I gestured toward the house, currently crawling with crime scene techs. "He told me there was a moving strap hanging in the pantry. That you and Willa used it to pull the refrigerator away from the wall so she could clean behind it." The jut was less prominent as I went on. "Said she was a nut about roaches and rats. Constantly set traps back there."

Kevin's mouth jerked. "She is."

"He said the gun was in a potato sack hanging on the wall behind the fridge."

His shoulders dropped, and he took a step backward. "I didn't know."

Mike stepped up beside me. "Where are your other guns?"

"The ones for hunting were in the safe. I gave your people the combination. They've already taken them." He nodded at one of the vans. "I kept my shotgun under the couch, but they got it too."

"Pistols?"

"One in the bedside table." He rested a hand on the porch rail. "I swear to you, Chief. I didn't know about that other pistol. I ain't seen it in twenty-five years. Ricky took it out west with him and told me he left it there."

Mike nodded, but the set of his mouth told me he did not quite believe the man.

"He told me that is what he had planned to do," I said. "He changed his mind."

"Did he say why?" Kevin asked.

"No." I moved closer to the old man. "I don't know if he knew. He stayed with a friend the entire time he was out there. Lived in this man's cabin—operating on instinct." And whiskey, but I left that part out. I had the feeling that most of Ricky's time in Colorado had been spent in a blackout.

Kevin returned to the rocker and dropped into it like a man defeated. "I'm . . . I'm just glad he's still alive."

"He didn't mean to make anyone think he was dead, just gone for a while. He was afraid for his life."

Kevin pointed in the direction of the field. "Rightfully so. So who's that?"

I glanced at Mike, who picked up the conversation. "We aren't sure yet. All we have is speculation." He straightened his shoulders. "Do you know anything about a cabin owned by Chase Rhone? On Lake Martin?"

Kevin's eyebrows went up. "Yeah, if he still has it. It's where he kept Jill for the first few weeks after he took her. I went there a few times, but it's been more than twenty years."

"Can you show us where it is?" Mike asked.

The old man shrugged. "Sure. Bring me a map of the lake."

A half hour later, the sheriff department's helicopter landed at the Turney house, and Mike handed the pilot the map. After a huddled discussion, the pilot picked up his radio, and Mike returned to his cruiser. He pulled two bulletproof vests out of the trunk and tossed one to me.

"Put that on, if you're coming with us."

I looked from the vest to his face. "You're letting me ride along?"

He shrugged into the vest and worked on the straps. "I shouldn't, but I have a feeling about this one."

I didn't argue. I put on the vest—which felt oddly familiar and comfortable. Few police officers were comfortable wearing a vest, even though for some it was daily gear. It was more that they got used to it as another piece of their gear. At one time I had done that as well—fastening down the Velcro straps felt like coming home.

The helicopter seated four, and within a few minutes we were airborne and headed southwest toward the lake. The pilot had also notified the marine teams of both counties, and they were on their way by boat.

Central Alabama in the fall was gorgeous, especially from the air, but I registered the beauty this time without truly appreciating it. My mind was on the man who had taken on the challenge to kill me without pulling a trigger, and I couldn't quite shake that we were walking into dangerously unknown territory. In my experience, cornered animals kill, and cornered humans even more so, no matter what their qualms about such an act in the past. Desperation and fear win out every time.

The helicopter passed over the marine teams as they sped across the lake, and I was impressed with how fast they had gotten their crafts into the water. We would beat them to the cabin, but not by much. We set down in a small clearing near the shoreline, about fifty yards from the cabin. We jumped out, and they took off again, not wanting the valuable bird to become a target. We took cover in a small copse of trees, and even after the teams pulled up in their boats, I stayed out of the way. Mike and I knew I was a risk, and he warned me to stay put "until I was needed."

How I might be needed remained a mystery.

I watched as he conferred with the teams, who then scattered into the trees on either side of the cabin. They moved quickly and efficiently, taking up positions and falling silent. I turned to look at the cabin, my eyes widening as Clarissa walked out onto the porch and sat down on the steps, as if a helicopter had not just landed on her lawn.

Even at this distance I could see the bruises on her face and arms. One eye was purple and swollen, and she stared out over the lake.

The wind stirred my hair, and around me the few fall leaves remaining on their branches rustled. Waves from the lake lapped up on the shore and created a steady creaking noise from the dock. We waited, then Clarissa looked up at the sun and closed her eyes as she called out. "Anytime y'all are ready. It's not as if you're invisible or that we didn't hear the helicopter."

I really liked this woman.

Mike called out from a position on the other side of the yard. "Clarissa? Are you all right?"

She pointed to her eye. "I've been better, but I'm OK."

"Is Chase Rhone inside?"

"Yes. He, on the other hand, is not doing well. He's been shot. Definitely needs help."

Four officers darted out of the woods and circled around to the back side of the cabin.

"We went to your house. We saw the blood," Mike said to Clarissa.

She ran her fingers through her hair and shook out the curls. "That's his. I'm bruised, not bleeding. He knew I was the only one who would help him. So, of course, I did."

"Who shot him?"

"His sister. Willa."

I could almost hear Mike choking. "His sister shot him?"

"Yes. And his friend Owen. He's probably dead. Could y'all come on up? I'm tired of shouting."

"Is he armed?"

"He is, a pistol, but I doubt he has the strength to use it."

Two of the officers who had gone behind the cabin moved down the outside walls and gave a thumbs-up.

"Clarissa, we're going to approach."

"That's fine. Is Star with you?"

Mike stepped out of the trees. "Why?"

"Because Chase said he only wanted to talk to her."

"Why?"

She shrugged. "Something about a feral cat with nine lives. He's mumbling a lot."

Mike stopped, and even from this distance I could see him fighting to hold his face solemn. Once under control, he looked at me and mouthed, "Up to you."

I stepped from behind a beech tree and headed up the hill. Mike fell into step beside me, and Clarissa stood as we trod closer. I could see the bruises on her face in stark relief now, along with a number of others up and down her arms. She saw my examination and shrugged again.

"Believe me, I had worse when we were married. Right now he's feverish and grabby. He's not trying to hurt me. Not anymore. But I couldn't leave him to die alone. And it's not like I have the strength to walk five miles to the nearest house."

"He's just desperate."

She nodded. "And he knows he's dying."

"An air ambulance is on the way," Mike said.

Her lips pressed together. "Thank you. I'm not convinced they'll be in time." She motioned for us to follow her inside. Mike drew his gun as we entered and held it down to his side.

The cabin had more than one room, but we only made it inside the door. Against a far wall, the man I assumed was Chase Rhone was propped up on a couch. Perspiration and oil plastered his dark hair to his scalp, and rivulets of water streamed down his face, neck, and chest. He was bare chested except for the thick white bandages that swathed his abdomen and one shoulder. Blood and sweat stained both. Random blue blotches marred his grayish skin, and deep hollows surrounded both eyes. His hands lay in his lap, one of them clutching a blood-soaked cloth. The other one caressed a 9mm automatic.

The moment should have been solemn, but this man had tried his best to kill me. Twice. I couldn't resist. "Man, you look like death warmed over."

Mike shot me a scolding glance, but Chase Rhone coughed out a laugh, a sharp bark, then coughed for real and spat into the cloth. The 9mm danced in his other hand, but he neither gripped it nor let it go. Clarissa put a hand on his forehead, then shook her head at us. She sat in a nearby straight-back chair, her body sagging, a woman weary of life.

Mike raised his pistol. "Rhone, drop the gun."

Chase ignored him, addressing me once the coughing fit had passed. "And you look like something the cat dragged in. No wonder that old cat made a home with you. He recognized one of his own." He spat again, then sagged against the back of the sofa.

Rhone had to be in his late fifties now, but he appeared much older, and I realized the dark hair was streaked with gray. I could see that he had once been a remarkably handsome man. And, around the mouth and eyes, I could see Jill. She had her mother's blue eyes, but the shape was his.

"Have you seen Jill?" I dropped the humor from my voice.

He gestured weakly at Clarissa. "On her tablet. Press conference."

I stepped closer to him, despite Mike's growl. "She's quite the success. You should be proud of her."

He gave a single nod, then flinched as if that hurt. "Has her mother's spirit." He swallowed hard. "She was my love. I waited for her. For the right time. But then she—" Rhone gagged and closed his eyes for a moment. "I never forgave her, y'know."

One more step, and I would have the gun. "Genevieve?"

"No." He opened his eyes and stared at me. "Willa. For shooting her. For killing my soul mate." His eyes narrowed then, and the glare in them turned sharp. "Like you. For doing it again. For digging her up and killing her all over again."

He lifted the gun, pointed it at my chest, and pulled the trigger.

Clarissa screamed, and the gunshot deafened me . . . but it wasn't Rhone's gun that fired.

Suicide by cop is a real thing, and it happens more than most people realize. The people who do it take advantage of the intense training police officers endure and their skills in self-defense. Officers are usually not allowed to fire at a suspect unless they are threatened, or in defense of someone who is.

Chase Rhone knew exactly what he was doing when he asked for me to be present and when he refused to relinquish his gun. To his dying breath, the man could not pull a trigger to kill, either himself or anyone else. He had to maneuver other people to do it for him.

His pistol was not loaded. He pulled the trigger on an empty chamber. But he succeeded in ending his life. Just as he had manipulated his nephew into a kidnapping plot and his sister into raising the child he had sired and stolen.

Still . . . it had been a long time since a gun had gone off in such proximity to me, and the thought that Rhone might shoot me after all had its effect. My knees buckled, and I sat down hard on the cabin floor.

Mike knelt beside me as the other officers swarmed the cabin, clearing it. They escorted a sobbing Clarissa out. Mike stared down at me, speechless for a long time. As I finally blinked a few times and looked up at him, he shook his head. "I really cannot take you anywhere, can I?"

EPILOGUE

Present Day
Pineville, Alabama

JILL WENT BACK to Chicago for a while, to find solace in her own place with her own friends. But she returned between Willa's arraignment and trial to find comfort with Kevin and Ricky, even staying in the farmhouse for a couple of weeks. Despite all that happened, her bonds to them remained strong. Kevin, while no blood kin to Jill, had been the only father she had really known.

The Marshalls, true to form, closed ranks and refused all contact with the press, especially after it came out that it had been Owen who had followed me when I left the Marshall compound and thus Owen who had killed Zebulon Rhone. Willa had arranged to borrow the car from her cousin Zebulon, and Owen had kept it stashed at the compound, knowing I would eventually interview them. Willa had also given Owen the varsity jacket in an attempt to frame Ricky for the murder. Jack Marshall provided DNA in order to prove that Willa had been plowing under Owen's body, but Margery put a lawyer between them and everyone else. They even refused to see Jill at first, until everyone's DNA had been processed. Even then her homecoming had not been what anyone had hoped, and I doubted Jill would visit Gen's family again. They had their closure but not much else.

That DNA sample, however, proved to be most enlightening, forcing yet more secrets out of the closet. When the lab contacted Mike with the results a few weeks later, he called me into his office and spread the reports in front of me, waiting silently as I read and absorbed them. I sat, simply staring, for several minutes.

As expected, Jill was, indeed, the child of Chase Rhone and Genevieve Marshall Eaton. But Ricky's DNA had markers that indicated he was, in fact, Owen, Jack, and Gen Marshall's half brother, the child of Kevin Turney and Margery Marshall.

Making Jill and Ricky kin by blood as well as by love.

Speaking of love . . . Richard Lee Turney and Clarissa Newton married in early December. He had joined a twelve-step program, and he included continued sobriety in his wedding vows to her. The first stop on their honeymoon was Chicago.

The one outlier in it all was Nicholas Eaton. While Chase Rhone had claimed Genevieve as soul mate, his behavior had been anything but compassionate and romantic. Nick Eaton, however, had loved his wife beyond measure as well as her child, and he had proved it each day of their time together. So it came as no surprise to me when he requested a meeting with Jill. She was reluctant at first—she had no memory of him at all—but finally agreed. But their common bond, a love for a woman who had treasured them both, broke the barriers, and she left his office as a friend.

Then there was Michael Luinetti, who stayed angry with me for exactly three days. By that time I was back at the trailer, cleaning up, making repairs, and removing the last of the listening devices. Those had been traced to a purchase Owen had made for his company, but by the time the tech guys had tracked it all down, everything had already been blown to flinders.

I had also done a great deal of soul-searching, talking to both Gran and God about my next steps. Perhaps Mike was right about the danger and how my acting as a PI stood as an obstacle between us. Or maybe—with the case in the spring and this one complete—it was time for a different stage in my career. My father's law firm would welcome me back to do their investigations—little danger there—although the idea of spending most of my time behind a desk did not entice me. Other firms had offered over the years.

In an intriguing personal turn, my ex-husband, Tony, had merged his law firm with a national group. I had insisted that his alimony payments be based on a percentage of his annual income, which he had agreed to because his income was stable. Now it skyrocketed, as did his payments to me. I knew this because I had already received his motion to have them reduced and changed to a set payment.

A motion I had forwarded to Jill for advice. Her response left me howling with laughter. Her law firm had a branch in Tennessee, and she referred it to them. These folks salivated at the idea of taking on Anthony O'Connell, even in a minor negotiation, and could not wait to get their hands on the case.

Life always came full circle.

Which was the same thought I had when Mike knocked on my door one chilly afternoon. The leaves had all fallen, and they circled on the ground in bursts of wind. Cletis, who had taken up full-time residence in his heated house outside my trailer, greeted Mike with a yowl that alerted me just before the knock. I could hear him murmuring to the cat before I unlocked the door.

I stared at him. "Aren't you still mad at me?"

He squared his shoulders. "I am. But I have a proposition."

I stepped back. "By all means, come in." I gestured to the recliner, and he sat on the edge of it. I pulled the door closed, then perched on a bistro stool. "So what's up?"

Mike hesitated, then took a deep breath.

"That bad, is it?"

His mouth twitched. "Don't do that. I'm already nervous enough."

I crossed my arms and leaned back. "Oh, now you *have* to spit it out."

Mike shook his head. "Do you know how impossible you are?"

"I've been told, but I don't seem to be able to do anything about it."

"You know why I'm mad at you."

"Something about almost getting killed."

"Because you take too many chances. And don't keep me informed."

"If I told you, you'd just try to stop me. And I don't want to get you into trouble."

"Did it ever occur to you that I've been grown for a long time? I can manage my own trouble."

"Yeah, but the problem is you keep trying to manage me. And as you repeat often enough, that's what gets you in trouble. I'm not a cop. I cannot tell you everything without putting you at risk."

"So maybe you should be a cop."

"Um—" I stared at him, my heart beating faster. *Did he really mean . . .*

He stood up. "Don't tell me I managed to render you speechless."

"I'm just trying to decide if I heard you right."

He stepped closer. "You did."

"You want me to be a cop."

"Yes. Specifically *my* cop—" His face flushed. "I mean a cop for the Pineville PD."

"Um—"

He held out a hand, palm facing me. "Listen for a minute. Don't talk."

"OK."

"Stop it."

I held up my hands in surrender.

"I've been talking to the city council. Something Miss Doris said triggered an idea, and I took it to them. Two of the biggest cases to break in this area in the past year have been yours. Cold cases. And it took an outside investigator to break them. Someone who had worked such cases for a long time. So I asked for the budget for a cold-case unit. Not just someone who worked old cases on occasion. Someone who specializes in them. This morning they approved the money. And they want you to run it."

I stood and moved toward him. "So you're offering me a job?"

"Yes."

I reached out and slid one hand into his. As always, his mere touch made my breath catch. "That means I would be employed by the Pineville PD. You'd be my boss. I'd report to you."

He smiled and squeezed my fingers, tugging me a little closer. "As a matter of fact, yes."

"So I really would be *your* cop."

The red flushed deeper, and his voice dropped almost an octave. "Only if you really want to be." He leaned toward me and put his arm around my waist. I could feel his breath against my temple, the warmth of his body encompassing mine.

"Michael?"

"Yes?"

I placed my hand on his chest, pushed up on my toes, and brushed my lips against his. "I do."

His eyebrows arched. "Keep that answer in mind, will you?"

"Oh, I will. Kiss me back."

And he did.

ACKNOWLEDGMENTS

As with Star's first book, *Burying Daisy Doe,* I needed guidance, support, and lots of prayer as I completed this one. As with most writers, I reached several "This is the worst thing ever written; why am I even trying?" stages along the way. My three "Js"—Julie, Jack, and Janyre—talked me off more ledges that anyone can imagine. Without them, this book would never have been finished, and they are due my eternal gratitude.